BOILING POINT

BROOKLYN BOYS #3

E. DAVIES

Publisher's Note: This is a work of fiction. Names, characters, places, and incidents are a product of the author's imagination. Locales and public names are sometimes used for atmospheric purposes. Any resemblance to actual people, living or dead, or to businesses, companies, events, institutions, or locales is completely coincidental.

Boiling Point / E. Davies. – 2nd ed.
ISBN-13: 978-1-912245-32-1

For H., A., and J., who told me that I can. Look, ma—I did!

1

———

CEDAR

Watching my ex-boyfriend Nathan have his pick of the club's men was exactly as awful as I'd expected.

Any attraction to him was long since gone. I wasn't clinging on to the hope we'd find a second chance together. As usual, he'd ditched me for the dance floor the moment we walked into Friction. I'd always felt like the ugly duckling in the club compared to the handsome and charming Nathan.

No different from the rest of my life, really. If only I could get away from him and start afresh—but I'd long since shelved that hope.

"How's your night going?"

I recognized the guy asking—the bouncer at the door who'd let us in must have just gotten off shift. He'd changed out of the stern jacket. Now he was in a regular bomber jacket and collared shirt, leaning on the bar and waiting for a drink.

He wasn't hitting on me, or he would have noticed me at the door earlier. It was clearly a pity conversation, but hey, I'd take it.

1

Better than the weirdo in the Smurf costume who'd been leering at me. I didn't bother questioning the costume—this was New York.

"Pretty good, thanks." I smiled at him, not about to dump my problems on him. Nobody in Brooklyn meant it when they asked that question. "You off work now?"

"Yup. Where's your friend? Don't you two come here together a lot?"

I made a face. Was he hitting on Nathan through me? Wouldn't be the first time. "Sorry. He's off dancing with some guy."

"Oh." The bouncer turned toward me and folded his arms. "I thought you two might be…"

"We were." I didn't lose my temper with him. The few friends I had hung out here, or at the diner next door. Gossip spread like wildfire through a midsummer meadow. I didn't need to make my life any more awkward than it already was.

His brown eyes turned warm and sympathetic, and he pretended to hoist his foot up to his mouth while I laughed. "Sorry. This is why they don't let me talk much. So, uh." He ran a hand through his short brown hair and pointed toward the staff room door. "You wanna hit up the bathroom? Nobody will bother us."

Simple, direct, and so straightforward it took me a moment to realize I was being propositioned for sex. I took a moment to look him over—broad and rugged, and a surprisingly cute smile I never saw when he was working at the door. He seemed kind of nice, but so not my type.

But I could use whatever the hell he was offering. I couldn't afford to be picky.

"Why not?" I shrugged. It wasn't every day one got a private bath-room to use, after all. "My dating life's shit. I could use a quickie."

"Great." It was done like a business transaction: offer, acceptance, and no doubt a swift conclusion. I reached out as if to shake hands on it, my hand shaking as I missed his grip. Thanks to my condi-tion, my damn coordination was shit, and a lot of bouncers thought I was drunk even when I was stone-cold sober.

He didn't seem fazed as he took my hand instead, lacing our fingers and leading us away from the bar. His fingers were so much bigger that mine were forced apart, but it felt kind of nice, too. He had a callused palm—like mine, but broader.

I'd never been through the door next to the bathroom, but he led me straight through without stopping. I only glimpsed a break room for a moment before he pushed me through another door and into a bathroom. It was a single cubicle and definitely staff-only, since it was clean and stocked with toilet paper.

I licked my lips, but before I could get nervous, he sprang into action. One big hand rubbed my crotch while the other arm snaked around me, pulling me in close.

"Sexy, aren't you?" he growled into my ear. "I noticed you when you got here."

Well, that was a lie. He hadn't even tried to flirt earlier in the *I'm at work, but later?* way. But I was okay with being his last resort as long as I got off, too.

"You gonna fuck me?" I growled back, challenging him. I could use a good distraction, and standing here flirting wasn't doing it.

"After you suck my dick."

Sure. That was a deal I was happy to make. I sank to my knees in a practiced move—from long hours gardening, not a full little black book—and waited as he unzipped his pants. He stroked himself hard and fast, and then rolled on a condom.

That was my cue to take over. I would have felt bad about tuning out if he'd seemed into me at all. But both of us were clearly just going through the motions, so I was free to daydream away.

My hard-on didn't care that it was all a drill. As long as I got drilled, I could pretend I was making him happy. And that he was making me happy.

My hands shook as usual, but I managed to grab his knees without him noticing and slid my palms up his thighs to get to where I needed them to be. It only took me a minute of warming him up before he was grunting quietly, grabbing the back of my head and thrusting.

He spat on his fingers and gestured for me to turn around.

Okay, this was gonna be rough. Thank God I'd kept the toy collection when Nathan and I split up, or there'd be another kind of splitting going on tonight.

Before long, once I'd breathed away all the pain and tightness, his fingers buried to the root inside me didn't feel like enough. I didn't even have to tell him I was ready. He pulled out his fingers and pushed in his dick without hesitation, sliding past the tight ring of muscle.

I choked back my gasp as I gripped the porcelain sink. My sweaty palms slipped on the edge, so I gripped harder, curling my fingers around the edge until my fingertips brushed the rough underside.

He was already fucking me, moving slowly at first. "Yeah, baby. You feel so good."

Honestly, I wished he'd shut up, but my body still reacted like I cared about it. I loosened my grip with one hand to stroke myself.

I had no idea how long this was gonna last. If he finished fast, I wasn't gonna awkwardly stand here, trying to get off while he looked bored.

It wasn't the best sex I'd ever had, or the worst. It was just pretty average. But contact with an actual warm body did things for me that my own hands couldn't seem to. When he bothered brushing my nipples and pinching them lightly, it helped me along real fast.

With enough careful maneuvering, I made sure that I came into the sink. He pushed me out of the way to do the same a minute later, beating himself off with one practiced hand.

We cleaned up without saying anything. As I zipped up my pants again, he said, "Thanks. Hope your dating life gets better."

I half-smiled. "Yours, too." We left the bathroom and I glanced towards the small break room-cum-stockroom, but nobody else was back here.

"Well, for my money, you're a good fuck. I'm sure you won't have a problem finding a guy when you're ready."

If only that were true. I was more than ready, but where were the half-decent guys? Probably running a mile when they saw Nathan hovering nearby me. How come *he* got to move on with his life, but I didn't?

I'd known what I was signing up for when I started going out with him, I reminded myself. I was always gonna be the loser compared to him. He had a rich dad who could buy him a charity sector "career," million-watt smile that opened doors, and distaste for manual labor or any kind of hard work. Opposites had indeed attracted—briefly—and starting a charity with him had seemed like a good idea.

Until now, anyway.

"You too," I told him. I respected that he hadn't wasted my time with mind-games or pretended he was interested in me for more than a night. It was an efficient use of both of our time.

Tonight's Mr. Right Now slapped my ass to send me out of the backroom and saluted me with two fingers.

I hadn't yet decided whether to get another beer, but I'd barely reached the bar before the guy next to me elbowed my ribs.

"Do you know that bouncer? Dude. He's such a dick. He nearly didn't let my friends in, you know!" He pointed toward a group of guys in the corner, glaring at me like he expected me to take the bouncer's side.

Sure, I'd sucked the bouncer's cock, but I didn't even know his name. I wasn't about to stand up for him. "Yeah? That sucks, man." A quick glance at his friends told me why the bouncer had considered barring them. They were drunkenly leaning on each other as they tried to dance.

"Yeah." The guy stumbled off, leaving me shaking my head.

Everyone seemed to be looking for a fight all the time. Plants were the only exception, which was why I loved them so much— and felt guilty when I constantly mishandled them. Whether I was dropping a tray of seedlings or breaking off a whole cluster of unripe tomatoes, I really could find any way to screw up, as Nathan loved reminding me.

If only we hadn't started this stupid urban gardening charity and I hadn't set my heart on changing the world with his help. But it was too late to back out now. If I walked away from Plant for the Future just because my ex was a little bit unlikeable, that would make me a pretty crappy example of charity work.

Didn't mean I had to stick around and watch him, though. Nathan still hadn't picked a guy, but if I snuck out now, I could get away before he showed off his catch of the day. It was always under the pretense of making sure I knew he was leaving so I could get home safe.

I made it out of Friction without being noticed, which was… good, right?

The diner, Bubbles, was right next to the club. When I pushed open the door, a woman in a fake-fancy coat and sneer burst through it, glaring back over her shoulder. She ran into me, and her high ponytail smacked me in the face as she whipped her head around and redirected the laser-like glare at me.

"Ladies first. Don't you know any manners?" She acted like she'd taken offense at my very existence, not just my getting in her way.

I shrugged but didn't say anything, and stood aside so she could step around me and leave.

It was gonna be one of those nights. If nothing else, I could count on one thing: the bacon here would send me home with a full belly and smile.

Unlike every man in my life, bacon couldn't let me down.

2

RICKY

"And why aren't you going to the wedding with that nice girl? She might catch the bouquet! Sure, she can't cook, but you've got that covered. She can stay home with the kids."

"Whoa. Okay. Mama," I protested again, stirring the pancake batter hard enough it splattered across the counter. I jammed the phone between my ear and shoulder to wipe the counter clean.

Frustration knotted my stomach until I felt half-sick. The stupid wedding wasn't the worst part—it was the lie that I'd been perpetuating for years. For the millionth time, it was coming back to bite me in the ass.

My last ex-girlfriend must have called Mama—again—to complain about my dumping her six months ago. Little did either of them know that Madison was gonna hold the "last ex-girlfriend" title forever.

I tried not to choke on my words. *I need to tell you, but I just can't.* The fear that paralyzed me from head to toe when I considered it was all too real. It was easier to keep putting it off and putting it off.

"I'm at work," I said instead. "Look, I'll stop by next weekend and you can try to change my mind."

My mom was eager for grandkids and a daughter-in-law, but I was done with girls. I'd tried my hardest to like them for the last decade. When that had failed, I had pretended. But I was at my breaking point now.

I was ready to be free of this lie. Someday soon, anyway. So far, I'd tried to hook up a few times on Grindr, but with no success; either I'd gotten nervous and backed out or the other guy had ghosted me before we met.

Gay V-card: still intact. Frustration: very much intact. And it looked like my frustration was only just starting.

Think of the devil and she shall appear. There she was, leaning in the doorway, arms folded, cracking her bubblegum.

"Mama, Maddie's here. I don't want to keep a lady waiting." I almost gagged as I said it, but it worked.

"Oh, you go talk to her, honey. Call your mama again soon!"

"Love you," I mumbled and hung up.

"You really left me in the lurch, Enrique," Madison launched with. "My cousins are *all* making fun of me now."

"Sorry," I said again, on autopilot. That seemed to be the most frequently-used word in my relationships.

It didn't satisfy her. "And I'm gonna be in some 'shabby chic' bridesmaid dress, Ricky. You don't even know how embarrassing that is. Single *and* broke." Madison persisted, huffing as she adjusted her ponytail. She stayed in the doorway, berating me from afar.

I flipped the pancakes on the stove while grabbing a handful of hash browns. That was one more skill I had on autopilot, which brought the number to two—cooking hangover specials and apologizing to my exes. Way too often, those were simultaneously used skills.

I sighed. It was obviously another way to get money out of me, but I *did* owe her for the lie I'd told her. A real man didn't get a woman's hopes up when he knew damn well he was incapable of being who she thought he was.

Another in my list of failures.

"You need another loan? Wallet's in the office," I told her. We both knew it wasn't a loan.

Madison rewarded me with a smile. "Thanks, baby." As pretty as she was when she smiled, I'd always seen her as if through a thick pane of glass. Pretty to look at, but it didn't *do* anything for me.

Not like guys did. And *that* was something Madison never needed to find out.

When Madison emerged, flashing me a grin and tucking bills into her pocket, I eyed her. "Is that a hundred?"

"Hundred-twenty. Tax, baby." Madison blew a kiss as she headed through the kitchen. I silently gestured after her, but it was no use. I was a sucker for a guilt-trip, and she knew it.

My life was ridiculous. Here I was, working at the gayest diner in Brooklyn: owned by a gay man, in the heart of the gayborhood, and next to one of the most popular gay bars in town.

Yet I wasn't quite out. Not ready yet, I'd told myself for months now.

It had clicked sometime last year—okay, in high school—but a guy had responsibilities. I had to *try*, and if at first you don't succeed, try again. But the harder I'd tried to attract women, the more they'd turned me off. After Madison, I'd given up.

Not that I could admit that to Mama. I was the only son—only kid at all. It was my job to marry a nice woman and give her grandbabies. On the other hand, I couldn't keep it up in bed long enough to make those mandatory babies. Real catch-22 there.

I'd been putting off the inevitable coming-out conversation with Mama for months, too afraid of the consequences. And coming out to anyone before Mama just felt wrong. She was the most important person in my life, easily. Especially since Dad died.

"Maddie?" Jared, the diner owner, stuck his head in. "You can't be back here."

"Sorry, baby." She stretched onto tiptoe to kiss his cheek and bat her lashes, her charm suddenly turned up to eleven.

Jared rolled his eyes. "City won't like you being back there. If you're visiting Enrique, stay outside the staff areas."

She rolled her eyes when he turned his back and mimed a blowjob, poking her tongue into her cheek and then smirking. She mouthed, *Gay*, and then stormed out.

Humiliation was the first wave of emotion that hit me. Then anger, and then fear. Did she know about me? She *had* meant Jared and not me, right? God, if she ever found out, she was going to lord it over me like she was a tabloid photographer with a scoop.

I pressed my lips together hard, my cheeks flushing at the stark reminder of why I was living a double life. It was the kind of thing you never think you'll wind up doing, but then you open your eyes one day and realize that you're not telling anyone the truth.

And, worse yet, you realize that you *can't*. Not without sending it all tumbling down… like a house of matchsticks on top of a barrel of oil.

Jared reappeared a minute later with another order for me. After he slapped it on the counter, he leaned there and looked at me without saying a word.

My cheeks flushed again. I hated myself for giving anything away at all. I wanted to pretend it was all just fine, and we were going through a rough patch, and I was gonna settle down with a nice woman like her in the end.

But my life wasn't a damn movie. Why was I still holding out hope for a damn happy-ever-after ending with a white picket fence, two-point-five kids, a dog, and a woman who made me smile?

That was all I wanted. Someone to make me smile. The thought was a knife twisting in my gut, and it drove me to action as I broke Jared's gaze.

"I'm fine," I insisted, slapping the order next to the lineup of them above the stove. I kept on plating both pending hangover specials and slid them at Daisy through the serving window instead.

Jared eyed me. "Okay. I'm out for the night, then."

"See ya, old man." It was a running joke between us—even though he was only a decade older than me, thirty-four seemed an eternity away to me. How the hell I was gonna get there without this house of dominoes crashing down around me, I had no idea.

A few minutes of peace and quiet followed before Daisy interrupted by sticking her head into the kitchen. "Hey. Kid's saying your bacon's no good."

Literally the last thing I needed tonight was a complaint from some obnoxious kid who'd turned twenty-one last week and his clones, all drenched in Axe and the smug certainty that a line cook had no real power over them. "God." I rubbed my face and threw my towel on the counter. "Really?"

"He's right," Daisy said, smirking at me as she tapped her order pad against her hip. "That bacon was awfully… limp."

God only knew what Madison had said to her about me. Probably too much. My temper flared. "Right," I snapped and moved past her. "Which table?"

I didn't have any illusions of being a hulking great dude who could tower over patrons and make them apologize for insulting my cooking, but goddamn, that bacon had been nice and crispy on the way out.

"My meat is *not* limp," I lashed out verbally and folded my arms as I reached the guy's table.

More than a few strangled giggles nearby didn't improve my mood, and I shot a glare around. The implied threat of spit in their food made everyone stop laughing. If they were spying, they did it more subtly, at least. Good. I didn't need this getting back to Jared.

"Oh." The guy in front of me had frozen, but the bacon dangling between his fingers and halfway to his lips was…

Well, it was distinctly limp.

I swore under my breath. There went my argument. "The damn thing died on the way out, then. I *told* Jared our new supplier is crappy. You try getting the shit they're sending us to crisp up. It ain't easy."

The idea that I was *bad* at my job—the one thing I had going for me—made me almost see red. Sure, I was bad at everything in life, but I'd fooled plenty of other people into thinking I was at least half-decent at this one thing.

Lots of other people liked my bacon, I reminded myself. It *couldn't* be bad. Right?

The guy had gone so quiet that I expected him to mutter an apology, but instead he pushed himself to his feet and put the bacon back on his plate. "Okay."

I blinked a few times. He wasn't even batting an eye as he locked gazes with me.

Despite myself, I noticed that he was... well, hot. He was blond and shorter by a few inches now that he was standing up, but his spiked hair made up for the difference. And he had a quiet strength in the set of his jaw that contrasted against the shake in his clenched fists.

Shit. I'd crowded so close to the table that, now that he was standing up, he was just a few inches away. I hadn't expected the closeness to awaken something else in me that was quite different from anger... or maybe way too close.

I wasn't sure if I wanted to shake him by the shoulders, or push him down on the table and satisfy his hunger a whole different way. His clothes fit way too well, and he smelled faintly like beer. Maybe he'd been out at Friction tonight, trying to pick someone up.

That could be me, if I weren't such a fucking coward. *I'm not a coward,* I insisted to myself, letting the bite of my nails against my palms keep me grounded. It was an empty phrase when it wasn't backed by actions, though.

He'd noticed the way I was looking at him. His gaze was fixed on my lips, and when he caught me staring, he licked his lips deliberately.

Shit. I couldn't back down now, but I couldn't step any closer. We were already nearly touching. Brain cells I didn't know I'd had were suddenly waking up, just to check that we weren't accidentally touching somewhere.

Oh my God. I want to be touching him, I thought, and then tried to get my thoughts to shut up long enough to say anything.

"Okay what?" I finally croaked.

"Okay, I'll try, then. You invited me. And it's quieter back there. People are watching." His voice was so soft I almost leaned in to hear it, but I could see every word on his lips. Could almost imagine them against my lips, too. Especially in some other context.

Fuuuuck. I really should've paused to clean the pipes on the way out the door to work tonight. Being late was better than stuck here, horny and pissed off while a brash little twink challenged me in my own kitchen.

And he was cute, too. Slouchy hoodie, clingy thin t-shirt, skinny jeans—such a hipster. Right to the thin layer of stubble along his jaw and the bright brown eyes set off against his spiky blond mane.

But he was right—I'd told him *you try*, and now he was stepping up to the challenge. I couldn't deny that his boldness turned me on as much as it irritated me.

"Fine," I hissed and stood back, gesturing toward the kitchen.

A few people shifted as if to stand up and watch through the serving window. I whirled on them, resisting the urge to flip off our customers. "This is none of your business," I told them, and luckily, they did all settle down and pretend not to be nosy bastards.

Good thing there weren't any regulars, or they'd already be

standing at the window with stopwatches, ready to start a competition.

I stormed after the guy. He had an awkward way of walking, like he wasn't quite steady on his feet. "I don't even know your damn name. Why should I let you in my kitchen?" And it was *my* kitchen when I was on shift. I had more seniority than most others there, having been hired when Jared bought the place a few years back. Fresh outta my work training placement, I'd jumped on a steady job.

I'd tried to fool myself into thinking my eagerness to work here hadn't had anything to do with the clientele or neighborhood. But this guy was making circuits in my brain connect that I hadn't even known were there.

"Cedar."

It took me a minute to remember what I'd just asked. "That's your name?"

"Yep."

"What kind of name is that?"

"Mine." He didn't waste words, and somehow, I liked that. He had a casually confident attitude—he reminded me of a sleek, graceful panther compared to my... well, puffed-up one-toed pigeon squawking over a crust.

I tried to calm down. The last couple minutes had just raced out of control before I could think about what was going on. My heart raced despite my deep breaths. What I should've been doing was saying, *Get the hell out of my kitchen, Cedar.*

Instead, I found myself reaching out for a handshake. "Ricky. You can't do better than me at cooking. It's my kitchen." What I wanted to say was that it had been a stupid bet to throw out there.

All I'd wanted was an apology—but not even from Cedar. He was right, the bacon had been limp.

It hit me like a ton of bricks: I wanted an apology from myself for being such a damn coward once again. Instead, every time something went wrong, I seemed to double down and make the situation explode.

When Cedar turned away and ignored my hand, it was hard not to feel slighted. Anger prickled under my skin again, and I tightened my jaw. Screw this—rejection stung. I folded my arms awkwardly instead, leaning on the counter as Cedar approached the hot stove.

"You shouldn't even be back here," I told him, keeping my voice hard. No need to let him see that he was getting to me with all his limp meat jokes and quiet superiority complex.

"I'm not gonna start a fire. I went to cooking school for a semester. Long enough to know how to cook a damn strip of bacon and keep it… erect." His lips flashed in a slight smile.

Fuck. I'd thought the last thing I needed was some random customer to turn out to be better in the kitchen than I was.

Turned out I was wrong. The last thing I needed was actually that same guy to keep teasing me with sexual innuendo, making me remember how fucking weirdly strong the attraction to him was.

"Mm." I grunted and tensed up even more, shoving my hands under my armpits and chewing on the inside of my cheek to break the moment. "Fine. Show me your tremendous skills."

"I will." Cedar grabbed hold of the flipper, then looked around for the bacon.

"Fridge." The word had barely fallen from my lips when he moved.

I could see the mistake before he even made it, but it was way too late for me to intervene. Cedar moved to grab the fridge door, but his hand was still too close to the flat-top. He stumbled, and the back of his hand smacked the surface.

"Fuck!" Cedar gasped, yanking his hand back.

I grabbed him by the shoulder and waist, dragging him to the sink. I held on tight to his shoulder and slammed the water tap on, then shoved his wrist under the water.

Cedar whimpered but went limp, no longer resisting me now that he'd figured out what I was doing.

Fuck, it turned me on to have his body pressed against mine, fitting tightly against me like he was made for me. My chin rested on his shoulder and I thought I smelled something orange or lemon-y. Must be his aftershave.

I wrapped my other arm around his shoulders for a comforting and strong hold. All the while, I kept holding his hand under the cool water, trying not to cut off circulation with my grip but also not giving him a chance to slip free. "You're gonna be fine, man. It was just a brush."

Heat was tingling down my body, making my toes curl into the thick-soled work shoes I had on today. My cock was pressed up against a round, perky ass, and I was damned if my body didn't notice.

"Yep," Cedar choked out, showing more grit than I'd expected. Instead of getting hysterical, flailing the burn everywhere, and breaking out the lawsuit card… well, he was squaring his jaw and breathing deeply.

I slowly let go of his wrist when I saw that he wasn't going to try to pull away from the water. "You keep rinsing that off, hey?" I was still pressed unnecessarily close, and my body was going to respond to this in a few seconds if I wasn't careful.

I needed to get away from him before something happened that I regretted.

A quiet gasp from nearby drew my attention. I pulled back and turned to the doorway. Of course it was Daisy. She was just hovering there, eyes wide, both hands over her mouth.

"Fat lot of good you are," I told her with a glare. "New table?"

"No, I just…"

"Wanted some good gossip. Scram," I told her in more of a snarl than I'd meant to. The fear wasn't just a simmer under my skin—it had hit a raging boil, sloshing over and making me lash out.

Madison was gonna hear about this in three minutes, if she hadn't already. Great. The last thing I needed was all of her friends making fun of my floppy bacon—and how stiff this cute little twink made it.

Daisy turned on her heel and left without complaint, thank God. I cast another look around the kitchen and through the window to see if anyone was lurking nearby.

Nope. Good. We were alone.

"Thanks," Cedar murmured, his voice small and hard to hear over the gush of water as he leaned on the counter. He didn't meet my gaze.

"Course. My own damn fault." I kept a close eye on him to make sure he wasn't about to faint. His hand was doing well under the water so far—no blistering or anything. Thank God I hadn't been frying anything at the time.

Cedar jerked back from under the water, grabbing paper towels to wrap around his hand and inspect it. "It really wasn't. But I'm fine."

"Yeah. Some cooking student you are," I scoffed, letting out my breath as I sagged with relief. Thank God the burn wasn't bad, or I would have been beside myself with guilt and frustration. "You should be running that under water for a few more minutes."

"I'm fine." He shook his hand off and pressed his thumbnail lightly into the red skin, then sucked in his breath. Obviously not that fine, then. "They kicked me out after the first semester." His voice was quiet and precise. "I kept fucking up my hands."

"Oh." I felt ten times worse for letting my anger get the best of me. If I was going to stop being such a coward, I needed to stop lashing out. And maybe apologize. "I'm sorry."

If it sounded clumsy, Cedar didn't mock me for it. He just smiled for a quick second at me and shook his head. "My fault."

Cedar headed for the door, and I tried to block his path. "Whoa. Stay and let me get the first aid kit." I wasn't used to begging someone to stick around—not in my bed, or my kitchen, or my life.

It was the least I could do—try to fix him up when I'd broken him. I could never seem to do that for anyone else, and now he was gonna walk out of here thinking that I was some egotistic young chef with his head too far up his ass to notice he was in a cheap and easy diner, not a Michelin-starred concept restaurant.

Why the hell did I care what Cedar thought of me, anyway?

In any case, Cedar was determined to ignore me. He brushed past, his citrus-tinged cologne making me breathe in deeply. "No way. Nothing you can do for me that I can't do at home."

There's one thing I'd like to do to him, but this isn't really the moment. I tried to put it to one side. "Let me call an ambulance."

Cedar just laughed, underscoring what I already knew about how stupid a suggestion that was. "Yeah, right. No. I'm out of here. Hope you figure out how to get your meat stiff again. I'll give you some credit: it's usually great here. I'll be back."

I had to give in to his wishes—he wasn't exactly severely injured enough to risk calling an ambulance, and if he didn't have health insurance, I'd ruin his life by doing it. And get in serious shit with Jared for having even let him back here in the first place.

"It's always great," I mumbled, glaring at Daisy when I reached the doorway and spotted her flirting with a table of obviously gay guys. *Good luck with that, honey,* I thought. Suddenly it all made sense: I'd bet dimes to donuts she'd let the bacon die on the way to dropping off Cedar's food.

As I stared at Cedar's retreating back, I tried to convince myself that I didn't care if he hated me. For maybe the first time ever, it didn't work.

Cedar had to come back to Bubbles soon, so I could make it up to him.

He just had to, right?

3

CEDAR

I hope I got away in time for Ricky not to notice my boner.

Goddamn, I'd had no idea my refractory period could be that quick. Not even half an hour ago, I was busting a nut in the staff bathroom sink at Friction, but here I was getting hot and flushed because some handsome bastard dragged me across the room and ground up against me.

To give me first aid, I reminded myself, quickening my steps through the chilly autumn air. The temperature drop made my lungs hurt. On the other hand, I could breathe deep without risking a lungful of weed, traffic, or sewage fumes. Ah, Brooklyn.

"Fuck this shit," I muttered, dodging the taxis to jaywalk and ignoring the honks they gave me. I wanted to get away from that diner as fast as possible.

Who the hell had I become there for a minute? Instead of meekly taking my scolding for criticizing the bacon—which *had* been floppy—I'd stood up for myself from start to finish. Like someone else had possessed me for a minute.

I tended to be a lithe young willow, bending in the face of any challenge, but for a minute, I'd channeled my namesake. I'd even challenged *him* to a cook-off!

What the hell? I hadn't had *that* many beers.

Just enough to make me clumsy as I opened the apartment door at street-level. I clattered up the staircase that wrapped around the side of my building.

It was a dim, depressing cube of gray stone—four floors, with four apartments on every level. Nathan and I had half the floor to ourselves, since we had neighboring units on the second floor.

Which had seemed like a great idea when we were dating. I knew it was a trap now, but I was well and truly caught in it. Nathan's dad kept funding the rent through Plant for the Future so that Nathan had an easy career. My job was to do the dirty work that we all knew Nathan never would, and if it covered the bills, who was I to leave?

Besides, if I left the charity, I'd lose my home and have to scramble for another at the same time as a job. A lot of people didn't want to hire anyone with cerebral palsy, even if I had the rare kind— ataxic, and relatively mild at that. I had the mixed blessing and curse of blending in with abled people, but intention tremor was a real bastard.

All it took was reaching out to shake hands, pick up a pen to fill out a form at an interview, or zipping up my coat afterward and just as they approached the destination, my hands would start to shake.

Physical therapy had helped, but it would never eliminate that shake. My parents had worked hard to make sure I felt "normal" as a kid—whatever that word meant—but the real world wasn't kind.

Leaving a secure job and housing at the same time was how gay kids wound up dead, homeless, or working street corners. Thank God my parents would never let that happen, but leaving Brooklyn wasn't an option, either. Sleepy upstate New York might as well have been Kansas in my mind. I'd do anything to avoid going home for more than an afternoon.

Nathan had me by the balls, and he knew it.

I glared at Nathan's door as I opened mine, kicking my shoes off with a violent shake of each foot. Once I'd stripped off my hoodie, I headed to the windows to open them up.

It was an automatic routine now, since I had to vent the moisture that had built up throughout the day from my precious potted plants. They made the place Instagram-worthy, but it took a hell of a lot of work to keep them happy without wrecking the place with mold.

With that done, I headed to the kitchen and yanked it open to grab the bottle of lemonade. I could seriously use a drink, but more alcohol wasn't a good idea.

My hand twinged when I curled it around the bottle. Not good. The burn could have been a hell of a lot worse—this wasn't bad enough to seek medical attention—but it pissed me off.

That one moment I'd managed to get an ounce of courage, I'd gone and fucked it up. What the hell would Ricky think next time I walked in there? And worse yet, that gossip-mongering waitress might be there. I'd noticed the way he backed off as soon as she got involved.

The worst part was that I couldn't just avoid Bubbles. Nathan and I went to Friction too much, and I liked a good hangover special at Bubbles afterward.

Plus, Billy hung out there. My gay fairy godmother, he'd taken me under his wing when he noticed me hanging out by myself. He'd been there for me when Nathan dumped me. He'd even let me crash sometimes when Nathan had asked to borrow my apartment to double the space he had for his parties.

It was weird to give up my apartment, but when we lived next door to each other... well, Nathan didn't often leave me a lot of choice. I didn't ask the details of his parties, and he didn't volunteer the information. A place to live in a nice part of Brooklyn was still a place to live.

"Ouch," I hissed when I caught my finger in the door while shutting the fridge. Tears welled up in my eyes, but I refused to shed them.

I was just the clumsy oaf I always had been. No wonder Nathan was banging someone else next door, loudly.

Thump. Mmmm! Creak. Moans mixed with the sound of furniture objecting to its violent treatment.

I sighed as I stared at my kitchen wall. The place had clearly once been an entire apartment to each floor, but had been hastily converted into four units. We each had one, an old lady who never opened the door had the third, and a bunch of college kids were in the fourth. The walls were still crappy as fuck.

My hands shook as I put the glass in the sink loudly and sank down the kitchen cabinet, pulling my knees up by my chest as I cradled my bad hand. I turned it this way and that, flexing my fingers. The damn thing hurt if a breeze so much as touched it, but I still had full range of motion, so I wasn't going to risk the medical bill.

Thank God I was done with garden maintenance for the winter.

Our mission statement was grand: reduce food insecurity and improve mental health in urban residents through rekindling a connection to nature. Not very long ago, I'd believed in what we did. Now, though? It felt like the charity was getting nowhere, and my whole life was on autopilot, too.

Walking away would sting more than my wallet. If I left the charity sector, I wouldn't be able to live with myself. There would always be more people in food deserts who needed help—or at least my manual labor—and I *knew* how to help them. Who was I to hoard that knowledge?

I rolled my head back against the cabinet. For the first winter of the charity's operation, after spending the summer gardening and educating, it had been a welcome break to fuck each other on every surface of both of these apartments.

Ah, young love.

At least the noise on the other side of the wall had stopped, so presumably Nathan had no more stamina than he ever had.

Good, because I really didn't want to jerk off to the sounds of my ex banging some random guy. But I was still gonna need to jerk off, and with my right hand in this state, it was going to be a tricky prospect.

I slid slowly down the cabinet until I lay on the floor, staring up at the ceiling and feeling sorry for myself.

Why couldn't I ask that hot guy from the kitchen, Ricky, to help? He had a strong grip and a no-bullshit attitude. He was cocky as fuck, and something about me just came unglued when a confident man so much as looked at me. Let alone dragged me halfway across an industrial kitchen by my wrist. And it was Ricky's damn fault I needed to jerk off again.

He could have shut me in the stockroom with him and I happily would have…

I looked down at my dick and sighed. Yeah, I'd have to deal with that problem. My orgasm earlier at Mr. Security Guard's hands— or my own, really—had been less than satisfying. One of those *blow your load and shrug it off* feelings of release, and not bliss by a long stretch.

I could save that thought for tonight. I was *not* going to jerk off while lying on my kitchen floor like the desperate loser I was starting to suspect I might be. I could at least treat myself to a bubble bath first.

I sighed and clambered to my feet, wincing when the back of my hand brushed the cabinet. I was going to be acutely aware of my clumsiness now, wasn't I? Like I needed any more reminders. Instead, I started the tub running. While I waited for it to fill, I headed to the bistro table that served as my dining table, then tucked myself in next to the palm plant that was almost bigger than me. That baby wasn't gonna get sold—not for anything.

Pretty much everything else here would fund next year's seedlings, and then we'd start the cycle again: planting, giving away the produce, holding cooking classes, advocating for policy changes that never seemed to go through, and working until our hands bled.

Well, mine, anyway. But I believed in what I did—or I had, once. If you did what you loved, you never worked a day in your life, everyone said. I'd stopped believing, but I kept on working. You didn't need to believe when the cause was good enough. Action made a bigger difference.

And what choice did I have?

"Fuck off," I mumbled when there was a knock on the door. "What?" I yelled instead of voicing my real thoughts.

"Just wanted to make sure you got home!" called back Nathan.

"Well, I did!" I snorted under my breath and shoveled more rice into my mouth.

It sounded kind of nice of him, but more likely, he'd wanted to make sure I'd heard that he got lucky. He had this weird ego about it, like he needed to brag about all of his hookups to make sure they counted toward the notches on his bedpost.

The hallway door closed again as Nathan no doubt returned to his own apartment. Man, had he even given the other guy a chance to shower? He'd never been considerate to me, either.

It was a timely reminder, though: as soon as I found any kind of direction Nathan didn't like, my funding would get cut off. Easier to go with the tide, even if it whipped up into a great swell some-times. I was making a difference with what I did, even if I had too many nights like this—staring into the semi-darkness of my apartment and questioning what the fucking point of it all was.

Ricky had made a bright spot in that darkness, at least. However weird the situation, he'd made me smile. His anger had fizzed away and revealed a guy who gave a shit about me. I knew beyond a shadow of a doubt that Nathan would have laughed and left the kitchen, had he been next to me at the stove.

I had to go back to Bubbles. Get back on the horse—or else the next time Billy dragged me out for brunch at the diner, it was gonna be awkward as fuck.

I wasn't gonna apologize, or make Ricky apologize. I hadn't done anything wrong. Possibly violated a few health and safety stan-dards, but whatever. And although he'd been kind of a dick about my muttered complaint, he'd also instantly taken care of me when I hurt myself.

No grudges or resentment, just a begrudging kind of shell around him. I wasn't used to being taken care of like that. I'd expected him to lash out and gloat about it, but even afterward, he'd only been… exasperated. Not pissed off.

Wait. It was Ricky that was intriguing me enough to want to go back to Bubbles. He'd looked at me like I mattered—not like I was good for nothing but manual labor. I'd almost forgotten what it was like to be treated like I mattered. Like I could stand up for myself without being terrified of the results. He'd admitted that he was wrong as soon as he'd seen that bacon. Nathan never would have.

And he's a lot cuter than Nathan.

What the hell?

It was way too soon to be a crush. I'd stood way too close to him twice and exchanged a few sentences with him. That was it.

Something under my skin had uncontrollably ignited at the way Ricky looked at me—both out in the dining room at first, and then later, when he'd dragged me to the sink.

It was hard to deny that I got hot just thinking about that moment. I hadn't found anyone who so much as made me look twice in their direction in a while now. In the summer I was too busy with my plants, and in the winter I stayed in my little nest of green things and tried to pretend winter would go away quickly.

Why didn't I just move somewhere it was green all year round? That was my dream. But that brought me right back to the fact that had kept me in this situation until now: the people who needed me for my skills, or at least my work ethic, were here.

It wasn't a small goal, but small goals didn't make an impact on the world. If I was going to sacrifice my own quality of living and dedicate maybe decades of my life to this work, it had to be a big goal.

Don't get me wrong, I didn't wake up every morning eager to get up. That had changed some months ago—before the breakup, even. I ignored the sneaking suspicion that I was just trying to rationalize my way back into loving what I did.

I could talk myself out of a good thing all day long.

"Hey." That was Nathan knocking on my door again.

I groaned. He was going to piss off our neighbors or landlords, and we'd done that enough already with his parties and my plants. Pushing myself away from the bistro table, I yanked the door open. "What?"

Nathan looked taken aback for a minute, but he grinned. "I take it you didn't get lucky."

"Yeah, I did." I kept my hand out of sight, against the wall next to the door. "Twice." I could fib just a little—I *had* gotten lucky that second time, even if it wasn't in the way he meant.

Nathan's jaw dropped. "No way!" He didn't seem pissed off, though. He just grinned and high-fived me. "Finally! At the same time? Or with the same guy? Different guys?"

I mimed zipping my lips. "What did you want?" I wasn't letting him inside to pace around my apartment and talk about grant shit until I fell asleep. Plus, the bathtub must be nearly full now.

"Big meeting on Monday. You good?"

"Of course." I didn't have much of a schedule to check. "Text me that shit. I'm going to bed."

"Gotta rest that ass up, you big slut." Nathan grinned and gave another congratulatory thumbs-up. He waved and headed for his door as I shook my head and shut mine.

If fucking only. The chemistry between me and Big-Dick Bouncer hadn't been anything to brag about. Me and Ricky? Yeah, there was something there, but I wasn't sure what. Did Ricky want to throttle me or show off his manly cooking skills? Or fuck me?

One bubble bath and some much-needed solo time later, just as I was blissfully naked and crawling into bed, I got a text from Billy.

Brunch tomorrow!

I whimpered and typed a short, *OK*, before I plugged my phone in and put it on Do Not Disturb mode. I was about to get stung by the angry hornet called life again, and all I could do was sit there and wait for it to strike.

My one saving grace: after working late tonight, hopefully Ricky wouldn't be on an early shift the next day. I was already going to have to face Billy's interrogation on what had happened to my hand. No doubt someone at Friction had seen me sneaking off with the bouncer, too.

But Ricky would be off. Maybe I could keep a little bit of face egg-free.

4

RICKY

My phone went off way too fucking early in the morning.

I moaned as I rolled over, slamming the screen with a knuckle and pressing it to my face. "Yeah?"

"Hey, bud." It was Jared, sounding way too awake. Going to bed at a normal time did that to a person. "Goddamn, I'm sorry I woke you up…"

"This is overtime, isn't it," I sighed. I rubbed at my eyes and squinted at the clock. This was supposed to be my day off, and it was ten-thirty. "Let me guess… Troy can't make it in today."

"Got it in one." Jared didn't sound happy, and neither was I.

"What's his excuse this time?" I yawned and swung my legs out of bed, already getting ready on autopilot.

"A sick baby."

I coughed and choked on my snort, then grabbed a gulp of water from the bottle at my bedside table. "Baby as in boyfriend, right? Not small human?"

"Anyone's guess," Jared said drily.

"Where do you find 'em? The rest of the staff, who aren't perfect like me?"

"Some back alley, obviously. Even further down the barrel than you," Jared teased.

"Hey. I'm a prime barrel-aged fluid... like whiskey." My brain wasn't working well enough to make a better joke out of that.

"I don't wanna know how old your fluids are," Jared told me, and I burst out laughing. "Just wanna know if you can make it for eleven, man. If not, I can cover—"

"Nah," I told him. Jared sounded stressed despite his jokes, and I could help out, so why not? I grabbed a plain t-shirt and jeans. All my work clothes were a little ratty, because they didn't last long anyway, and nobody expected a greasy spoon cook to be wearing a tuxedo. "Be right there, old man."

"God bless you, punk. You're the cream at the top of the barrel."

"My cream is grade-A," I agreed and hung up before Jared could make a noise of shock or horror. I couldn't wait to see his face when I got in.

A quick mug of coffee and bowl of cereal later, I was back on my feet and ready for another day of work.

At least Jared hadn't found out about the incident with the drunk guy, Cedar, last night. And nobody in the world had found out about what I did in the shower later while thinking about him.

No sirree. That could stay firmly in the *not thinking about it* box on the shelf of *nuh uh, never.*

The morning was brisk, and my fingers tingled with the chill. Soon would come the first snowflakes, and then we'd be back to the long, bitter cold of east coast winters. I wished I'd grabbed gloves by the time I pushed my way through the front door of the diner and headed straight to the back.

I didn't quite get all the way there before a table in the corner caught my eye.

Fuck. There was Billy, along with…

Along with Cedar.

I nearly stopped dead on the spot. I hadn't expected him to be back in today, and he looked bright-eyed and bushy-tailed, too. Luckily, nobody at that table had spotted me, and they didn't really know me well anyway.

Those were the regulars—some of them friends with the owner, Jared, or his boyfriend, Shay. Hangers-on and friends gathered there for brunch most mornings, but there was a small core group.

I couldn't believe I hadn't noticed a cutie like Cedar before. But then, I didn't tend to see *who* I was cooking for, since I was stuck over the grill during my shift.

I couldn't resist a casual glance in his direction, and then I couldn't look away. He was smiling, laughing at something Billy said, and his teeth flashed as he tilted his head back. His Adam's apple bobbed. God, I just wanted to lick it.

"Hey." Jared strode up to me and clapped my shoulder. I nearly jumped out of my skin but played it cool, jerking my chin at him. Jared led me back to the kitchen. "Thanks so much for making it here, man."

"Sure. Sure, no problem." I gulped and tried not to look like I was fleeing.

I had nothing to worry about, right? I'd wanted Cedar to come back here. And now that I knew he was a regular… it wasn't my last chance to see him. Something deep in my chest liked that.

But I couldn't really apologize and check on him while the other guys were around. Plus, stuck over the grill during brunch rush, I wouldn't get the chance anyway.

Wait. There *was* something I could do.

I smiled at Jared and made small talk, teasing the old man and continuing our conversation from that morning—which quickly got raunchy—until he fucked off out of my kitchen.

I made sure I was set up with supplies, and changed the frying oil. I wasn't gonna let Madison throw me off my game today. If she came in, I wouldn't let her snide comments about *guys letting her down* get to me.

Work came fast and hard. Three tables arrived almost at once, and I found myself up to my elbows in batter. By the time I finished up all of their food, we'd settled into a steadier pace.

I peeked out of the kitchen to check on the table of regulars. A few of the hangover specials had been for them, including one for Cedar.

He hadn't been scared off from my cooking, then. I smiled to myself and grabbed an extra plate.

Next time Jess came back to the serving window, I flagged her down and leaned in through the opening, dodging the heat lamp before it scalded my cheek. "This is for the blond guy." I handed her a plate of crispy bacon. "Don't put it on the bill. I've got it."

Jess blinked at me a few times and looked around. "The blond girl at the counter? Someone got a crush? That looks like her boyfriend next to her, babe."

"No. The blond *guy*. Table twelve, sitting with Billy and, uh…" I squinted, cheeks flushing as I recognized Adam. I'd nearly hooked up with him once. Thank God it hadn't worked out. "Adam and the other regulars. Blond guy in the blue shirt," I emphasized again, firmly. "Don't tell him who sent it."

She followed my gaze and shrugged. "Ohhh. That blondie? You got it." She scooped up the plate and headed that way, and I ducked out of view. My heart raced as I found a position by the stove where I could lean back and duck down just a little and see Cedar's reaction.

God, I felt like I was passing notes in high school. *Do you like me: Y/N?* More like, *Will you sue me: Y/N?*

I heard the raised voices and laughter going on at their table, but it wasn't derisive. There was definitely teasing.

Then it went quiet for a bit before it picked up again. When I leaned back, luckily nobody was staring my direction.

The guys were looking around the restaurant, and Billy had his arm slung around Cedar's shoulder.

I tried to ignore the knot that twisted in my stomach. The guys were all affectionate with each other here. It meant nothing, least of all any kind of claim on him.

"Enrique?" That was Jess, waving her hand through the window to get my attention. "The waffles?"

"Shit." I had a job to do, and staring at him like a lovelorn teenager wasn't getting it done any faster. All of our tips relied on me, and I was letting them down. "Sorry."

I sprang into action, and I swear to God, I'd never been keener for the iron to beep its finishing tune. It was plated and ready to go before Jess was even back to scoop it up.

To keep myself from staring at Cedar and watching them play

guessing games about which customer might like Cedar enough to send him a complimentary plate of food, I wiped down the counters.

"Ricky?"

The soft voice from the kitchen doorway made me jump. "Jesus! Everyone's sneaking up on me today." I tossed the towel over my shoulder, trying not to spin toward the voice like I'd been waiting to hear it.

Cedar leaned in the doorway. Fuck, that blue button-down shirt brought out the warm brown of his eyes, and his smile sparkled. Those cheeks were dimpled. With his arms folded like this, I could tell he had some muscle on him, but not how much.

I badly wanted to know how much.

"Hi, Cedar." The name slipped out, and it felt perfect on my lips. Just as soft as his skin when I'd gripped his wrist yesterday, and just as warm as his body pressed up against me.

Fuck, what was getting into me?

"Thanks for the bacon. Much stiffer today. Have you been here all night? They don't have you chained to the stove, do they?"

I licked my lips and tried to ignore the shiver of desire at the idea of Cedar chaining me to anything. I didn't need another day of struggling to hold back a boner at work. "Uh. No, no, this is just overtime." It took me another second to regain my composure. Then I smirked. "And yeah, my meat always is. You were too drunk to know better."

Cedar snorted with amusement. "I oughta know a floppy bit of meat when I see it." The way his gaze flicked up and down my body told me everything I wanted to know about his sexuality.

I glanced behind him, catching sight of the table. Everyone was leaning around each other to watch—Billy had half-risen to his feet to stare, too. At my glare, they all pretended not to be, but I could see them sneaking glances anyway.

Right. There was still the minor issue of… well, *me*. If this were a girl, I'd already have her giggling and twirling her hair and ready to give me her number.

But the stakes were too high right now. I couldn't just flirt with him until fantasizing about my favorite actors stopped working and then drop him. I wanted… what, exactly? Cedar to keep coming back? Forgiveness?

And I didn't want to do it in front of everyone else, but I also felt like there was something too precious going on to let slip away. None of my Grindr attempts had ever held this umami.

"I… I'm glad you liked it." My voice came out croakier than I'd expected. "I don't want to leave anyone disappointed who walks out of here when the kitchen's mine."

Cedar slowly straightened up and dropped his arms to his sides. "Oh, I wasn't disappointed," he told me softly. "I've always liked my food here. Now I know who to thank for that."

The flash of redness on his hand as he moved his arms caught my eye, and I hissed through my teeth. Before I knew what I was doing, I moved toward him to take his hand.

"This okay?" I raised it for a look, turning his hand this way and that, our fingers hooked together like we were holding hands.

To my surprise, Cedar didn't push me back, or yank his hand away, or even tense up. He relaxed and opened his posture, facing me fully now as I raised his hand to my face—so, nearly to my lips.

If we were flirting, I would have kissed the burn to make it better. It was a weird moment when I realized what I was doing and how comfortable I felt. And how much I *wanted* to take it further. I wanted to flirt with him, and I didn't know how.

"It's feeling better," he murmured. "I've been rubbing burn cream on it."

"Good. I was gonna tell you to do that." I felt responsible for the whole damn thing—*was* responsible for it, really. I made the voices in my head shut up and raised his hand to my lips. I pressed my lips lightly against the pink skin before winking. "There. All better."

Cedar blushed and stuttered for a moment, then shook his head. "P-Perks of being a clumsy asshole: I've got a great first aid kit."

I cracked a smile, but I didn't like the disparaging tone in his voice. "We've all got our faults."

"What's yours?" His voice was soft and curious, like he genuinely wanted to know.

This wasn't supposed to happen, was it? Some random guy walking into my kitchen and sweeping me off my damn feet? But here I was, not myself, yet feeling myself more than I ever had. It felt like the air was sucked out of the room. How the fuck did I handle this?

I hadn't let go of Cedar's hand yet, and all I could focus on was the way his palm felt—rough and tough against mine, nails dirty and cracked. A working man, then, despite his nice clothing.

"Enrique? Order up," called Jess from the window, in a tone that clearly meant *I'm pretending not to see this but you're gonna spill the beans later.*

I winked at Cedar and let go of his hand. "Perfectionism."

Cedar snorted. "Classic interview tactic."

"If I'd known it was an interview, I would have dressed better." I sprang into action, grabbing the slip of paper from the window and slapping it above the stove.

"I think you're dressed fine." Cedar let that comment hang in the air for a few moments, and I could feel him looking me over, even if my eyes were on what I was doing. "Anyway, I'll let you get back to it."

"Cool, bro." It took every ounce of strength I had to play it cool and answer like this was some friendly chat.

I heard him chuckle quietly, and then he vanished from the doorway and suddenly I could focus again.

Jess cleared her throat meaningfully and leaned through the window.

"Oh, shut up," I told her, turning my face away to hide my blush. "And don't you *dare* tell Daisy, or Maddie, or…"

Jess chuckled quietly. "Those homophobic claptraps? Wouldn't dream of it."

"Whoa." I looked over at her, my jaw dropping.

"I'll tell you later." Jess turned to stride for the door and welcome another table, and I sighed. That was it for my downtime, probably.

At least this shift kept me busy so I couldn't moon over Cedar. I firmly did *not* let myself peek through the serving window again at Cedar, even when I heard raised, teasing voices greet him at the table.

God only knew what he'd told them all, and what would get back to me.

What the hell was I playing at? I had no idea, but I'd never met a good flame I didn't want to cook on. Even if I was both chef and meal, I couldn't step away.

5

CEDAR

Ricky didn't even look at me on my way out of the kitchen, but he hadn't been able to look anywhere *but* me not even thirty seconds earlier. That was the definition of hot and cold.

The sudden frost didn't fool me, though. Together with his behavior last night, I knew this much about him: for some reason, he didn't like others watching us flirt. I had to resist the urge to glare at the cockblocking waitress as I headed back to the table.

For a second, I let myself hope that conversation had moved on without me. Reality, of course, said *no way*. Everyone was rapt with fascination and clearly just waiting for me to return. Had they been watching?

My hands shook, so I stuffed them in my pockets and then recoiled, trying to ignore the pain that seared through my system. By the time I'd learned not to let my hand brush anything, I'd be healed.

Like walking into the lion's den, I took my seat at the booth again. They barely waited for my ass to hit the seat before launching into the interrogation.

"Okay, tell us now: was that his way of asking you out?" Teasing laughter from everyone followed Kev's question.

"Oh my God. Did Enrique hit on you?" Billy gasped. "I thought he was straight!"

"Was it him that sent the bacon, anyway?" Adam wanted to know. I'd only told them I thought I might know who it was. They'd inferred it must be him. "Or someone else?"

Even Charlie joined in: "Do you know him?"

I groaned, but I couldn't deny that a small part of me enjoyed the questions. Since the breakup with Nathan, I hadn't really been the center of attention for my love life. Even during our relationship, everyone had carefully avoided comment. Now I knew they'd thought he wasn't right for me, but I hadn't wanted to hear it, so they hadn't tried to get it through my thick skull.

Well, I was determined to listen to their opinion of a future beau this time. Wisdom of herds. Maybe it could keep me from making another mistake quite that epic.

"I dunno, what do you guys think?" I asked in return when I could finally get a word in edgewise. I shrugged. "All I know is he sent the bacon. I ate here last night and it wasn't very good. He wanted to make up for it."

"Oh." Billy looked disappointed at the lack of gossip, and I tried to hide my smile. I wasn't gonna lie, but I also wasn't gonna rush to fill in the rest of the details. "Well, that's not at all exciting."

"He's straight?" I asked, glancing around at them all. That was the much more important bit of information, because either my eyes and dick were deluding me or... or he was closeted, and that could turn into a mess real fast.

It wasn't like this was an unsafe place to work if you were straight.

I suspected Ricky was the only supposedly straight guy around here. He'd be welcomed with open arms. But whatever was going on in his family or personal life to keep him there? That was a lot harder to dodge.

Already, I wanted to know the guy's story. There wasn't a doubt in my mind he'd been hitting on me. I could still see those dark eyes looking into mine as he raised my hand to his lips and brushed his lips along the skin. Gentle, not rough.

And he'd rushed forward to take my hand like he hadn't been able to stop himself. I'd just let him grab my hand, too. God, if any guy tried that at a club, they'd get an elbow in the ribs.

"Straight? As far as I know," Kev hummed. "I can find out." The guy had once been an escort, and even now he kept tabs on most of the gays in the neighborhood. If he didn't know someone, he still had connections he could leverage to find out. "I'm sure word's gotten out if not."

Adam was staring at his coffee mug like he was hoping not to be picked on in class.

I raised my eyebrows as soon as I noticed this, but I let him get away with it. Maybe his new boyfriend didn't know about some history between them, after all. That face sure said *history*.

"We could ask Jared or Shay," suggested Billy. "If anyone knows, it's them. I'll make some enquiries." As much as I told him there was no need, he wouldn't be dissuaded. "Darling, even if you're not curious, *we* need to know now. And I'll tell you, sending you extra bacon is more than Nathan ever did for you."

I grimaced at how true that was, but shook my head. Because at the same time, it wasn't at all. "How about his dad paying my rent?" I pointed out. I wasn't just careful not to talk smack about him because we were still friends and it was a small community, or because it wasn't a nice thing to do. And it wasn't even my usual skilled conflict avoidance kicking in.

No, I needed Nathan, and they all knew it as much as me.

Billy sighed and raised his hands in a silent gesture of surrender while Charlie put his arm around my shoulders for a moment.

"Doesn't mean you can't find a cuter boy to smooch," Kev informed me with a grin. "Even if it's not Enrique."

"Enrique," I echoed in a murmur. Everyone here seemed to call him that, but he'd introduced himself to me as Ricky. The wave of laughter that followed the word took me aback, and I blushed as I looked around. "What?"

Kev made popping sounds with his tongue and waved his fingers around my face. "Every time you say his name, little hearts pop up around your face like that. I think you want one specific boy, don't you? And his name starts with E… and ends with nrique."

I leaned away from him and smacked his shoulder, but I was laughing as hard as I was blushing. He was too fucking right, so I couldn't argue. I *did* sound like I was writing our names together with a heart around them. "I don't do straight boys."

"Mmmmmhmm." Billy couldn't have sounded more dubious. "Nobody does until a straight boy bats his pretty little lashes. And then it's *well, just this once…*"

"No," I insisted, sticking out my tongue at him. I didn't care if it was juvenile. "I'm not gonna end up in a sticky situa—"

I couldn't even finish the word without another burst of laughter from everyone.

"Oh my God. You're all a bunch of pervs," I told them, my cheeks burning.

"Come on. If he wanted to get sticky with you, you can't tell me you wouldn't tap that," Billy told me, craning his neck to try to see into the kitchen again. "He's hot." Everyone else nodded, and I felt weirdly defensive that anyone else had even noticed.

Fuck. I had no right to be jealous. But the fact that I was anyway told me that I needed to do something more than just hover in the doorway of his kitchen letting him feel up my arms.

The delicate bit of the situation was figuring out how to do so without everyone's eyes on him. If he was straight, or bi-curious, or just figuring it out… well, he didn't need that kind of scrutiny.

"You've noticed he's hot." Billy leaned in, a wicked grin on his lips now.

The ground could open up and swallow me any time now, please. "I… haven't *not* noticed." I sure remembered the painfully pleasurable sparks that had flashed through me when he pressed his lips against the burn.

Adam was still weirdly quiet throughout this whole conversation. Kev had noticed, too. He looked over at him and elbowed him, making a *you okay?* face. Adam just nodded and sipped his coffee, but Kev gave him an extra side-eye.

I wanted to know what the hell that was about, too. "What?" I asked him. "You think I've got a chance?"

"I think… you might," Adam told me. There was something he wasn't saying, and it was driving me crazy. Had they slept together? Did I care? I could do one degree of separation, right?

"If anyone knows, it's him," Kev agreed, grinning at me. "Mr. *Straight until the right roommate moves in.* Maybe you just need to move in with Enrique, huh?"

We all shared a laugh at Adam's expense as he flipped us off, and I was glad the heat was off me.

Billy moved on to talking about the latest goings-on at Friction while I pretended to pay attention. In reality, I had a lot more on my mind—like how I could get some more attention from Ricky —or Enrique, whatever he went by here.

I was half-considering downloading Grindr just to check the vicinity for Ricky-like profiles, but no way could I pull out my phone and do it right now without them all noticing.

This was going to be a project, wasn't it? Oh, well. It was nearly winter. I could use one.

I managed to wait until I was the last one remaining, and it was no small miracle that nobody noticed what I was doing.

The little bacon incident seemed to have been forgotten by everyone by the time it was two o'clock and they were all heading off to take care of errands, get to work, or spend time with their boyfriends being all gross and coupley.

Not that I would have minded being gross and coupley.

Even when Jared and Shay came in, nobody remembered to ask them about Ricky's sexuality, and I didn't even risk looking back at the kitchen once. No need to remind them. As far as they were concerned, it was all a joke, and as far as I was concerned, they could keep thinking that.

I was serious about finding out, though.

"Hey," I flagged down Jared on the way by. "I wanted to talk to you about that charity event sometime."

"Hey, Cedar! Right!" Jared dropped into the booth opposite me and gave me a big smile. "Breakfast with drag queens?"

"Yeah!" I was surprised he'd remembered, since I'd brought it up before the summer started. Everything had gotten out of hand over the summer, as usual, but now that it was fall I had a chance to get back to it.

I could use up fresh local produce, show people how to cook with it, and raise funds for a couple charities at once. Neil ran a local LGBT hotline, and he was a pretty cool guy. He always needed more funding, and he was happy to partner up to promote this kind of event.

We could probably even get a small grant for the event, or use it to show the impact of our actions. Drag queens got tips and more exposure to audiences who already loved them. And customers got a tasty breakfast and entertainment.

Pretty much everyone won, and those were the solutions I liked best.

We just needed a spot to host it, and where better than here? I hadn't brought it up with Nathan yet, but we each pursued our own projects pretty freely. He wouldn't have a problem with it.

"I've been thinking about that," Jared told me. "Saturday morning or Sunday morning? I think we can let you take over the restaurant." I stifled my gasp. Those had to be their high-income days. Jared just smiled at me and ignored my shock. "Wanna come by tomorrow after the brunch rush? We can iron out the details."

"Wow. Thank you. My main concern is costs," I admitted. "Our budget is tiny right now."

"We'll figure it out," Jared promised. "We'll make sure everyone wins here. My customers love having a show with brunch. I've got some buddies I can hit up in the drag scene. And I can ask the staff to help. A lot of us are gay here—well, as you know," he laughed.

"Enrique?" I hoped it came out innocently. "I mean, of all the cooks here... his bacon is the best. It'd be cool to have him on board." I resisted the urge to giggle. *No stiff meat puns in front of his boss, Cedar.*

Jared shook his head. "Straight, but he's always been a good guy. He'll say yes if I ask. He does have a knack with a frying pan. He's working tomorrow morning; we'll pull him into the discussion."

"Great." I reached out to shake hands, my back straightening. I didn't need to wait around for Nathan to schmooze with grants organizations. I could raise funds myself, my own way. Nathan was gonna love this plan. "Mind if I talk to Enrique about it first?"

"Go ahead." Jared still seemed to suspect nothing as he waved toward the kitchen. "It's slow again right now."

I waved and saluted as I left cash on the table to cover the bill and headed back to the kitchen. My heart raced as I even approached the kitchen. It still felt like our little secret that I'd been back here just last night.

And apparently, I couldn't stay away.

"Hey," I greeted when I saw Ricky lean on the counter and wipe his forehead with his sleeve as he grabbed a drink of water.

Ricky sputtered and turned to me, then looked at the clock. "You still here? Are *you* being chained to a table?" He grinned at me, and that grin made my knees just melt.

I leaned in the doorway, fanning myself. Sure was hot back here. "I waited for everyone else to leave," I admitted with a sheepish smile. God, he was pretty even when he was sweaty and grease-streaked.

I wanted to see him pour that water bottle over his head and shake the droplets off. Shit. Maybe I *was* crushing on him. That was an oddly specific image, and now I couldn't seem to banish it from my head.

"Why?"

"I wanted to talk to you again," I admitted, and then drew a breath. "And ask for your number."

"It'd be easier to look me up on Grindr," Ricky countered, grinning.

I made a face. "I don't have Grindr."

Ricky blinked a few times at me. "I thought… everyone did." It wasn't the same way someone like Kev might say it. There was a hint of uncertainty there, like he wasn't quite sure what he was saying was true.

"Nope. Some of us want the hot, no-strings-attached sex, but not the *what u doin*," I imitated the text speak in my sleaziest voice.

"Where do you find that, then?"

"Next door, if I'm lucky." I drew a breath. Now was my chance. "Here, if I'm luckier." Ricky blinked a few times at me as I kept my eyes locked with his, making it completely clear what I meant. "And I'm pretty sure you owe me some help." I turned my right hand to face him. "It hurts to bend my fingers, you know."

After he stared at me, a grin finally flashed across Ricky's face and stayed there. "Well, you can have my number."

Yes! I resisted the urge to pump my fist in the air as he approached. By the time I handed over my phone, he was standing *right there* in my personal bubble where he had last night.

And this time, instead of looming over and glaring at me, he was playing with me, swaying in toward me until our knees brushed and then stepping back.

As Ricky gave the phone back with his digits in it, he brushed his fingers along my hand again. "You sure you're okay?"

I'd do anything for that touch again. I raised my hand a little, but he didn't reach out to take my hand like he had earlier. "Yeah." I affected a grimace. "Hurts a little, you know, but... I got used to it in culinary school."

"That's right," Ricky murmured and then flashed me a smile. "You're a tough cookie. I didn't expect that."

"You like it?" I murmured, pocketing my phone.

Ricky hadn't stepped back yet. "I do." His gaze flickered between my eyes and then dropped to my lips for a few long moments before he dragged it back up to meet my eyes.

I wanted to kiss him so fucking badly. He was right there. But... not here, where all his coworkers might see.

Ricky abruptly stepped back when I heard footfalls behind me, approaching the kitchen. "Text me," he told me casually and winked. "I'd better get back to work."

"And I do have to go home eventually," I added with a laugh. "There's a charity thing I was wondering about if you could help, but that's cool. We'll wait. We'll talk later, huh?" I waved and turned, nearly bumping into Jared on the way past. "Thanks, man!" I added, but I didn't slow down to wish Jared goodbye.

I needed to get out of there before I turned around and grabbed Ricky by the cheeks and hauled him in for a bruising kiss.

It had been so fucking long since I'd felt this kind of *want* burning through every inch of my body. It was a tidal wave that was sweeping me away from my senses, making me want to do stupid things.

I didn't want to wait another minute, but damn it, Ricky was at work for probably hours more. And I had to finish putting the garden beds to winter on our south-facing site. But if this was what chemistry felt like, holy shit... I was gonna text him first thing tonight.

But first, I had to tidy up my apartment, get the plants contained to one corner of the place... and maybe move my bed against the wall. Not that I was deliberately getting back at Nathan for keeping me awake with his conquests, but if I *happened* to, I wouldn't complain.

It felt like I was getting in way over my head, but I hadn't been excited about anything in so long that I'd almost forgotten what it felt like.

What could go wrong?

6

CEDAR

"We can't keep going unless we get a miracle grant, Cee. And unless you got one to pull out of your ass..."

Since listening was not what I wanted to do, I focused on what information my other senses were feeding me. The scent of earth and the delicate roots I could feel in my hands, even through my gardening gloves, grounded me.

Nathan had never been easy to get along with. He was even less so now that he was my ex. We'd continued to run Plant for the Future because we worked together so well, but it took a lot of tongue-swallowing on my part.

"No. You're the grants expert," I conceded. I was the hands-on guy, and Nathan took care of the fancy stuff. For a charity and personalities like ours, it just made sense to divide tasks like this.

"I am." Nathan crouched by me and handed over a watering can. "And I say we've gotta prioritize the healthy eating angle. You know the public health sector loves that shit. We'll be rolling in grant money. And I have another idea."

At least at this time of year, I didn't have to worry about snapping off stems by gardening while I was distracted. My hands had never been great at doing what I told them to do when I wasn't watching closely.

Nathan's argument didn't sound quite right to me, but I didn't know enough to challenge him. Besides, Nathan's dad still funded our little project by paying the rent on not one, but *two* studios in the same crappy building. He hadn't wanted his precious son being stuck living with me if things went south.

Almost like he'd had the foresight I hadn't. It had blindsided me, and now I found myself stuck. Having my boyfriend as my neighbor had been great, but having my ex as my neighbor was awful.

Plant for the Future—a much less creative name than we'd first thought it was, over a bottle of bargain basement wine—was still as directionless as it had been for the last two months. Sure, we had a few projects on the go: a couple rooftop gardens, slices of volunteers' backyards, one community garden in the center of a square of cramped housing, and a boxcar on an old building site.

We just hadn't figured out how to best sell our goals to get other people to give us money. So we hobbled along with some online donations, a couple grants, and Nathan's daddy's money to fund most of our personal expenses.

"What's the idea?"

"You won't like it. First, the public health angle. You in? We'll be rolling in cash, my man."

I sighed, pushing my gloves off my hands after I patted the earth into place in the bed I'd been turning over for winter. Selling plants at backyard flea markets was one of our best income streams, which said a lot about urban hipsters and our grant funding.

With the autumn nearly over, the outdoor growing season's bounty was done. I was about to be limited to a few cold frames and greenhouses, plus the indoor space in both of our apartments, to grow houseplants.

I winced at the sensation of the glove sliding over burned flesh. Even though I cradled one hand in the other, Nathan didn't seem to notice, which was no surprise.

"Fine," I told him. It wasn't worth the argument with him—it never was. "What else are you suggesting?"

Nathan smiled like he always did when he got his way. "Great."

All I had to do was tune him out and daydream of Ricky. Wasn't like I was gonna argue against his ideas, anyway. Plus, I was too busy hauling compost to the repurposed locked salt bins at the end of the garden. With this day's work done, the beds would be ready for next spring.

"If we work with the HOA, they'll even help us out and give us some of their community land…"

I snorted. Knowing them, they meant a patch of solid clay in a shitty beer bottle-filled corner of the neighborhood, which would only get vandalized and filled with old tires and broken car seats. I'd come back to a spot only to find ripped-out plants and barren beds once too often.

"No more new sites," I reminded him. "Not without help."

"Well, we might lose the hotel rooftop anyway. You'll have time then."

I pressed my lips together. He was right. Was it really worth the argument? "Make the offer," I finally gave in. "If they accept, we'll figure it out."

We couldn't really afford to buy plants on our already slim operating capital, but I could make do with seeds. Maybe trade a promise of produce for fresh plants. I was good at keeping people blossoming. It was just what Nathan needed, because he tended to tromp all over my carefully-tended relationships with people.

Nathan actually making concessions and trying to meet halfway was rare enough that I didn't want to discourage him. It wasn't worth the thrill of victory in another argument with him. I didn't often taste that thrill, really, but I didn't mind. Life was about more than scoring points on a scorecard, right?

"Fab." He kissed my cheek on the way by and strode to the entrance of the garden, tapping at his phone. By the time I'd joined him, he pocketed his phone. "Done."

That seemed like a suspiciously fast email, but I let it go. Of course he knew I'd give way if push came to shove. He'd pre-drafted it.

I swallowed back my indignation again. I was nowhere near the doormat he thought of me as, but I had no other options—yet. Until I figured out an exit route, I wasn't dumb enough to burn my bridges.

"You wanna do something for dinner tonight?"

My phone went off and I grabbed it so fast I almost dropped it in the garden bed. I'd texted this morning to ask if Ricky wanted to come over for dinner, and I almost hadn't expected a response.

Yes! It was a message from Ricky. *I'd love to! I'll bring the wine?*

"Nope," I told Nathan, popping the "p" as I grinned at him. "I've got plans."

"Who with?" Nathan chased me almost all the way to the end of the garden. "Is it the guy you hooked up with? Is that a thing now?"

He didn't even sound pissed off about it. A jealous ex was nothing to laugh about—Nathan could get scary when he was jealous. But he sounded like a puppy, eager to know everything. Kind of like he *wanted* me to move on to some other guy.

"No, it's not," I told him with a sigh. Why was I even telling him anything? Damn it, what was going on between Ricky and I was strictly between us.

"Ooooooho. Check him out," Nathan crowed. "Before you know it, you'll be joining in my parties."

I didn't ask too many questions about them. Frankly, I didn't want to know. If he showed up at my door in wildly different moods, he was high on life, I'd told myself. "Riiiight. No thanks."

"Is he hot? Of course he's hot, you like hot guys. Short? Tall? Gimme details, man."

I rolled my eyes at him. "If we didn't work together, this would be weird."

"If it were weird, we wouldn't work together," Nathan countered.

He had a point. I sighed and shook my head. "Look. No details until I know how it's working out. And *don't* try and sneak peeks at him, or I'll take him out to… I dunno, Manhattan. Somewhere far away from you spying."

"Fine. No spying," Nathan promised with a sigh. "Just show up for the meeting."

"Duh," I snorted as I tapped out my response to Ricky. Like I was gonna get distracted and spend my weekend fucking him. Actually, I'd love that, but I had to not fuck up this evening first.

My chances weren't great. After all, I was... well, *me*. This could only end in disaster.

7

———

RICKY

The moment I finished up work, I grabbed my jacket, patted down my pocket, and pulled out my phone. There—exactly what I was looking for. Among the screen of notifications, there was a message from a new number.

I waved a distracted goodbye to everyone still at the diner and shouldered my way out through the door, swiping to unlock my phone and read the message.

Hi, this is Cedar. Since you've cooked for me a few times now, want to come over for supper tonight?

My heart leapt into my throat as I pocketed my phone and waited to cross the street. I already knew what I wanted to say: *Yes!*

But if I went over to his house and had supper, I might have to have sex with him, and… so far, every time I'd tried, I'd run off like a scaredy-cat. Then again, I'd never felt so drawn to someone I met on that hellhole of an app.

Once I was on the other side of the street, my mind was made up. Why the hell wouldn't I accept? I'd wanted to spend more time with Cedar for some reason I didn't fully understand yet, and here was my chance.

Cedar and his beautiful, big, brown eyes. And his blond hair that made me want to ruffle it. And his soft voice that so contrasted the iron-solid resistance he'd met me with that first night.

And his poor, burned hand because *my* ego had gotten out of control. And his poor dick if he couldn't jack off for a few weeks…

Yeah, at the very least, I owed him one.

I'd love to! I'll bring the wine? I responded, carefully reviewing my text to make sure there were no typos before I sent it. I could grab a cheap bottle on my way over.

That's kind of you, thanks! Does 6 work?

I made a face. That was pretty early for me, but at least we'd have more time in the evening together before he kicked me out.

Or not.

I wasn't sure which prospect worried me more.

OK, see you at 6. Send me your address! I answered, my breathing quick and pulse shallow as I pocketed my phone again. My palms were even sweating.

It was no big deal. I'd had tons of these kinds of dates with girls. Well, not tons. Mostly I took them out to eat—nobody wanted to show off their apartment on the first date unless they were looking for sex.

Was he looking for sex?

"Oh, my God, Ricky," I mumbled, rubbing my forehead as I nearly stepped into the street against a red light. "Get it together."

How was I supposed to dress for this, anyway? Too formal and I'd look like an idiot. Too casual and I'd look disrespectful.

I decided I'd treat it like a casual date restaurant vibe.

As soon as I got into my crappy little apartment above the thrift store, I stripped down and jumped in the shower. The water sometimes ran hot and cold and there was mold I'd been studiously ignoring creeping up the caulking, but at least the pressure was good.

I scrubbed my hair and body with my usual minty soap, going over everything twice to make sure that scent of grease that clung to me was completely gone. I was usually blind to the scent, but others noticed, and by the time I hopped out of the shower, my nose had acclimatized to fresh mint.

I could faintly smell the grease on my clothes as soon as I picked them up, so I wrinkled my nose and dropped them back on the floor as I went to find fresh, clean, *nice* clothes.

That left me with a short-sleeved button-down. Too cold for winter. I threw a cardigan over top and nodded at myself. That plus dark jeans would look nice.

"Hot stuff," I told myself, pointing at myself in the mirror as I clicked my tongue and winked.

After a couple hours in front of the TV mentally rehearsing my best pickup lines, I was ready to go.

The weekend after Thanksgiving, the air was growing chillier as winter approached. As I walked to the address Cedar had texted me, I kept my hands tucked into my pockets. My mom had adopted Thanksgiving instantly, though our food was never like the standard American feast. She'd always put on a feast, but the last few years had been quieter—especially since Dad died.

When a dingy gray apartment building came within sight and the address matched, my heart leapt back into my throat and suddenly all I cared about was making the right impression.

I couldn't have made a worse first impression, so why the hell was he inviting me over for supper now? He must really be having trouble getting himself off with that hand.

Get in, flirt over supper, do the job, get out.

I gave myself handjobs all the time. I could do that for him. No sweat. Right?

I climbed the stairs slowly since I was a couple minutes early, drawing out the time until I reached the second floor and pulled open the shabby hallway door.

The hallway was dark, and I shivered. When I reached number five, I knocked on the door and gulped, brushing myself off and folding my hands tightly behind my back.

For all I'd joked earlier, it *did* feel like a job interview.

Or maybe like I was interviewing for a porno. I stifled my giggle as Cedar pulled the door open, and instead managed a grin and a little wave. "Hi."

"Hi." Cedar waved back in a little motion close to his shoulder.

It was exactly as awkward as I'd expected, so I stepped inside and half-hugged him, hoping the physical closeness would make it feel less stiff and formal.

He felt good against me. I breathed in and noticed that citrus smell again. Definitely aftershave, because his cheek was baby-soft and smooth against mine as he pulled away from the hug.

"Hi. Great to see you."

I offered the bottle of wine. "I thought I might have to use this as a weapon if I met anyone in the staircase."

Cedar burst out laughing, and that grin looked great on him. He shook his head and thanked me as he took it, turning over the label. "Chardonnay. Great choice."

"You would have said that if I brought anything, wouldn't you?" I teased.

Cedar chuckled again and nodded. "I'd never turn up my nose at free wine. But this will go well with risotto."

"Oooh." I was instantly impressed, yet wary. Risotto was hard to get right, and a lot of people fucked it up in a creative variety of ways, even in our culinary classes. Still, this guy had been in culinary school himself, so maybe he'd picked up tricks. "What kind?"

"You'll have to wait and see," Cedar teased. "Mainly because if it doesn't work, I have store-bought."

It was my turn to burst out laughing. I followed Cedar to the kitchen—which was only a few steps away, since this was a Brooklyn-sized apartment. "I hope it works."

Cedar stirred the pot and gestured for me to have a seat at a cute little bistro table that was jammed into an alcove of plants.

"Oh, wow." I stopped to admire the lush greenery. A few of them were flowering, but even without flowers, it looked picture-perfect. Especially with purple paper napkins folded and tucked under crisp white plates, and wine glasses already set out. He'd even lit a candle on the table.

This might be the most mature dinner date I'd ever had, and I was back to being nervous. Definitely a date, not a just-friends thing.

I licked my lips and took a seat. "Let me know if I can help."

"You cook all day," Cedar said with a smile and a shake of his head. "It's my turn to… uh, hopefully wow you for the right reasons."

"You put up with my floppy meat," I said with a grin.

I could have sworn he murmured, "I hope it won't be." When he winked roguishly at me, I must have gone beet-red, because he laughed a moment later. "Sorry. That was inappropriate for a first date."

Okay. Definitely a first date. I stifled the squeak before it could emerge and casually folded my hands on my knees instead. I'd never had a girl over for dinner myself, so I was operating pretty blind here.

I found myself watching eagerly as he brought over bowls of risotto, carefully plated with sprinkles of herbs across them. "You're good," I complimented with a grin.

As soon as he put the plates down, I spotted his hands shaking. By the time he jerked his hands back, my hand was already halfway to his wine glass, and I caught it easily and set it upright again.

"Shit," Cedar muttered, shaking his hands and glaring at them before he flopped into the seat opposite me with something less than grace. "Damn it. Sorry."

"It's fine," I shrugged and grinned. "Didn't start on the wine early, huh?"

That was the wrong thing to say. Cedar frowned at his plate for a moment, but before I could apologize, he looked up at me and smiled. "Nah. I'm just nervous about you being here."

"O-Oh." And I was off to the blushing races again. Judging by the heat in my cheeks, I beat him to the blush, but he wasn't far behind. We locked eyes for a few long moments before I scrambled to my feet. "Wine!"

"Right! Yes."

There was a definite nervous tension between us while I poured wine, like both of us were eager to make a good impression. Cedar was more eager, though; as soon as I sat down, he asked questions about my job and where I lived and what I liked to do, and at least that gave us a starting point for our conversation.

The risotto was actually good, too—not too soft, not too firm, and filled with veggies that gave it pops of texture and flavor. I'd always thought there was something extra-attractive about a woman who could cook; as it turned out, it was the cooking skill I'd been attracted to. From the first forkful, now that I knew he really could cook, I could barely keep my hands off him.

When I turned the questions back on him, I found out that he worked at an urban gardening charity, whatever that meant, and his family wasn't far away, just north of the city. From the sounds of it, he spent most of his time with plants and not people.

It kind of surprised me, and I felt bad about it. For a good-looking guy with such a twink vibe, I'd half-expected him to be hanging around the scene all the time. But not everyone was like that—I sure wasn't.

"And that's why I was looking for your help, actually. Cooking for the charity event."

"Sure." I shrugged. I liked to give back when I could, and contributing my skills felt better than handing cash to Madison and watching her walk off with it. Honestly, it was a little flattering—and a lot relieving—that he'd thought of me after the limp bacon incident.

"But you went to culinary school?" I pressed as I set my fork in the empty bowl. Clumsiness alone didn't seem like a good reason to drop out. Everyone called themselves clumsy. "God, that was really good. Only for a semester?"

Cedar frowned and nodded, looking down again. "Fucking hands. I've—I've got a condition. I've always been a little uncoordinated. My doctors were worried I'd cut a finger off one day, and you can't graduate to being the person who cooks the food without being the person who preps the ingredients."

"Oh, shit." I hadn't really thought of that. Everyone was just expected to be *able* to learn the process from the ground up. Knowing how to get a good cut of meat or highlight a vegetable's flavor was part of the next stage, but you were supposed to be able to demonstrate it, too.

Every exam in school had been a literal trial by fire, and though I'd passed, I'd never had much sympathy for those who didn't. Or maybe I'd had a little too much, and I'd squashed down my own fears about joining those who got kicked out of the program.

"Yeah, so," Cedar said with a shrug and a little smile at me. "I admire people who can do it."

"I really shouldn't have challenged you last night, man." I couldn't express enough how awful I felt for doing it, especially knowing that I was rubbing in his face something that was clearly painful for him. "God, I'm a dick sometimes."

Cedar grinned. "Be that as it may, I'm the one who took you up on it."

"I like that you called my bluff," I confessed, watching as he took his glass and stood up.

There didn't seem to be a sofa or living room in this tiny place, but the bed in the corner was made up as one with cushions piled all around the edge of it. Sure enough, he moved over to it, so I picked up my glass and followed.

"You did?" Now that I was watching it, I noticed that Cedar cradled his glass by his chest for extra support.

"Yeah." I settled down next to him, pulling my legs up beside myself. We were almost touching, but not quite. The last few inches of space between us somehow felt bigger than any chasm, because of what it would mean if I did take the leap. "I like someone who's as strong-willed as me."

"I'm not sure I'm that guy." Cedar smiled at his glass and then looked up at me. "I don't know what got into me that night. Well, I remember what got into me, I just didn't enjoy it that much. So I was pissed off at him, and my ex, and myself, I guess."

My gaze sharpened and I caught my breath. "Nobody hurt you, did they?" I wanted to pull him into my arms, or else break the face of anyone who took advantage of him. The protective instinct was so much stronger than I'd anticipated.

"No, no." Cedar reached between us to tangle our fingers lightly and smiled at me. "I just wasn't that into the guy that night. It was *okay*. But then when I stood up next to you…" he trailed off.

He didn't have to tell me. I'd felt the sexual chemistry simmering between us, like we were either gonna shout at each other or fuck each other silly. It had made my mind spin, and even now, it was having the same effect.

It was either the proximity or the wine. I tipped back my glass and leaned over to put it on the table next to us. I tried to convince myself that this was the moment I'd been aiming for—where I could make someone feel good.

But I was so fucking scared of getting it wrong, and I couldn't figure out how to express my reservations in words.

The banging on the front door made me lurch to my feet. "Shit!"

Thank God I'd already finished my glass—but Cedar wasn't so lucky. Wine went all over his pants.

"Oh, fucking—fuck off!" Cedar raised his voice to yell at the front door. "I'm busy all night!"

"All right, all right. Text me," shouted back someone in the hallway, and then a door slammed.

I stayed halfway on my feet, not sure if I was supposed to make a run for it or sit down or what.

"Sorry," Cedar groaned. "My neighbor's a dick with boundary issues. He can't imagine I might be *busy* doing something that doesn't involve *him*."

At least there wasn't a jealous ex—or worse, current boyfriend. I let out my breath and laughed, then groaned as I patted his thigh. "You wanna change out of those?"

Cedar blushed and squirmed to his feet. "Yeah, I kind of do." His glance strayed to the dresser and clothes rack in the corner, and then he looked back at me with a mischievous smile. "If you don't mind."

I hadn't meant he should change *in front of me*, but there was nowhere else in the apartment aside from awkwardly going into the bathroom, and I was planning to see him naked soon anyway, so changing his pants surely wasn't a big deal…

I just dumbly nodded as I watched him. Still standing in front of me, he unbuttoned his jeans and unzipped them, then pushed them down slowly, peeling them off his thighs.

By the time he stepped out of them, my dick was hard as a rock. I tried to casually cover it with a hand, but the boner was unmistakable.

Apparently, I *really* liked seeing a guy strip in front of me. And now he was just in boxer briefs, so tight that they left little to the imagination. I could see the outline of his cock, and… I might not have a lot of practice at it, but I'd judge that it was stirring to life.

"I like your legs." I raised my hand from my dick to my mouth to cover it a moment later, realizing how fucking dumb that sounded.

But Cedar just grinned and sat next to me, taking my other hand and resting it on his thigh. It was hairy and firm and warm under my palm, and I found myself rubbing my palm in a slow circle over his thigh.

Should I go down toward his knee or up to his…

Okay, he was definitely getting hard. I didn't mean for it to, but my hand went still as I stared.

"This okay?"

Cedar's voice brought me back, and I yanked my hand away quickly, rubbing my neck and adjusting myself. "Yep, yeah. This is good. Of course. I mean, I'm fine. You're hot. That's hard to handle. I need oven gloves."

Fuck, my lips could zip themselves ASAP, please.

Cedar's hand rested on my shoulder, and then he kissed me, which cut my desperate ramble off.

The kiss was good. *Really* good. His lips were perfectly smooth and soft and warm, and instinct alone made me push forward and kiss him back. I was making out with him now, and I wanted so much more of it.

Instantly, I found myself wondering how he'd react if I sucked on the tip of his tongue, or bit his lip, or drilled him into the bed while he whimpered into my mouth…

Whoa. The thought turned me on so much I could barely stand it.

"I want…"

"Mmhmm?"

I drew a breath and choked back the thoughts of what I wanted. I didn't have nearly enough experience—any at all—to know what to do with a dick that wasn't mine.

What if I fucked it up again? And hurt him? I could bite his dick, or chafe it, or hurt him if I fucked him too hard, or… there were a hundred possibilities, and my brain was screaming at me that they were all likely to happen immediately.

Or worse, what if we fucked and I liked it, and I wanted more? And I ended up dating him and I had to tell Mom she was never getting grandkids from me? I was gonna hurt someone somehow if I kept experimenting like this, and Cedar was the most likely victim.

I stood up before I knew it. "I want to take it slow." I tilted my chin up at him and smirked. "I'm not as cheap as a bottle of wine and a meal. Even if it is a damn good meal."

"Oh." Cedar's cheeks flushed, and I instantly felt bad for making him feel bad. "Sorry, I'll get some pants on again, and—"

"No, no. I should be getting home. Sorry. Early shift tomorrow."

"Right. Cool." Cedar shifted from one foot to the other as he stood up and trailed after me to the door. "Thank you for coming over, though. It was—I had a really nice time."

He sounded confused, and I didn't blame him. I would be, in his shoes. I was running away instead of fixing any of my problems, and now he was gonna think I was a stuck-up, cockteasing prick. Or worse, a scaredy-cat.

"No, thank you," I told him. "It *was* a great meal. Almost as good as mine," I winked.

Cedar rolled his eyes but cracked a smile. "And no floppy meat here."

My gaze flickered down to the hard line in his underwear, and I was keenly aware of the pressure in my own pants. No, there sure wasn't.

A moment later, he seemed to realize the innuendo in the moment and he blushed, hooking his thumb awkwardly into his underwear waistband like he could cover himself up with his hand.

"I'll… see you around?"

"Yeah," I managed. If I hugged him, I was only gonna kiss him, and if I kissed him, I was gonna press my body against his and run my hands down to that cute little ass, and…

We'd be back in that bed in three seconds flat.

I gulped another quick breath and waved as I took off down the hall to the sound of my own footsteps and my thoughts bouncing around my head like an echo chamber, magnifying with every step.

You're an asshole, and he deserves better. This is better for everyone. If you can't do him right, don't do him at all.

So why did my brain scream with every step for me to turn around and throw myself at his forgiveness one more time?

It was as though I'd left something of mine behind at his place… like the fragile hope that I might *one day* be good for something, or someone.

8

____

CEDAR

I spent about eight hours feeling like an asshole before I woke the fuck up—along with my alarm clock—to a revelation.

"He's scared." The words were the first out of my mouth, like my subconscious had been trying to impart them to me in my sleep.

I hadn't been horribly misreading Ricky at all. It *had* been a date, and it *had* been going well.

And then I'd gotten naked, and he'd approved of that idea at first... before I saw some thought process kick in behind those sweet, dark eyes of his, and he shut down and ran away.

He'd grinned about not being that easy, but Ricky struck me as the kind of guy who needed an excuse so he didn't show weakness.

I ought to spend today running errands and getting the house clean. But I'd scrubbed this place yesterday, before the date, so...

I could spend all day mooning after him, or I could go after him and see what was going on. I already knew he was going to be at Bubbles, and that Jared wanted to rope him in to help with the event.

Hopefully Ricky was still up for it—the event *and* me.

My stomach churned with nerves. I was so damn awkward that I wouldn't blame him if he wanted to hold out for someone more… well, suave. Not a guy who spent half his time handling manure or plucking broken beer bottles out of the dirt. Not really glamorous stuff.

Then again, he hadn't seemed turned off when I talked to him about the charity yesterday.

All I could do was go meet Jared and keep my fingers crossed that Ricky didn't give me the cold shoulder.

I'd felt a connection last night—I knew it. For once in my life, I was determined to hang onto a good thing.

After a morning watering the plants and taking inventory of what I could sell at next weekend's thrift market, I changed into one of my nicest shirts—plain cream, with thin brown vertical stripes. It made me look taller, and I needed all the help I could get.

Spiking my hair with gel didn't take long. I never could stand a fussy hairstyle. No time for that when every day was full of practical stuff to worry about.

Okay, I looked as pretty as I was ever going to. It was time to see what these eyelashes could do for me.

"I love the idea. I think you can raise a couple hundred bucks from a raffle, easy. I'll ask the waitresses and see who wants to work that day," Jared told me. "The queens will be happy to pitch in, too."

I'd just had a great, crisp bacon sandwich, Jared wanted to help with the fundraiser, and Ricky was on board to cook. Everything was coming up roses. So why wouldn't Ricky look at me?

"What do you think?" I asked Ricky, leaning back in the booth and folding my arms.

Under his boss's scrutiny, Ricky loosened up and looked up from the table. He looked at Jared more than me, though.

God, those eyes were pretty. *Focus, Cedar*, I told myself. I was here on business, not pleasure. Okay, maybe a sneaky bit of pleasure, but that didn't seem to be what he was after today.

"I think it'll go great." Ricky was near the end of his shift, so Jared had sent his coworker in to take over his kitchen early. Was that why he was in a mood? He'd been looking at the kitchen for the last twenty minutes, more than either of us.

Surely he didn't *want* to work in the kitchen when he could be here planning events, just to prove that he was the best in there... or did he? I was never gonna be able to get in his head and figure him out.

"Thanks for the eloquent opinion," Jared teased Ricky.

"Welcome, old man." Ricky tipped him a wink and a nod. "Can I head home? All that overtime's left me kinda tired out."

"Sure thing. Growing boys need their rest," Jared retorted.

Ricky flipped him off and slid out of the booth. "I'll cook for it," he promised me. For the first time all meeting, he made direct eye contact with me, and the moment that jolted between us was... fucking electrifying.

Exactly like it had been last night, when I'd been kissing him and his hand had crawled up my thigh.

Before he froze and ran like a frightened rabbit, anyway.

"Good," was all I managed. After a second, my brain switched on. "I mean, thanks. Thanks, man." I blushed.

"Welcome." Ricky turned and headed for the kitchen, grabbing his jacket.

Well, no need for me to stick around here then. I had a guy to intercept. "Thanks for your time, Jared." I shook hands with the diner owner and grabbed my notes, bundling everything up into my pockets as I made for the door.

I was going to lay an ambush.

I didn't have long to wait. All I had to do was lean by the brick wall next to the diner, just out of sight of the windows at the front. When Ricky stepped out into the chilly air, he looked around as if expecting to see someone he knew.

Like me.

"Hey." I stepped forward and then held my palms out when he leapt backward. "Whoa. Sorry!"

"You make a habit of ambushing strangers?"

That stung. We weren't strangers, were we? He'd been to my house. At the very least, we were on our way to becoming friends —or so I'd thought. "Um…"

Whatever Ricky saw on my face made his expression crumple. He stepped toward me now, his hand resting on my arm. "Or only your friends?" He jerked his chin at me and gave me a cocky little smile, like he'd been planning to say that all along.

I let out my breath and rolled my eyes at him. "Only the guys I really, *really* wanna kiss."

A few seconds passed as Ricky's jaw dropped and he stared at me. He didn't look offended or weirded out, or even turned on. He just looked… surprised. Finally, just when I was worrying that he'd been replaced by a robot whose programming had failed, he snapped back to life. "Look, why don't we talk about this in…" he looked around. "The thrift store?"

It was my turn to stare at him, blinking a few times. "If… you want? I mean, whatever floats your boat."

Ricky clapped me on the shoulder and led me at a brisk pace to the thrift store. It was just quick enough to make me feel like I was being smuggled away from Bubbles and Friction—and everyone who knew him.

It made my gut twist. Was I going to be the secret in his life? How long could I endure that? Did I even want to get involved?

Feeling like a secret made me feel dirty, and despite all the time I spent in the dirt, it wasn't a feeling I was used to. It wasn't the comfortable kind of hard-work-induced dirt that lived under my nails from April to September.

It was sneaking down staircases in the morning because the boy I was dating didn't want anyone to know that *he* was dating a "crippled trade school dropout." I'd overheard his dad call me that once as I hid in the bathroom of their fancy mansion the first time I visited.

To give him credit, Nathan had told his dad not to call me that, but not another word about it had passed between them. Ah, Nathan. Still fucking with my head even months after our breakup. *Give this guy a chance,* I reminded myself. Comparing Ricky to my ex would lead nowhere good.

"Okay," Ricky breathed out when we were inside. He looked around and then crooked his finger, leading me to the back corner of the store where the really tall clothing racks blocked the view from the door.

Now I was positive I was being hidden, and my patience was wearing thin. My voice was sharp as I asked, "What's this about?"

"Privacy," Ricky muttered. "Trust me. You don't want some of the people I know getting on your case."

I wasn't sure why anyone would be angry at me for talking to him, but I had an idea. It all made sense now, and it wasn't that I was a horribly awkward, lame date who'd forgotten how to kiss a guy.

It was all Ricky.

"You're closeted."

Ricky flinched and folded his arms, inching closer to the racks like he wanted to disappear in the folds of the fabric. "And if I am?"

I was surprised that I didn't feel more disappointed. I mean, dating straight guys was out of the question. I'd been out since high school; I didn't have time for that shit. It was always one of my lines in the sand. But apparently the tide had come in, because all I had to do was step towards him and put my hand on his arm and…

Line? What line? It had been washed away by the force of whatever built between us whenever we touched.

I felt compelled to step closer, to touch him, like a physical connection between us could bypass the limitations of my words. Language could only go so far, and I'd never been so afraid of saying the wrong thing and shattering this delicate moment.

"Look," I murmured, running my hand up his arm toward his shoulder. Although he tensed up, he also breathed out, like he couldn't decide whether to be nervous or like it. "I've never dated someone in the closet. But you're into me, aren't you? I don't care if you're bi, or gay and in denial, or... I don't know... I just don't care. I wanna get to know you."

Ricky hesitated for a few long moments before he stepped away from the rack again, and right into my personal space. That intense expression on his face turned me on every damn time— like he was taking a risk just standing in front of me.

And for him, he probably was. He was challenging his own sense of order in the world, and maybe his friends or family. Even Jared had told me Ricky was straight. Why was he hiding it from him, of all people?

"I liked the date last night," Ricky admitted. His voice was slow and hesitant. He reached up to cover my hand with his own warm palm, rubbing his thumb along mine. "I liked your cooking, and talking, and..."

I grinned when he trailed off and went a funny shade of pink. "And getting my pants off." Ricky swatted my hand and I tried not to laugh at him. I rubbed my other hand across my chin instead, smoothing away my smile as I kept a hold of him.

"Okay, fine." Ricky tossed his head like a straight guy never would.

Someone had picked up body language from being in Bubbles, around all of us. Or maybe he was giving himself permission to let loose.

"I liked that a lot, and... uh..." Ricky trailed off, stepping closer. He lowered his voice almost to a mumble. "And..." he broke off again, huffing slightly like he was trying to figure out what to say.

I leaned in, my hand gliding around to the back of his neck. It felt strangely like I was pulling him in for a kiss. His breath was hot on my neck, and I wanted to melt in his arms. Let him drag me into this clothing rack, or over to the sink in the kitchen, or any flat surface in my apartment.

My heart was thumping. I tried to figure out what he was going to say before he could say it. Was he about to ask me out again? Or tell some deep, moving story about why he'd gotten scared off? Nobody had hurt him, had they?

Footsteps behind me came around the corner.

Ricky half-screeched and jumped backward. He stumbled, tripping over the lower bar of the rack and grabbing a handful of hangers to keep his balance.

I couldn't grab his arm in time to keep him from faceplanting into a row of dresses, my hands bouncing ineffectively off him a couple times before the stupid things got a hold of him. At least I grabbed enough of his weight that he didn't tear half a dozen dresses at once.

I snuck a peek behind myself at the college kid who'd just walked around the corner. She was pretending to be glued to her phone, but her shoulders shook in silent laughter, so it didn't really preserve our dignity.

Ricky kept his face in the dresses for a second before following my gaze and looking at the woman who had scared the shit out of him.

I just barely heard him mumble, "Fuck." He let out a quick huff of breath and straightened up, rubbing his face against the fabric of the closest dress like he was deliberately clutching them all to his face. "Yeah. That's definitely silk. Nice. But I don't see anything here my, uh, my mom would like. Let's go."

He grabbed me by the hand and towed me away, letting go as soon as we approached the door of the thrift shop. It took almost all my willpower not to burst out laughing at the incredibly smooth coverup.

"Go where?" I managed, my voice strained. I had the feeling that if

I made fun of him now, he'd only make a break for it. He'd been on the edge of something, after all, and I didn't want to shatter that mood.

"My place." Ricky cast me an indecipherable look, that vulnerability from a moment ago gone. "It's more private, and… nearby. And I think we have unfinished business from last night."

Well, if he was blowing hot and cold, this was a straight-up tropical wind. And I was dying to know what he'd been about to say.

"Let's go."

9

RICKY

Apparently I wasn't the world's biggest asshole.

For some unfathomable reason, Cedar not only wanted to talk to me, but he wanted to follow me home so we could continue our conversation away from the risk of... well, running into people I knew.

"I live here," I told him, stepping out of the thrift store and turning to the door right next to it to unlock it.

Cedar blinked at me a few times, but he didn't ask any questions. "Cool," was all he said, shoving his hands in his pockets, wincing, and waiting casually behind for me to unlock the door.

"Hold on." My heart thudded as I bent over to grab the mail from the ground, keenly aware of the view that gave him of my ass. And a part of me... kind of liked it. I looked over my shoulder as I fumbled to scrape a pizza leaflet off the ground, hoping he was enjoying the show.

Oh, yeah. Cedar was checking my ass out. He was even tilting his head, one hand on the doorway, the other hovering dangerously close to my ass. He glanced up and met my eyes with an unapologetic smirk.

"I was gonna smack that ass, but I didn't think I knew you well enough yet. I want to respect your personal space."

I didn't know how to tell him that I didn't want him to respect any kind of personal space. I wanted him crowded up against me, just where we'd left off last night. I swallowed hard, crunching a junk flyer in my hand as I led the way upstairs. "That's… nice of you."

"I know. Self-control, right?" Cedar fanned himself and shut the door after himself. "Oh, it's dark in here." The hallway light had burned out ages ago. I usually raced up the stairs before the door could swing shut behind me, but I knew the staircase well enough now to do it in the dark on the way down.

"Grab onto me if you're—" I burst out laughing when Cedar cupped my ass. "Yeah, you could do that."

"Well, if you're inviting me."

Cedar hooked a finger through my belt loop, his footsteps clunking up the stairs behind me. I could feel the cold breeze down the back of my pants. More lights on and he could get an even better view of my ass.

I juggled my mail under the other arm to take my phone out, and a moment later, turned on the flashlight pointing down at the steps. "Just a couple more."

Cedar didn't let go, even at the top of the stairs. Only once we were inside the crappy—but surprisingly spacious—apartment did he let his finger slide out of my belt loop. "Good thing I had my guiding light… globes."

I snorted with laughter and dropped my keys on the table by the door, then gestured around. "This is it."

No studio apartment in Brooklyn that real people my age could afford was ever impressive. Even Cedar's was a little sketchy outside, even if the plants made it look way homier than my place.

Cedar didn't judge. He just cast one look around and smiled at me. "Cool." He seemed much more interested in staying close to me.

Right. We were alone together, in my apartment.

I couldn't just run away if I didn't like something. I should have felt cornered, but I didn't. Instead, I felt somehow safe in my own space. *My* turf. Maybe that was what had possessed me in the kitchen—that was my turf, too.

"Are you all right?" Cedar asked. "You looked pretty startled back there."

I sighed and shook my head, heat rising in my cheeks. "I'm sorry. Thought she was… someone else." Did I really wanna admit I'd thought my ex-girlfriend was about to bust me for being gay? Just because I was hanging out in a bunch of clothing racks, my hands wrapped around another man's shoulders?

No, I did not. That could go without saying.

One more glance around and Cedar found the couch. He headed for it and collapsed, then winced.

"Sorry." I winced, too. "I should have warned you. The springs are kind of…"

"Springy." Cedar ran a hand along the underside of his balls and flashed his palm. "It's okay. No blood."

I laughed. "Only one of them pokes through, and it's on the other end. Water?"

"Gah!" Cedar shuffled closer to me. "No, thank you. I mean, yes to the water. No to the impromptu Prince Albert piercing."

"Oh!" I cringed as I grabbed water glasses. "You had to take us there."

"I took us there." Cedar was laughing, but he sounded a little nervous now. These first few minutes of being in a new romantic interest's apartment were always awkward, in my experience. At least that much was the same when it was a guy.

I came back with water and set the glasses on the coffee table, then sat next to him. Avoiding the spring gave me a convenient excuse to... well, get in his space and stretch my arm along the back of the couch, behind him. "So, uh..."

"What were you going to say back there?" Cedar burst out with, looking over at me. Those bright eyes were so earnestly curious, and it was frankly adorable.

I smiled at him, resisting the urge to wrap my arm around his shoulders just yet. It was hard to think past the sudden shock of thinking Maddie was going to tear into me—and worse, Cedar. He looked too sensitive for one of her bad moods. I didn't want my mistakes to ruin anyone else's days.

Least of all, Cedar. I liked him.

Oh. That was what I'd been about to say.

"Um..." There was no way around it. I drew a breath and looked at him. "I liked our date a lot. But when it went further..." I trailed off, embarrassment making my toes curl. I grabbed my water glass to give me something else to look at.

"You want to slow down?" Cedar asked softly.

"No! No." I wasn't gonna chicken out of this. "I'm just not, uh... I mean, I'm sure I can make it up as I go along. I can give you a good time. How different can it be?" God, how much I hoped that was true. I didn't want him to come into Bubbles and laugh at me every day if it didn't work out.

Cedar sat up straighter and I could see it click in his expression. Wonder in his voice, he surmised, "You've never been with a man before."

I groaned and rolled my head back. "Yes." I pretended to pour the water over my own head. "Is it hot in here, or am I just waiting for the floor to swallow me up?"

Cedar laughed and plucked the glass out of my hand. When I looked at him, he cupped my cheek with his hand.

Oh.

That felt nice. The warm pressure of a man's hand against my face, and the firm grip he put on my chin a moment later when I tried to look away…

I could do this. I could look at him and listen to whatever he had to say. My heart might be racing, but there was nothing unpleasant about this. Quite the opposite—it felt like I was on the edge of a cliff, but I wanted to take the step.

I wanted to *so* badly.

"We can pick up where we left off," Cedar said softly.

My arm slid off the back of the couch to rest along his shoulders, and he smiled as if encouraging me. "Yeah." Oh, that was a little croaky. I swallowed and tried again, louder. "Yeah. I'd like that."

Cedar fit so nicely under my arm, and fit even better when he slid closer, his hand coming to rest on my thigh. All I had to do was hold him as he ran his hand down my thigh to my knee, and then up to my chest—carefully bypassing my crotch, which was good, because I was getting hard with lightning speed.

Despite how damn unsure I was that I could be any good, and how eager I was to prove that I *could* be good, and how surprised I was that Cedar even wanted to give me another chance…

I was also excited. Almost out of my mind with excitement. Was this the day I'd finally have a guy under me, his arms and legs wrapped around me? Oh, God, I hoped so.

"Kiss me," Cedar whispered.

There was something I knew how to do. I set aside all the fears in my head and pulled him in for a hard kiss.

Our lips met with nothing of the soft exploration we'd tried before. This time, it was a passionate spark that had been waiting a day to ignite. And ignite it did, until I found myself biting his lower lip, sucking the tip of his tongue, pushing him back against the couch.

Cedar nearly smacked me in the face as he tried to grab my shoulders. I laughed and dodged the black eye, then helped him lie along the couch—head facing toward the good end, of course.

"Sorry," he whimpered.

I just grinned at him. "Keeping me on my toes, huh?"

The embarrassment shifted to relief, and Cedar smiled up at me. "Toes or knees. Either works."

"Oh!" I grinned. I shifted until I straddled him, jamming one knee in the gap between the couch cushions and the back of the couch. The other foot pressed against the floor, which wasn't great for comfort, but gave me great leverage. I'd made love on this couch before, and I knew what kind of angle and force I could get in this position. Hence the broken spring.

We were still fully-clothed, though. That was a problem.

Before I could pull back, Cedar slid his arms around my lower back and pulled me down against him. "Come here."

I obeyed, finding myself awkwardly propped up on an elbow a moment later, but my lips were just inches away now. It was strangely intimate as he leaned up, his lips just begging to be kissed.

How could I ignore that? I kissed him until his lips were swollen and he was panting, open-mouthed, whimpering every time I ran my tongue along his lip.

It took all I had to ignore the fact that Cedar was as hard as me, but eventually, I couldn't keep my hands to myself. I ran my hand between our bodies, my palm up toward me, and I felt his bulge against the back of my hand at the same time as my own.

Oh, that pressure was good. I rocked my hips forward, which pushed my hand down against him, too.

"Yes," Cedar whispered. "Do you want to touch me?"

Did I want to feel up the hot guy who was sprawled across my couch, rocking into my hand and moaning into my mouth with every kiss we shared? "Duh!" I grinned down at him.

Cedar laughed. "Points for enthusiasm." But there was a shy tone in his voice, like he wasn't quite used to being admired. Which made no sense, because he was fucking gorgeous.

I tilted my head and put that in the figure-out-later category. I was way too busy with things like getting us naked. If I was gonna pop my gay cherry now, that was the first step.

And it was further than I'd managed to get with any guy. Shirtless was about all I'd managed, all three times I'd tried on Grindr.

His shirt came off first, and then I fought mine off and tossed it out of the way. Now to ditch our pants.

"Whoa." Before I could unbutton my jeans, he put a hand over mine and smiled up at me. "Take your time. We've got all day, right?"

I swallowed hard. I wasn't used to taking my time in any area of life. When I saw an opportunity, I leapt on it—metaphorically or not. "Right," I agreed nonetheless. "But you want me, right?"

"I want to have fun with you," Cedar told me, looping his arms around my shoulders and scratching my back lightly. "That doesn't automatically mean dicks in butts."

"Oh." Foreplay, then. That was the *I like you, but not that much* option.

Cedar saw the expression on my face and laughed. "You don't have to look like a wilting flower, you know. There's a lot of ways to have fun when you've got two dicks to play with."

Okay, he had my attention again. I tilted my head. "I won't find out about those until we get these out of the way, though."

"I see what you're doing there." Cedar grinned at me. "But fine. Get us naked if you'd rather."

Oh, wow. Now that he'd put it out there, *out loud*, it hit me what I was doing.

First time getting naked with another guy. And this time, I was *not* going to flee.

"If you're nervous—" Cedar started, his voice soft, but I shook my head and cut him off.

"Nah. It's just new. Doesn't mean it's bad." I shed my pants as fast as I could, wanting to get it over with. I left on my underwear for now, which didn't give me much privacy. My cock was straining against the fabric, and I was hungry for touch.

That hunger was going to get me through this. *You and me, little buddy,* I thought, rubbing myself gently. *We're gonna find out what the big deal's about.*

Cedar unzipped his jeans and pushed them down, but with me straddling them, he needed my help to get them off. It took a fight with his feet before I managed to fling them aside.

"Hah! Take that."

Cedar dissolved into laughter. "Sorry. I don't usually wear skinny jeans, but…"

With the jeans gone, I turned around again, settling over him where I'd been a minute ago. "But?"

He looked a little embarrassed but gave me a sly smile. "I was hoping you'd like them."

With Cedar's warm body between my thighs, it was hard to focus on anything else. "Sneaky," I chastised him. "I didn't even know you were coming back today." Or else I might not have run away yesterday.

"I hope it wasn't… too much." Cedar gazed up at me. "I don't want to push."

He was so accommodating—a far cry from the way he'd introduced himself, all grit and quiet determination. I hadn't expected that side of him, but it showed in his little mannerisms. Maybe that had been the unusual moment for him, then.

"I need to be pushed sometimes," I told him and ran my hands up his thighs, over his hips, and up his sides.

"Mmm—ooh!" He squirmed as I reached his ribs, and I grinned at him. "Oh, no!"

"Oh, yes." I tickled under his armpits and Cedar gasped, squealed, and nearly bucked me off. That was some surprising strength he had. I had to grab the back of the couch to hold on. "Okay, no," I laughed.

It suddenly occurred to me that I didn't know the last time I'd laughed while getting naked with someone. But I wasn't grimly focused and half-terrified of the inevitable difficulties facing me. No, I was still half-hard, shifting my weight this way and that just to feel him under me.

"Tickle the pickle, not the pits." Cedar waggled his brows at me, and I laughed again.

I'd thought I would be more nervous, but Cedar was making it all easy—and *fun*. This felt fucking great. Why the hell had I waited so long?

The way I'd had to shift my weight had lined our cocks up against one another through our underwear. I snapped back to attention, my breath catching in my throat at the heat that crawled along my skin until my nails dug into the back of the couch.

Cedar stretched out along the couch again and rested his hands on my hips. He pulled against me slightly, encouraging me to move.

I leaned forward, bracing myself on my elbows again so I could grind our bodies together.

Instinct kicked in. The rapidly hardening bulge I was grinding on felt amazing against me, and judging by the moans falling from Cedar's lips, he felt the same.

"Yeah, Ricky," Cedar whispered. "That's it."

I thrust against him, my heart thumping with excitement. "I don't wanna give us friction burn."

"Then get us naked," Cedar told me with a grin. "Let precum do the job."

I was about to feel another man's dick against mine, and I couldn't move fast enough to strip my underwear off.

Cedar laughed, but it wasn't mean-spirited. It never was when he laughed at me. He just seemed to be taking pleasure in how much I was enjoying myself.

It made me relax, and it made the part of my brain that got defensive and competitive just shut off. Instead, I could focus on both of us and how I could make us feel good.

I took a little longer to work Cedar's underwear down, enjoying the sight of his cock just slightly obscured by the thin material. When I finally eased him free of the fabric and pushed them down to his knees, he took over and kicked them off.

Okay, now I was naked with another guy and it was fucking fantastic.

"You good?" Cedar asked, his hand running up from my thigh to my chest. He rubbed gently, then looped his arms around my shoulders again. It was a gently possessive move—enough to indicate that he wanted me, but not that he was stifling me.

I was still free to go if I wanted to, but I wanted nothing less.

"So good," I whispered, letting my hard length bump and brush his.

Cedar's mouth dropped open as he squirmed. "Oh!"

I grinned. It took a little work to get us lined up right without using my hands to keep everything steady, but it was a pleasurable kind of work. Every time the head of my cock slid across his own ridge, both of us shivered with pleasure.

This might not be sex, but it was pretty damn good anyway. I dropped my weight onto him to help keep us lined up just right, trapping our cocks between our stomachs as we ground together slowly.

When I worked my hand between us and grabbed both cocks, it was impossible to hide my grin. "This is awesome."

Cedar's laugh was light and musical again. "Isn't it?" He beamed up at me. "Oh, *yeah!*"

With his encouragement, I ran my hand along both of our shafts at once, and then tightened my grip and thrust into my fist.

Cedar did the same, choosing an alternating pace that quickly settled into a rhythm with mine.

Holy shit, I could probably come just like this. The usual pressure was gone—the fear that I wasn't gonna keep it up, which inevitably led to the reality.

"You're so hot," Cedar panted. He raised his hand to my cheek and cupped it. "Kiss me?" He sounded uncertain, like he wasn't sure I wanted it.

Of course I did. I leaned down, catching his lips with mine and sliding them together slowly. I hoped I could show him with a kiss exactly how much I wanted him despite all the bullshit in my brain.

The chemistry between us had started out explosive, but it was settling into something gentler—something that didn't make me want to run. The fear that I wasn't going to be good enough was gone now.

Cedar didn't seem to mind taking it slowly as I learned my way around sex with a guy. Did that mean he wanted to do this again already? Work our way up to sex?

"I want you," I whispered, glancing down at his pretty, swollen shaft and then meeting his gaze. How better to show it than… well, treating him?

Before he could form an answer, I shifted my hand until it was wrapped around him alone. I jerked slowly at first, testing different pressures and speeds to find what made him moan the loudest.

It was almost hypnotic to watch him squeezing his eyes shut, my name spilling from his lips along with a combination of swear words and senseless moans.

Cedar bit his lip hard, and then mumbled, "Mm'gonna come."

"Good," I breathed out. I pressed closer to him, kissing along his jaw and behind his ear. The more foreplay I tried, the more I found myself loving it.

Fuck, I liked it as much as—more than—I'd ever enjoyed sex before.

A whole new damn world was opening up, and it started here, by making Cedar feel an ounce of the pleasure I did right now. It was turning me on so damn much to watch his reactions to my hand.

If he was this sensitive even to my hand, what about my mouth? Or toys? Or me, deep inside him? Did he like it hard and fast, or slow and gentle? I wanted to try it all.

"Yes!" Cedar gasped, like he was reading my thoughts. "Don't stop!"

"Never," I whispered. If I'd known what this was like last night… well, we both would have missed work today.

He came in a hard, fast jet of passion and then several more, crying out so fucking beautifully. I couldn't tear my gaze away from his face. It was enchanting to watch him completely lose control, all at my hand.

Cedar mumbled, "Oooof. Wow." He peeked through his lashes at me and then offered a shy smile. "Good?"

"I—that was—it was—" I stuttered. "I just—I had no idea…"

"That was the first time you did *anything* with a guy?" Cedar whispered.

"Yeah." I gulped. Was it that obvious? "Was I… okay?" I couldn't pretend not to care about the answer.

Cedar's smile was real, and so beautifully sincere. "Yeah. You were wonderful. You're a natural. Do you want a turn?"

"Well, I… if you want." In truth, I could barely contain my excitement. I was already on the edge, my cock throbbing with need.

Cedar saw through my attempt at coolness and grinned. "Sit up and enjoy." He grabbed my hip with one hand and wrapped the other around my shaft, gently running from base to tip.

Having another guy touch me wasn't just not-weird, it was a total thrill. He knew how to handle a hard cock, gently and quickly tightening his grip as he sensed how damn close I was.

"Did it turn you on?" Cedar whispered, twisting his wrist with each upstroke. "Watching me?"

With pleasure tightening my muscles and tingling through my fingers and toes, it was impossible to hide the truth, even if I'd wanted to.

My thighs shook as I grabbed the back of the couch with one hand and the side with the other. "Yes," I confessed, rolling my head back. "Makes me wanna do everything with you, or to you, or for you…"

"I want you to come on me," Cedar whispered. "I'm gonna make you. Is that okay?"

"*Fuck*, yeah." I wasn't a lunatic who'd make him stop now. I needed release, and I wanted it to be at his hand, right here and now. Getting to add my mess to the streaks already coating his stomach and chest? Perfect.

And it made me feel weirdly possessive, like I was claiming him as mine.

Which made me realize I *wanted* to claim him as mine.

And that was a thought I could save for later.

Because… I was about to come.

All. Over. Cedar.

"Fuck!" My body bucked and arched as I threw my head back. The orgasm hit me harder than any quick jerk-off session in the shower as my body tightened from head to toe and then shuddered uncontrollably.

I cracked my eyes open and gasped. I was used to closing my eyes to try to maintain the fantasy, but the sight was even hotter than any I could conjure up. Watching my own cum shoot across his pretty, smooth skin just blew my mind until words just failed me.

All I thought was, *I want this, with him, again.* I might not know a lot about myself, but I knew that in my very bones.

When I finally gasped and relaxed, Cedar slowed his strokes and then gently rubbed his thumb along my length to clean me up. He wiped his hand on his stomach and giggled. "I think I'll need a shower."

"Shit. Mine kinda sucks," I told him. "But you can if you want?"

Cedar hummed and took my hands before I could scramble up off him. "Kiss me first and tell me how that was."

I relaxed and grinned at him, leaning over him to peck his lips a few times. "That was…" I pecked his lips again. "Fucking awesome."

Cedar laughed and tangled his hand in the back of my hair, meeting my lips for one nice, long, slow kiss.

It was good. It relaxed me and brought me down from the orgasmic high without the guilt-fueled crash I was used to experiencing after watching gay porn.

This was nothing like those experiences. It felt tender, and loving, and addictively intimate.

"Okay," he whispered, smiling a smile that was just for me. "Now we shower."

And maybe—just maybe—I could persuade him to stick around for round two. Or had he gotten what he wanted already?

I O

CEDAR

Ricky was right—the shower *was* shitty. It alternated between streams of hot and cold water, but never seemed to actually produce a mix of the two.

Typical for a Brooklyn apartment, though. At least he was giving me a chance to clean up, and he even set out a washcloth and towel for me on the counter before telling me he was going to make coffee.

I wasn't imagining his excitement, right? He'd sounded eager when he asked me what my favorite kind of coffee was and rushed off to make it.

"Brr," I mumbled, stepping out of the shower and instantly regretting it. Heating was also a little lacking in this place. We'd been too hot and sweaty earlier to notice, but now I sure did. I quickly wrapped myself in the towel and scrubbed myself dry.

"Coffee's almost ready!" called Ricky from outside the bathroom door.

I grinned, wrapping the towel around my waist and tucking the end in, then pulling open the door. "Perfect."

Ricky jumped. "Oh! So are you." He'd gotten dressed while I was in the shower, but he left his shirt off—a touch that I appreciated.

Oh, I definitely wasn't imagining the way his eye wandered down my body, taking in my damp, bare chest, and the bulge at my groin where the towel pulled tight across my barely-soft cock.

That had been some pretty great sex, I had to admit. A million times better than Mr. Right Now on Friday night. I was so hooked on Ricky already. What had gotten into me? Not even his dick—yet.

"Uhh." Ricky jolted to life again, his cheeks flushing as he waved up and down me. "That's a—that's good. A good sight."

Some guys said it was their first time before they bent over and took six inches without lube. Ricky, though? It was easy to believe that it was his first time. He was jumpy but excited, and whenever he wasn't trying to play it cool, overeager.

I remembered my own early explorations well, and it made me smile to see Ricky going through that with me.

"You're tongue-tied again?" I teased. "Haven't gotten it out of your system?"

"Well, we could always have real sex."

I liked that he was eager, but there was a little warning flag there. I eyed him sternly and headed for the couch, grabbing my clothes and sidling into them again. It was too cold to laze around naked. "Real sex?"

"Um..." Ricky followed halfway and then lingered between the kitchen and living room, leaning awkwardly against the half-wall there. "You know. Dicks in butts, like you said."

"I don't think sex is just…" I formed a circle with my thumb and forefinger and jabbed my other index finger through it. "I dunno. Some guys do," *Nathan*, "but that's never been me."

"Well, what else can it be?" Ricky sounded almost like he was challenging me, but I didn't rise to the bait.

I suspected he had a whole lot of insecurity about being so inexperienced. So the trick was to get at him sideways, without raising his defenses.

"Anything designed to turn each other on."

"What?" Ricky sounded genuinely dumbfounded for a moment. "But you have to get off."

Oh, he was so sweet and naive, but he would hate to hear me say that. "What about when guys can't get it up?"

"Then they're failures." Ricky muttered under his breath, "Or fags. Same difference, some say," as he turned to grab coffee mugs.

I nearly tripped, grabbing the couch to steady myself. My hand landed where I meant it to, luckily. The word hit me like a punch to the gut, but I sensed Ricky wasn't throwing it out there to hurt me.

I hadn't asked about his relationships, but I was going to have to now. "Before I take offense, I'm gonna ask you to clarify that." I tried to stay polite, yet firm, and pushed back against my instinct to smooth things over and let him say whatever he wanted.

I'd done that too many times with Nathan, and now I was trapped in this bizarre, semi-dependent relationship with him. Never again.

I followed Ricky to the kitchen.

"Oh, there's that little spitfire." Ricky grinned at me, but he wouldn't look my way. He was making a big deal of pouring the coffee, but that wouldn't work forever.

I just leaned on the counter and waited.

Finally, Ricky sighed and slid one mug toward me, wrapping his hands around the other and turning his back to the counter to lean on it, next to me. "I've always known what was wrong with me. I just didn't want to admit it."

I bristled again but swallowed it. What he was saying had more to do with him than it did with me. "Wrong?"

"You know what I mean," Ricky scoffed, bringing his mug to his nose to inhale deeply. His shoulders fell a little when he breathed out again, and I gave him a few moments to calm down and think. I didn't want to push him.

Finally, Ricky turned slowly toward me, leaning sideways now. He was still looking down, but this was an improvement.

"I'm sorry. I don't want to imply that... that being gay is wrong. I just felt like it was."

I half-smiled and ran my arm up his side, taking note of Ricky's reaction. He breathed in sharply, but he didn't pull away or fold his arms or withdraw. "I know," I told him. "A lot of my friends did."

"But not you?"

I shook my head and shrugged. "My parents were fine with it. It was almost cool to be gay in school—not always, but enough of us thought it was cool that I got through. Maybe it's cause I'm twenty-two? But I never had a big, painful moment."

Ricky let out a long breath. "I'm jealous," he admitted. "And I'm twenty-four. I guess it's just about having the right family, and... I dunno. Schools? Friends? Luck?"

"Yeah?"

Ricky took my hand and I raised it, letting him press his palm against mine and run his fingers along the front and back of my hand. It gave him something to do besides sip his coffee. Every touch of our skin made me crave more. I wanted to cuddle him while he talked, but I could see how that might just scare him off, too.

"I've only ever dated girls. I tried to hook up on Grindr, but I got scared and ran away," he admitted with a short chuckle. Finally, he looked up at me, and I suddenly couldn't look away. "You were different."

I ran my hand up his arm and rested it on his shoulder, then walked my fingers to the back of his neck to play with his hair. "How?"

"I don't know. I was pissed off on Friday night. Madison—my last ex-girlfriend, I dumped her six months ago—was bugging me. I felt like shit. Then you came along, just so… self-assured. It drove me nuts, but I kind of liked it," he admitted with a laugh.

He touched my arm and then pulled my hand away from him. Before I could feel hurt, I realized that he was looking at the burn, his expression creasing with a guilty frown.

"It's okay." I smiled at him and set down my coffee mug, taking both of his hands in mine and swaying lightly, side to side. "I'm used to being a clumsy idiot."

"You're not an idiot." Ricky spoke with utter confidence that blew me away. "And maybe you're a little clumsy, but who isn't? It doesn't mean you're an idiot."

Now it was my turn to blush, and I couldn't quite look at him. "You wanna sit down?"

"Or come to bed with me?" Ricky counter-offered, gesturing towards the corner. A screen separated part of the room, and I'd guessed he had a bed back there.

"Yeah." I clutched my coffee close as I walked over, relieved to find a windowsill behind the bed that I could put it down on. Guaranteed I'd spill coffee in his bed otherwise. I was very conscious of Ricky behind me, but he didn't make any comments about my gait.

Once I'd scooted on and arranged pillows behind me to recline at a comfortable angle, Ricky joined me. He seemed a little awkward at first as he shuffled closer to me, and I laughed and looped my arms around him to pull him in.

"Oof," Ricky complained as he ended up with his head on my chest, but I didn't let him go.

I just gently stroked his hair. "Good?"

The tension drained out of Ricky's body when he stopped resisting and closed his eyes, turning his head so his cheek pressed against the middle of my chest. "Mmhmm."

This felt perfect. I hadn't actually cuddled with a hookup in so damn long, but I could already tell this was more than a hookup. At the very least, I wanted more, and I could tell Ricky did—if he let himself.

After a minute of just holding him, Ricky finally spoke up. His voice was soft, and against my chest, I could feel the hum of it through my body. "I always had trouble in bed with girls. I felt like that made me a failure. And failure isn't an option. So I had to try harder. And again. And again..." The frustration came through loud and clear.

"Did it ever work?" If he was trying to say he was bi, I was fine with that. Stereotypes were bullshit.

Ricky shook his head and finally rolled over onto his back to look up at me. His expression was sad, and more than a little guilty again. "Maddie was my last ex. I stopped trying then, but... I haven't told my mama yet."

I smiled at him as I combed his hair back, away from his eyes, and ruffled it. "Does your mama love you?"

I hated seeing the fear that flickered through Ricky's eyes. "Yeah," he said, but after seeing that look, I didn't follow up with hollow reassurances that she'd love him anyway. I didn't know that about her, so I couldn't lie to him.

Instead, I just hummed. "I like you, but... it's up to you what to do about that. I'm not gonna let anyone hide me behind clothing racks."

Ricky blushed and looked up at the ceiling, humming noncommittally. "And I'm not gonna let anyone be an asshole to you. Especially Madison. That's who I thought that woman in the thrift shop was."

Click—another puzzle piece in place. "Right," I breathed out. *Are you that afraid of her?* was the wrong question to ask. It would only make Ricky feel worse, if he was that conditioned to want a heteronormative relationship. Instead, I frowned. "I can run her off."

"You're way too sweet," Ricky grinned at me. "She'd eat you alive."

"Oh yeah?" I raised a brow. Something about him made my fighting instinct come alive like it hadn't for a long time. "I'd like to see her try."

Ricky sucked in a breath, his eyes wide as he gazed at me. I was about to ask what he was looking at when he grinned. "You're so hot when you get like that."

I tried not to compare, but I couldn't help it: Nathan had sure as hell never encouraged me to talk back to him. When I'd tried, he'd just run roughshod over my arguments and reminded me that I was the brawn and he was the brains of this operation. No wonder I felt so dumb all the time.

But Ricky didn't make me feel like that at all.

Instead, I smiled at him and winked. "I like you, too." I wanted to see if I could embarrass him a little without pissing him off.

He turned a funny shade of red and sat up next to me, fumbling with his coffee mug. "Cool. That's good. Me, too. I mean, I like me, but also you. Especially you."

I twisted to grab my own mug and cradled it close once I had a hold of it. The coffee helped clear my thoughts—and damn, it smelled good, too.

Wait, I knew that smell. "Isn't this the same stuff you have at the diner?"

Ricky looked guilty for a moment and then grinned. "Jared lets me get away with a lot."

"I can tell he likes you." I smiled at him. "He chose you when I asked about a cook for the charity event. You're definitely in his good books—and mine. Thanks for helping out with it."

"Tell me about the event, anyway. And the charity." Ricky was clearly trying not to acknowledge the praise. A lot of people were bad at taking compliments, but it didn't mean they didn't deserve them.

Talking about work gave us a chance to cool off, but it also brought us closer. Ricky seemed interested in the charity, and as I explained the different fundraisers we ran, he even seemed to pay attention.

As essentially a two-man operation, our charity didn't get a lot of support apart from Nathan's dad's pocketbook, so we needed every dime we could get. Last spring we'd run awfully short of money at a time when I'd needed to buy seedlings, pots, tools, compost… that had been a close call. I didn't want the same to happen this spring.

After the coffee was done, I wasn't feeling the urge to leave, though. Ricky wasn't even hinting at it, either. In fact, he put an arm around me, idly touching me as we talked.

I wasn't sure how to tell him this, but the more he touched my bare skin, the more aroused I was.

"Dude," I finally cut off his rambling about movies he'd watched lately. "If you keep feeling me up, we're gonna Netflix and chill, if you get what I mean."

From the sly look that crossed Ricky's face, I could immediately tell that was what he wanted. "Oh, really?"

"Don't you try bullshitting me," I teased, wriggling down the bed until I lay flat. "I can see it a mile off."

Ricky shook his head. "No getting away with anything around you."

"Oh, I'll let you get away with a lot," I promised him, raising my brows meaningfully.

Ricky slid down the bed and propped himself up on his elbow next to me, running his hand along my chest to play with my nipples. "Like what?"

I couldn't make my mouth form actual words, so instead I bit my lip hard and grunted. Well, that was making my boner come to life, that was for sure.

"Oh," Ricky breathed, running his finger ever so slowly down the center of my body. "Like this?"

"Please," I managed to gasp, reaching above me to grab the headboard so I didn't go straight for his dick.

It didn't take long before Ricky was pulling my clothes off again. He kicked his jeans off moments later. By this point I figured we might as well stay naked and save the energy next time. He looked eager to explore, but I still suspected he might try to rush things along.

He surprised me, though. Instead, Ricky took the time to explore my body with his hands, touching me gently—but not too lightly under my arms this time, despite the wickedly teasing glint in his eyes that showed me he wanted to.

"Oh, damn," I breathed out. "I'm so turned on." A glance over showed me that he was feeling just the same, that gorgeous, thick cock pressing into my thigh as he lay beside me.

"How'd that happen?" Ricky whispered, grinning at me. He tweaked my nipple harder.

I bit back my moan and grinned at him. "You just have to look at me and it happens," I told him just as softly, running my hand along his cheek and cupping it.

When I leaned in for a kiss, Ricky kissed back. This time, instead of dialing up the intensity, he held it just where it was. The soft, gentle air between us was exactly what I'd been craving.

I loved that despite Ricky's fears, he wasn't shutting me out, and I wanted to reward that trust in me.

This time when he reached down to stroke me, I pulled him over top of me instead and batted his hand away. "My turn," I told him, grinning up at him.

"Oh," Ricky whispered, grinning. "Okay. Thanks!" He braced himself on his forearms and peppered kisses along my forehead and cheeks, which was so fucking adorable I could barely stand it.

"Stop being so cute when I'm trying to get you horny," I murmured, my hand wrapping around both of our shafts. Damn, it felt amazing to have another man's cock against mine, hard and throbbing and needy.

I thrust gently against his cock, wrapping my other arm around his back to keep him where I needed him. The blissful high didn't take long—despite trying to stay still, he was soon thrusting into my fist, grinding down against me hard and fast.

I let him use my cock to stimulate himself. My cheeks hurt from smiling at just watching him learning so quickly what felt good.

"I wish I hadn't listened to my fear," Ricky whispered. His skin glistened with sweat, and his dark eyes were wide. Then, he smiled. "But I don't think any of the guys I tried to hook up with would have been as good as you."

Damn it, he knew how to make me blush. I would have covered my face if I could, but I was too busy grabbing onto his sexy ass for dear life.

"You're so damn hot," I gasped. Tendrils of pleasure crept through every sensitive nerve ending in my body. "I'm close already."

"I am? You are?" Ricky lit up with pleasure and grinned at me, like he hadn't expected to hear that I was liking it so much. "Yeah, baby. Come for me."

"Ricky!" I whimpered when I finally couldn't hold out any longer. For the second time that night, he was all that I could think of, and all that I wanted.

He came hard, grunting and screwing his eyes shut, but the most precious part of all was that he still peeked at me a few moments later—like I was too sexy not to watch.

I tried to cling on, half-afraid I'd never taste this again, and deeply afraid of what a life without the raw intimacy of Ricky's spirit and mine mingling might feel like. But try as I might, I fell over the edge into blissful oblivion and I couldn't regret that for one moment.

The climax felt too damn good, washing through me in bursts of pleasure that sparked my body to life. It felt like I'd been lying dormant all summer, only to burst to life now as winter crept across the city. A late bloomer, maybe, but no less sweet.

I barely remembered the rest of the evening as he cleaned us both up and pulled the blankets over us. It wasn't even a question of whether I'd stay the night or not.

The question of what would happen when Monday morning's harsh light crept in to disturb the precious moments we'd shared —that could wait. Sleep in Ricky's arms came first, deep and long.

11

RICKY

"Oh, man. I can't believe we slept in for so long!"

Cedar was hanging off the edge of the bed to grab his t-shirt from the floor, so I thought it wise to grab onto an ankle—just in case. His clumsiness was adorable, but a bump on the head might not be.

"I know," I agreed, keeping hold until he emerged, victorious, clutching a t-shirt in his hand. I patted his thigh and let go, kicking the blankets off myself, too. "And I gotta get to work."

"I haven't slept this well in ages," Cedar admitted, now scrambling to the edge of the bed so he could get dressed.

Come to think of it, I didn't have to get dressed *just* yet. I sat back and enjoyed the view—especially when he bent over and tugged on his socks.

Cedar caught me looking and snorted at me, but he grinned. "Perv."

"Guilty." I raised both hands. "Your fault for being so hot."

"So hot I needed a couple rounds to cool off?" Cedar smiled and came to sit on the bed, disappointingly fully-dressed but still adorable. "I really gotta go, though," he added, wincing as he looked at his phone.

"Sorry I kept you here." I smiled and leaned in to peck his lips. "You have a good day, huh?"

"Will do," Cedar said, his steps light as he bounced over to the door and tugged his shoes on. "See you!"

I heard Cedar flying down the steps and winced, listening until I heard the outer door open without any great crash and bang.

And like that, it felt like my life was that much emptier again. It seemed hollow somehow when I got dressed as I had a thousand times and got ready for work. Pouring one mug of coffee was lonelier than it ever had been.

Not quite sure what the hell was going on with my head, I headed into work early. At least I wouldn't be alone in a quiet, echoey apartment.

"Madison's here to see you again." That was Jess, judging by the sympathetic tone instead of the gloating I'd expect from Daisy.

I glanced over my shoulder and rolled my eyes. "Thanks for the heads-up," I said and braced for the incoming tirade.

I felt the cold wave sweep into the hot kitchen before Madison came to a halt in the doorway, arms folded. She stood imperiously, but where I'd once felt bad for her, I only felt… well, kind of amused.

"My mom's worried sick about me."

"Mine too. Join the club. I think that's a mom thing," I told her, keeping my voice blank and neutral as I turned the sausages on the grill.

Madison huffed and stepped forward. A throat-clearing from nearby made her scowl and step back into the doorway, not quite entering the staff-only zone. She looked pissed even from my peripheral vision.

"Yeah. Your mom is worried about me going alone to Atlantic City, too."

That drew my attention. Mama was worried about her? How did she know that, and what the hell was Madison doing now?

Madison gave a triumphant smile when I looked over at her. "Yeah. I called her."

I groaned and tossed my tongs down on the counter, turning to Madison and folding my arms. "Look. We've been broken up for half a year. Get over me."

"Get over *yourself*," Madison retorted, sneering. "You think I still like *you*? After everything?"

I knew what she was dangling over me: the last disastrous attempt at sex the night I'd broken up with her. My cheeks flushed, but I didn't turn away from her. "Yeah. Why else are you asking me for help every other day?"

Her eyes widened and lips turned down. A clear bid for sympathy, and I wasn't buying it. "I thought we were friends."

"I've loaned you, what, five hundred bucks? Pay me back and we'll call it friendship," I told her.

What the hell had gotten into me? Was I channeling Cedar's boldness now? He'd come off so easygoing, but sometimes he put down his foot. When he did, I wanted to bang him on the spot.

I was biting back a grin. Oh, man. Madison would be pissed if she found out who had replaced her. It had always filled me with fear at first, but Cedar had issued a clear challenge—*I'd like to see her try*—and I believed him. He wouldn't let her get into his head.

So why the hell should I?

"I'm done feeling guilty," I told her, turning back to the grill.

"Who is she?" Madison sounded half-hysterical. "Who is it? Daisy?" She whirled on her heel and glared behind her, then looked at me again. "Jess? Someone else?"

"Oh, hell, no. I'm not dating," I told her. "Least of all at work."

Madison's eyes narrowed. She'd clearly sensed that the money tap had turned off, though, so she tossed her hair and stormed out without another word.

Huh. That was easier than I'd expected it to be. No doubt she'd call Mama and put a word in her ear about me *not being myself,* so I'd call her at lunchtime and make sure she knew that things were well and truly over with Madison.

And not just because I had a new guy in my life, but even having that thought made me smile.

Fuck. It was written all over my face, wasn't it?

When Jared came to give me a break, I headed out to sit at the counter with my plate of food. Hopefully I'd get some time to think about how I felt about Cedar, and if it was worth breaking down that wobbly wall that stood between my double life.

Was I really enough for a guy like Cedar? Smart, driven, sweet. Not many people could run a charity—much less manage to share those duties with their ex in a mature, responsible way. But clearly Cedar was making it work, and that made me respect him.

And I was the kind of guy who'd let a girl blackmail him into giving her money to shut up about his limp dick. I'd cut her off at last, but it was still six months after when I should have. Cedar would never respect me if he knew about this.

Oh, man. Today wasn't my day to be left alone in peace and quiet, apparently. Billy slid in next to me. "Hey, Enrique."

I nearly groaned but just barely held it back. I offered him half a smile and echoed him. "Hey." Then I chowed down on a sausage almost whole, trying to make it clear that I was very busy eating.

"Those talents are wasted," Billy remarked, pointing at my mouth. I nearly choked and glared at him. He snickered and leaned in. "Or are they?"

Great. The gossip hadn't taken long to start.

"What?" I managed when I swallowed.

"You and Cedar? No?" Billy laced his fingers and propped his chin on his hands. "Cause if you're not into him, you're leading him on."

"There's nothing going on," I told him, my voice firm and steady. If there was one thing I could do, it was lie with a blank face. I'd lied to enough women, after all.

Not the time to pull the self-guilt-trip, Ricky.

"Mmm." Billy leaned against the counter. "He's not in a great place right now. I don't know how much you know, but his ex is a piece of work. Not that he's ready to hear that."

I looked over quickly at him, betraying my interest—and maybe my protectiveness. My eyes narrowed. "How so?"

"Nothing I know for sure." Billy blew out a sigh and shrugged. "Ask him yourself, if you're getting that close."

I rolled my eyes at his less-than-subtle attempt to pry gossip from me. "Thanks for the heads-up."

"Just… take care of him, okay?" Billy spoke quietly, for once in his life. "I'm pretty fond of him." He patted my back and stood up. "And don't worry. I won't breathe a word to anyone."

Fuck. Despite myself, I blushed and stared down at my coffee mug, jerking my chin in a silent thanks.

Billy's touch lingered on my back for a few moments before he headed back to his usual table, holding down the fort for the regulars.

I felt weirdly good about that interaction. Like I wasn't on the outside, looking in—as I'd felt like I was doing for my whole life.

Maybe I should go visit Cedar. I knew where he lived, after all. I could bring takeout and talk with him about our days. It sounded weirdly romantic when I put it like that.

Okay, it *was* romantic.

I was into him, and I didn't know who to talk to. My sole confidante was Adam—a guy I'd tried to hook up with on Grindr before he got scared off. We'd cuddled and watched Netflix—without chilling—and it had been pretty much the best experience I'd had on Grindr.

We'd texted a handful of times over the last few months, but now that he was in a steady relationship, I just felt weird about trying to be friends.

But Adam was friends with Billy, and part of the circle of regulars. Maybe others, like Billy, could give me advice.

I looked around and behind myself.

"Fuck," I breathed out. Nobody else was around besides Billy at the usual table, and he seemed busy with a book.

I left behind my empty plate and slid into the booth beside him, lacing my fingers together tightly around my coffee mug.

Billy lifted his chin in acknowledgment but didn't say anything, just inspecting me. Finally, he smiled. "What's wrong?"

I let out a long breath and folded my arms on the table, then plopped my forehead on them. I'd chatted a little bit with him about girlfriend problems before, and he'd always held back from offering specific advice.

But he could give a more experienced listening ear when it came to *this* problem.

Billy put his hand on my shoulder. "That bad, huh?"

"It's good," I told myself, trying not to sound like I was convincing myself.

"But?"

I looked sideways at him. *Don't make me say it out loud, man.*

Billy met my gaze and didn't say a word.

There was a whole exchange in that moment, and I realized what he was doing. He *wanted* me to say it. Maybe to admit it to myself, or just to get used to what it sounded like out loud.

I cleared my throat, my mouth suddenly dry. I wasn't going to look around first, but I broke that promise to myself almost immediately and sat up, checking to see if Jess or Daisy were within earshot.

The place was quiet, though. Monday was, after the lunch rush and before the slight uptick of evening footfall. Since Mondays were the quietest day at Friction next door, the overnight shift was crushingly slow, too.

Which was how my mistake with Madison had happened. And I'd known damn well it was a mistake from the beginning. The only way I could avoid repeating it was to admit it out loud.

"I can't," I muttered, shaking my head. "Not without telling Mama."

Billy cracked a little smile. "Mama's boy, huh? Classic sign."

"Oh, fuck off." Still, I smiled back at him, sitting up a little straighter. It was true, and I wasn't going to be ashamed of it. Not if Madison was going to try to use it against me.

"Uh huh." Billy patted my shoulder. "Well, if you aren't ready to say—"

"I'm gay." My voice sounded uneven, and then I found myself struggling to breathe through it.

Shit. There was no going back, was there?

Billy stared at me for a moment before he smiled, the missing tooth making his warmth shine through more, somehow. "Was it your first time?"

"Yeah." *Wait, how does he know that?* I stared at him for a second. "Did he tell y—"

First time saying it out loud, idiot. I plopped my forehead back on my arms as Billy laughed.

"Shoot me now."

Billy ruffled my hair as he finally cleared his throat and stopped laughing. "It's all right, kid."

I rolled my eyes. Twenty-four wasn't exactly a kid, but to him, everyone under thirty was.

"This feels like the biggest deal in the world now," Billy continued.

"I promise, you look back in five or ten years, and you won't even know why you waited so long."

"I already don't know." I grimaced, forcing myself to look up at him again. "Maddie? I knew that was a mistake. I'm an asshole."

"She's the kind of woman we're *supposed* to want." Billy didn't even look pissed off at me for leading her on like I'd expected. Maybe I was the only one beating myself up about that. "And boy, she's been milking it ever since."

"Does everyone know my business? Oh, my God."

"Jared's coming over."

It took a second before I realized what Billy was saying. He was giving me a chance to put myself together and play it cool to my boss if I wasn't ready to come out to him yet.

God, I owed Billy a big wet kiss. If I were into him at all, and not so into Cedar, and oh God, I was totally into Cedar.

I sat up straight just in time, rubbing my eyes and rolling my shoulders.

"Wakey wakey," Jared told me cheerfully, slapping my back as he arrived at the table. "Late night?"

"You could say that," I answered, ignoring Billy's smirk. "Break over already?"

Jared nodded. "Sorry. Go on, get doing what you do best."

Cedar was right—he *did* like me. As much as I worried about not living up to my potential, Jared trusted me with his kitchen.

If only I trusted myself half as much, I could have avoided half this mess.

"Thanks for letting me crash," I told Billy, flashing him a thumbs-up before I escaped to the kitchen.

I'm gay. My own words rang in my ears, settling like a weight in my stomach. However much Billy insisted I didn't need to tell my mom first, I knew damn well that I did.

I owed her that much.

Problem was, I wasn't sure I could face up to her disappointment. But I'd hit the end of the road. I also couldn't stomach trying my hardest not to follow my instincts.

He still hadn't texted back—not that I'd checked that before starting my break. I'd found myself thinking about him all damn day long.

Mama would like him. I knew that much. I smiled just thinking about introducing them, and it almost made up for the fear that had gnawed away at my insides for years. I knew she'd be okay with me—and us. But there was a difference between knowing and taking the plunge.

But Cedar wasn't going to hang around forever, and he'd already said he wasn't going to be hidden away behind clothing racks. I was ninety-nine percent closeted, even if I'd told Billy now. I had a long way to go. I felt like I was doing well, but compared to the level of *out* that Cedar was clearly used to, I had to look like a brick wall.

I could do better than that. I wasn't gonna be some asshole fucking him behind closed doors and refusing to hold hands in public.

And that meant taking a deep breath and gathering my faith in my family to stand behind me when I needed it.

If nothing else, Mama would have my back, right?

1 2

CEDAR

"Are you wearing *yesterday's* clothes?" Nathan hissed as he briskly walked alongside me. He plucked at my collar, which was definitely wrinkled.

We were heading to some fancy Manhattan accountant's place—a friend of his dad's, of course. The whole charity sometimes felt like it was Nathan's and I was just tagging along to do the hard manual labor.

But that was ungrateful of me and I knew it. They hadn't had to keep me on after the breakup. They could have dissolved the charity and reformed with Nathan and some other warm body who knew how to grow things.

I wasn't even an expert at that. I'd never taken classes or studied it. I hadn't worked in landscaping. The most hands-on experience with gardening had been in the backyard veggie garden with my parents, who had viewed it as physical therapy to help with my coordination.

"Yeah, I'm wearing yesterday's clothes. So?" I turned red with embarrassment as Nathan started the interrogation. I was only

119

surprised he'd waited until we met at the station entrance to do it, instead of texting me like usual.

Nathan rolled his eyes. "Well, it's not like I've never done that. Jacob won't care." His dad's friend had a buddy-buddy attitude that made me a little uncomfortable in an accountant, but I didn't have a lot of points of comparison. "It's just a surprise, coming from you. Sooo, is this the guy you were with on Saturday?"

"Am I gonna get the ninth degree every time I'm not hanging out with you?" I eyed Nathan, hoping he was listening to himself here. I had no time for controlling exes screwing with my future relationships.

Nathan held up his hands. "Whoa. Sorry. Touchy. What's wrong with you today?" He frowned at me. "Are you getting sick?"

The problem with being a people-pleaser was that the moment I had a bad day—or, hell, the moment I stood up for myself for once —everyone thought something was *wrong* with me.

Ricky likes it when I talk back to him. Here I was comparing them again. *He doesn't treat me like I don't know anything, either.*

"Nothing," I told him, trying not to become grumpy and prove his point. "I'm not sick. Fine: yes."

"Yes, it's the same guy?" Nathan's brows shot up.

It was hard not to get offended. "You don't have to look so surprised that someone actually wants to see me more than once," I told him, turning the corner to the office. I'd left the house without gloves either, and I was regretting that decision.

Last year, we'd walked here hand-in-hand. I hadn't noticed the cold at all. We'd been too busy giggling and kissing on street corners. That hadn't lasted, and I'd known it at the time, but I'd been staving off the inevitable.

"Okay, okay. I'll let it go. Well, we're almost here. You know the drill," Nathan told me, as if fumbling to get control of the conversation again.

"Let you handle the money stuff." I rolled my eyes. "Gladly. I'll sign whatever they say to sign and daydream."

"About your new boyfriend, huh?" Nathan said in a sing-song voice.

God, he could be annoying. I snorted with laughter. "Yeah, if you don't mind, I think I will."

I pushed my way into the accountant's office and smiled at the receptionist, trying not to let on how flustered I was. "Hi. We're here to see Jacob."

"Ah, he's waiting for you. First door on the right."

"Thanks, Veronica." I reminded myself to send her a Christmas card from the charity and waved as I led the way to the office. For once, Nathan was shadowing me, and it felt damn good.

It only lasted a couple seconds. Once we got to the office, I held the door for him and he swept through to greet the broad-shouldered, well-suited man who stood inside. Jacob always had impeccable skin and huge rings on his hands. Definitely not the kind of guy who I got along with.

"Ah, Nathan!"

"Jacob!"

They hugged like old friends, slapping each other's backs. Then Jacob reached out to shake hands. "You two are still doing well, I take it. You look well."

"We're doing great, going our separate ways in life... but still collaborating for a higher cause," Nathan answered with one of those charming smiles to smooth over the awkward moment.

"Oh! Oh, sorry to hear."

Nathan and I waved off Jacob's apology. It was just as well Nathan had dumped me before the summer started, really. Sometimes it just took someone doing what both people knew had to be done, and that was usually Nathan.

I settled back to nod, smile, and stare out the window as usual. I didn't understand any of the financial stuff that Nathan seemed to, and I didn't know any of Nathan's friends and family that Jacob inquired about. We'd dated for less than a year, and I hadn't really met many people in that time.

Turned out to be a good thing, or disentangling would get even harder, if that were at all possible.

If only I could distract myself by fidgeting with my phone. But I hadn't felt like bothering to plug in my phone—some nights, it was too much goddamn hassle, and we'd been... well, otherwise occupied. So my battery was at twenty percent already, and the more I fidgeted with it, the more it drained.

Dammit. I'd gotten the text from Ricky on my way out his door, but I'd had to head straight home. Hadn't even gotten into the apartment before Nathan called and told me to get my ass to Manhattan from wherever it was when I wasn't at home.

I wanted to send Ricky a quick text back and... what, invite him for dinner again? What was the next step here? Maybe coffee.

I stared at the message, but I quickly realized someone was saying my name.

"Huh? Oh, sorry." I signed the paperwork where Nathan pointed, just relieved that Nathan wasn't rubbing in my obvious distraction and teasing me in front of Jacob. As was immediately obvious to most who met him, he didn't have a lot of filters.

"I trust you submitted all the receipts," Nathan told me, and I nodded obediently. "After this, it'll be too late to get compensated if you forgot anything."

I nodded. "I gave you everything ages ago."

"Gotcha." Nathan looked at Jacob. "Then we're ready. Thanks so much for helping us get this done early."

"Early is better than late," Jacob cheerily told us, and then launched into another explanation of what accounts were due. He was telling us that he was going to go through everything and be in touch if there were any discrepancies, and if I wanted, I could sign off on it all and let Nathan handle the rest of it since I was clearly not paying attention.

Something about their tone of voice when they joked about me just signing off on it made me bristle. I was jointly responsible for these finances, even though it was Nathan's dad pouring money into the charity. If anything was fishy, I was on the hook—so to speak.

Nathan wasn't that kind of guy, was he? He was a very different person from me, and he didn't respect me, but he'd seemed so passionate about it. He'd gone from *Whatever you're passionate about, babe*, to being able to lecture a room on food deserts.

Which gave him a chance to be in the spotlight, but had I been mistaken when I assumed he gave a shit what we did?

That was not a Pandora's box I wanted to open just now.

"Great. That's a better policy anyway," Jacob told me briskly and dove straight back into a discussion about employee maintenance costs with Nathan.

The whole charity status thing just confused me. For all I grumbled about Nathan leading the charge, I never would have managed to set this up without him. All I wanted to do was play in the dirt, change the world in my own little way, and do as little paperwork as possible. I didn't mind fundraising and talking to people, but the official stuff was scary.

I felt a little guilty that Ricky had sounded so impressed about me running a charity when I wasn't really *running* it, per se. It was like I was claiming credit for something I didn't do. I felt weirdly like an impostor, and he was going to find out someday that I just liked playing in the dirt and having my expenses covered.

If I was changing the world, it was almost an accident. What right did I have to suspect Nathan of any funny business when he was dealing with everything complicated on my behalf?

"Then we're good to go."

I had no idea how long that appointment had lasted. It felt like hours when I had to occupy myself and look interested while not taking in a word. Blinking off the torpor that had set in, I thanked Jacob as if I'd been paying attention to the whole thing, shaking hands on the way out. As far as long, boring meetings went, that was pretty painless.

"Great. That went well," Nathan enthused as he blew out of the office so fast I almost missed the chance to say goodbye to Veronica. I hurried after him, my hand slipping on the handle as the door closed on my face.

Nathan grabbed it just in time. "Keep up. Jesus, you okay?" He cupped my face for a moment, inspecting me up close. His breath was warm on my face in the outside air.

I drew a quick breath and jerked out of his hold. "Fine."

It just felt weird when he touched me now. Not even like a

friend—I wouldn't complain if Billy or Kev or the other guys had done that. But knowing what I did about Nathan, I'd always been wary that he might just try to slide back into my good graces and bed someday without the relationship label to burden him.

To his credit, he hadn't tried it, but the possibility was always going to keep a wall between us.

Nathan frowned, still holding the door open for me. He shifted from foot to foot but stepped aside so I could get through. "God, your clumsiness worries me. One day you're going to get hurt. Can you get more physical therapy for it?"

I appreciated his concern, even if it made me feel resigned to this awful fate of having people do things for me. It brought me right back to days in the doctor's office as a kid, kicking my feet since I couldn't even reach the floor. I'd spent so many hours listening to my mom worrying to my specialists about my future with me right there sitting beside her.

I'd always just accepted that I was going to be handicapped, as they'd put it back then. Now I didn't feel that word was the same kind of burden it once had been. But I also didn't feel like I could reclaim it—my disability wasn't severe.

I was mildly affected, according to the scale they used, and my cerebral palsy only affected my speech, balance, and arms. So many people had more to overcome than me. I felt like I had no right to complain about my life.

But there wasn't much more that could be done for me besides paying more attention to my surroundings. The speech therapy hadn't been the most fun, especially as a kid, and I'd hated the physical therapy. I was done with all that crap now.

"Nope. I don't usually shut the door in my own face," I told him, my annoyance slipping through just because my adrenaline was still racing.

Dropping, crushing, or batting things off surfaces now and then was almost in the normal realm of clumsiness.

Normal. How I hated that word. My parents might not have been worried about my being gay, but they'd always been afraid for me not growing up *normal.* It was funny how much I resonated with Ricky's experiences on a totally different axis.

Nathan was quiet for a minute as we walked side-by-side to the train station. "Sorry," he finally said. "I didn't realize you were lagging behind me. I feel like shit. I forget—"

"It's fine," I cut him off. No point in chewing him out when he already felt bad, and it wasn't the worst thing to forget. Once upon a time, I'd been over the moon when the other kids forgot there was something different about me.

Ricky took extra care when he gave me my coffee. It hadn't escaped my notice that he'd kept his hands close to mine when I'd picked up the coffee mug last night. Not in an annoying, hovering-over-me way that made me feel incapable of functioning, but in a... supportive way.

Holy shit, that was it: he was *supportive.* I'd never felt that from Nathan, even as we embarked on the same charity journey together. I'd always felt like I was rushing to try to keep up with impossibly high expectations.

I wanted to see him again... today.

As I pulled out my phone, I saw Nathan shuffle closer as if trying to get a look at the screen. Swallowing my sigh, I pocketed it again. "You're heading uptown, right?" He'd said something about meeting friends on our way here.

"Yeah." Nathan sounded distinctly disappointed. *Gotcha. Snoop.* I rolled my eyes to myself. "Well, you'll be heading that way, then," I pointed across the street at the uptown line with a bright smile. Which would give me a chance to text Ricky *without* him getting in the way.

"Oh, right." Nathan skidded to a halt and sheltered his eyes for a look up and down the street. "See you later, huh? Some of my buddies will probably come back with me after drinks."

"Maybe." I didn't want to invite him over to meet—and scare off—Ricky. I especially didn't want to see him deciding which of his new friends he'd fuck loudly.

"Unless you're out with your boyyyyfriend—"

"Go away," I grumbled good-naturedly and headed down the steps of my station as he laughed.

I stepped to the side before I went through the turnstiles and pulled out my phone for a quick text.

Sorry, first chance to text now. What a day. Off work yet?

I was barely through the turnstiles when my phone chirped with a response. I tried not to squeak out loud and failed, ducking my head like I had no idea where the noise had come from.

Yup! Was thinking about you all day :) Got stuff to catch up on. Want to meet?

Oh my God, even better than I'd imagined. He wanted to see me. I hadn't pissed him off.

I'm on my way back now. 45 minutes, at my place?

He seemed way more comfortable in private, and it only seemed fair to alternate meeting spots. Besides, my house was better-heated and prettier. Not to diss his, but... having an ex-boyfriend with a dad with deep pockets paid off.

One day, I'd make my own way in life. Until then, I'd at least enjoy a cockroach-free apartment. And if Nathan got home and loudly screwed some guy, well... that was part of city living. Maybe it would inspire Ricky and me.

I smirked at the thought and then lit up when my phone chimed again. I glanced down at it.

You're on! See you then :)

I pumped my fist as I trotted to the platform. There was a train there, and the doors were open, so I could be even quicker to get home and get supper started for us both, if only I could...

I stumbled and my hands shot out to catch myself on instinct. I immediately saw exactly where this was going, and was powerless to stop it.

My phone hit the ground and slid like a greased pig across the platform. *Please, please, don't—*

It slowed down just at the edge of the platform while my arms windmilled and I tried to catch my balance. Screw doing it without attracting attention—I'd already heard the gasps of people nearby. I'd take maintaining my balance without breaking my face. And maybe, just maybe...

Nope. The phone disappeared off the edge of the platform. Ironically, if it *hadn't* slowed down, it might have jumped the gap straight into the train. But that wouldn't be my luck.

I moaned and caught my balance against a pillar, covering my face with my hand so I didn't have to see anybody pretending not to have noticed a thing.

There was no way to play it cool. Ricky was on his way to my house, and no way could I afford to just ditch my phone and jump on the train anyway. I had to wait for some unimpressed subway worker to fish it off the tracks.

I was going to be so fucking late home, and Ricky was going to think I'd ditched him.

Tears of frustration welled up in my eyes, and I swiped them away, but they only insistently returned. The one small mercy left to me was that, when the train left, Nathan wasn't standing on the other platform watching me melt down in public.

I was fucked.

13

RICKY

My steps quickened as the dull gray concrete of Cedar's apartment block loomed into view.

I'd been just in time to grab the last decent-looking bunch of flowers from the bodega around the corner from Bubbles. It was impossible to look tough while gently cradling a bunch of flowers, but I'd resigned myself to the knowing smiles and glances from passersby.

It was nowhere near Valentine's Day, so they probably thought I'd screwed up. Wouldn't be the first time I tried to apologize with flowers, either.

The closer I got to the apartment, the more of a bad idea the flowers seemed. What if he hated them? What if he was ethically against cut flowers as plant murder? What if he thought it was too romantic?

God. Why the hell was I overthinking everything about this?

I trotted up the stairs and around the corner to Cedar's apartment, then dug out my phone to check the time.

Five minutes early. Better early than late, right? I wasn't going to fake forgetting something only to walk back and forth and arrive on time.

I drew a breath and knocked on Cedar's door.

Nothing. Huh. Maybe he wasn't home yet.

Just in case, I knocked again and leaned in, pressing my ear to the door to listen for any response. I wasn't aware that I was holding my breath until sparks danced on the edge of my vision.

I breathed in deeply and then muttered, "Fuck."

Well, I could wait around a few minutes for him. Right?

I sent a quick text. *Oops. Here early :)* Then, I slid down the wall and sat on the floor, grimacing at it and hoping I'd chosen a clean spot. Hallways in Brooklyn were no joke, especially external hallways. Only place worse to sit was a parking garage staircase.

Five minutes stretched into fifteen, and then twenty—not that I was religiously checking my phone. No sign of anyone coming or going down the hallway.

I knocked on the door again, just in case. "Cedar? You there?" I called out. He couldn't miss my voice from the hallway. Apparently he and his neighbor regularly chatted through the door, after all. "If you're avoiding me, I brought you a surprise. That's not even a euphemism for my dick." Pause. Nothing. "Oh well. Worth a try."

My pride gone, I called Cedar, but it only went to voicemail after ringing for a long time. And no answer to my text. Okay, that was weird.

Worry coursed through me as I imagined the possibilities: he'd been hit by a car. Or a bus. Or a bike messenger! Fucking bike messengers. I'd never trusted them.

Maybe he was running late—but if so, why not answer my calls and texts? Cell signal down in the subway was great these days. I could watch Netflix without a hitch. And the calls were getting through, not going straight to voicemail.

There had to be a mixup, right? Cedar was now thirty minutes late, not answering his door, and not answering calls or texts. I'd been dumped that way before, but Cedar wasn't that kind of guy.

Right?

I'd only known him for a few days, but he was starting to restore my faith in people. All I could do was trust him. And besides, if I walked away now and didn't get the chance to reconnect or at least find out what I'd done wrong…

That would hurt me too badly.

All I could feel was him cuddled up in my arms, his head on my bare chest, the scent of his shampoo tickling my nose.

One more call, and this time it went straight to voicemail. Shit. That wasn't good. Either his phone was off now or he was ignoring me. My gut instinct told me he was ignoring me, but that could be my self-esteem talking.

Footsteps!

I lurched to my feet, almost crushing the flowers but grabbing them just in time.

"Ce—" I started and then cut myself off. It wasn't him. Fuck.

The guy gave me a weird look, then looked at the flowers and back to me. Understanding blossomed over his face, and I prepared for myself for a *rough night, pal?* comment.

Instead, he grinned at me. "What are you doing hanging out

there?" He sounded kind of smug, like he already knew the answer.

I frowned at him. That voice sounded familiar.

Wait. Right, the shouted hallway conversation. This was the neighbor with no boundaries.

"Waiting for Cedar to get back. I think he's running late."

"He sure is. He was supposed to be on his way home when I was heading uptown. He's still not back? Are you sure?"

I shrugged as he brushed past me and banged on the door. "Cee! Your boyyyyyfriend's here!"

Well, everyone on the floors above and below had heard that bellow. I winced and resisted the urge to toss the flowers at him and make a run for it.

"I'm not…" I started a weak defense, but he just grinned at me.

"That's not what those flowers say."

I sighed and raised my shoulders in a defeated shrug.

"Weird," Nathan said when there was no answer from the apartment. "Huh. Why don't you wait in my place? I'd let you into his, but… you know, you could be a stalker."

Right, so he had a key. No wonder he had boundary issues. But Cedar trusted him enough to give him a key to his house, so I'd better play nice.

"If I'm a stalker, at least I have good taste in flowers." It would have gone over better if the price tag hadn't still been on the cellophane. I rolled my eyes and peeled it off, then tried to brandish them at him again, but the moment was gone.

"I'm Nathan." He grinned and headed down the hall to the next door down. "Come on. I'll text him."

"Already done, three times. And called him twice."

"Huh. That's not like him at all."

The apartment was weirdly clean, totally different from the place next door even though the arrangement was identical. Instead of plants, there were couches—meanwhile there was barely room for four people to sit down without someone ending up on the floor in Cedar's place.

"I know, right?" I frowned, my adrenaline spiking again as I followed him into his apartment, flowers in hand. Those things weren't going to last a lot longer without water. "You think he's in trouble?"

"Nah. Not unless…" Nathan trailed off, and my heart felt like it might flip-flop out of my ribs.

"What?"

"Nothing." Nathan offered me a smile that wasn't at all reassuring. "He can get a little clumsy sometimes. Maybe the cell service is patchy down there today, and a train got stuck under the river, and…"

"Not helping."

"Sorry." Nathan squeezed my shoulder. "Want some coffee? Come on, sit down."

He chatted about small talk: the weather, the neighborhood, sports. I could tell he was trying to keep me distracted from the what-ifs, and I appreciated that. There was an easygoing manner about him that made him charming, but my gut instinct also told me not to trust him.

Unlike my instincts about myself—which were generally programmed to *loser* no matter how well I did at anything in life—I trusted my instincts about other people.

A thudding sound from the hallway made me leap to my feet again. Distinctly the sound of a door slamming.

"I think that's him!" I took off out of Nathan's place without a backward glance and knocked on the door. "Cedar? It's me, Ricky."

"Ricky, huh?" Nathan was leaning in the doorway, watching every moment of this going down with a grin on his face like he was watching the twist in a movie.

The door flew open and Cedar stared at me, tears streaking his cheeks, shock written across his face. It was like he hadn't been expecting me at all. "Ricky?"

"Babe, are you okay?" Instantly, my protective instinct kicked in. Whatever had happened, I wanted to shield him from it. I nearly threw myself at him for a hug, wrapping him up in my arms.

"I lost my phone on the tracks and I could see it lighting up every time you called and then it went dead and I thought you'd be pissed at me—" Cedar wasn't even stopping for breath, so I pecked him on the lips to interrupt.

"No. I'm just glad you're okay. Jesus, I was starting to worry."

Cedar let out his breath and buried his forehead in my shoulder, hugging me back now.

"Not-boyfriend, you forgot these."

We both jumped—Cedar probably had no idea Nathan had been listening in, and I'd completely forgotten he was here. When I let go of Cedar and turned around, he was holding out my somewhat wilted flowers and wearing a shit-eating grin.

Cedar's quiet groan behind me didn't go unnoticed, but I couldn't do anything now except own it. "Thanks," I answered and grinned back at Nathan, taking the flowers from him. I plucked out some white flower and offered it to him. "For rescuing me."

Nathan snorted with laughter but took the flower and saluted me with it. "You're too sweet. Hold onto him, Cedar." He winked at Cedar and wandered back to his door, craning his neck over his shoulder like he hoped to see more gossip.

"God," Cedar muttered, backing up through the apartment door to let me in. "Of course he had to stick his nose in. I thought he was out, anyway! I was supposed to be here, and he was supposed to be out, and oh my God, I'm like an hour late…"

"Hey." I took him by the shoulder and offered the flowers. "For you."

Cedar stared at them for a few long moments and then looked up at me. It was hard to read his expression, and I was only going to be harsh on myself by trying.

"Even though I stood you up, and Nathan probably charmed you by being… well…" His eyes were wet again and he raised his wrist to wipe them. "Him?"

"What?" I frowned at him and then looked toward the wall that separated their apartments. "Nathan? Charming? Nah. He has a key to your place, so I figured you trust him."

"I do," Cedar said, sounding miserable. "But compared to him…"

Maybe I shouldn't have given him a thank-you flower. I'd go kick down his door and take it back, but I had the feeling the damage was done.

"Don't compare yourself to him," I told him, and then raised the bouquet to his face. He tried to turn his face away, but I managed to tickle his face with it. "Gotcha."

"Jerk," Cedar laughed, but his spirits seemed to be lifting. He finally accepted the bouquet and shook his head at me. "Why'd you wait around with Nathan?"

"I knew you wouldn't just dump me—I mean, ditch me like that." At his inquiring look, I groaned. "Okay, someone once dumped me like that, and I always felt like I was supposed to stick around longer and… I don't know, fight for her. Compete against whatever new guy she found."

Cedar shook his head and headed for the kitchen, pulling out a vase to put the flowers into. "Guys don't fight over me."

"They should," I told him firmly. I came up behind him when he filled the vase in the sink and looped my arms around his waist, pulling him in against me. "I'm sorry you've had a shitty day, but I promise you… I'm not into your neighbor."

"I'm not jeal—oh my God. I'm jealous." Cedar put the vase on the counter and buried his head in his hands. "Sorry I'm acting like a total weirdo. It's just… today *is* shitty."

The longer I held him, the more I could feel us both relaxing. It was so much easier to communicate how I felt about him by holding him close, rubbing his chest and humming gently so he felt the vibrations against his back and through his own chest.

Cedar's shoulders had dropped by inches by the time he squirmed sideways enough to reach the bouquet and place it in the vase. "Perfect."

"Not sure they are," I admitted with a laugh. "They were the last okay-looking bunch. The others were either wilting or decapitated. Sorry. It was a spur-of-the-moment thing…"

Cedar turned around in my hold and kissed me before I could keep apologizing. He didn't pull back, either—instead of the peck of the lips from earlier, he was kissing me slowly and deeply.

His eyes might not be watering anymore, but his lips still tasted salty. God, the poor guy really had had an awful day, huh?

I rubbed his back and shoulders, my hands wandering down to cup his ass and squeeze gently before I ran them up his sides again.

"Nnh—no tickling," Cedar pulled back and gasped.

I winked. "I wouldn't dream of it." I grinned wickedly at him but cupped his shoulder blades instead, holding him tightly. "You okay?"

"Better now," Cedar admitted softly. He groaned and rested his forehead on my shoulder. "Nathan's my ex, and I run the charity with him."

Ohhh! Everything made sense now—why Nathan seemed so familiar with him, and why he was so worried I'd been into Nathan and not him.

Wait, he was living next door to his ex? That had to suck.

"You been broken up for long?"

"All summer. I haven't dated anyone since, and I'm still kind of..." Cedar trailed off, blushing and resting his head on my shoulder. "Awkward about dating."

"Bet I'm more awkward," I murmured and smiled, kissing the side of his head. "Sit down?"

"Sure." Cedar towed me over to his bed, which was rumpled and unmade. "God, my place is a disaster, too. I was supposed to get home and have time to clean..."

"Shh," I whispered and collapsed on his bed, scooting over against the wall and beckoning. It wasn't at all a disaster. It barely looked touched since Saturday.

Cedar followed me without hesitation, stretching out alongside me and rolling over so we were squished together.

"Better?"

"Much," Cedar murmured. He sighed and rolled his head to look over at the wall. "He just gets all the hot guys, and I get... pity fucks. I thought for a minute that maybe..."

"No," I told him firmly, gripping him by the hip. Whatever was going on, he was rattled and it was showing. "I'm into *you*, man. I wouldn't wait around all that time if I weren't."

A smile touched Cedar's lips, and he finally cupped my cheek. "Thanks." He kissed me and then settled back against the pillows. "I spent the afternoon with Nathan at the accountants' not understanding a word they said, and then I had a clumsy moment and dropped my phone on the tracks, and... I just feel like shit about myself right now for letting you down, and causing a nuisance to everyone at the station, and crying all the way home, and now Nathan knows about you..."

I wrapped him in my arms and kissed the top of his hair. "Don't even worry about any of that. We're here, and that's all that matters."

For once, it wasn't about obligations or the show I was putting on for anyone else. All I wanted was to hold Cedar and spend time with him—even if we were just cuddling in bed all night long.

"We can get takeout," Cedar finally murmured. That sounded perfect to me.

"Yeah. Let's do that."

It didn't even occur to me to be worried that Cedar didn't want Nathan knowing about me. I was just too damn happy that Cedar was smiling again.

I'd do anything to make him smile.

CEDAR

I felt like grass in the spring. In a matter of a week, I'd gone from parched to revitalized, and there was only one source for that spring: Ricky.

The downside was that every damn day without Ricky there seemed to drag by. As wonderful as it was to spend Monday evening together eating Chinese takeout and laughing about stupid TV shows we watched on Netflix on my laptop, he'd had work super-early the next morning.

Tuesday had vanished into a black hole of work for me, negotiating the terms of the deal with the HOA that had been fighting us for months. Thank God Nathan hadn't breathed a word about Ricky yet—maybe my warning glare every time I saw him was working. Wednesday was much the same, but with laundry to do, too. I'd squeezed in time to stop by Bubbles twice, but I'd missed Ricky's shift both times.

We'd exchanged morning and night texts, and a few in the middle of the day. But every time I texted him and couldn't see his face or feel him pull me against him as he talked, a little piece of me withered. Text conversations never cut it for me.

By Thursday morning, there was an itch I didn't fully understand and couldn't cope with. I was so cranky that I couldn't even bring myself to joke around with the cashier when I went to grab groceries and the prices scanned up wrong.

That was it. I needed to be around Ricky, one way or another.

What time do you work today? I asked as I juggled my bags.

Just got off work! Half-asleep but I want to see you today, answered Ricky within moments.

I smiled at my phone. *I have groceries but can drop them off and be there soon.*

Come right over. I'll keep you warm and your groceries cold ;)

That was an offer I couldn't refuse.

Besides, the lack of action Monday night—which was entirely my fault for getting so wrapped up in one little moment that I'd felt shitty for the rest of the night—had left me aching for *something.*

Bonus: Ricky's apartment was just steps away from Bubbles, in case we got snackish. Not that I didn't trust him to cook, but I hadn't noticed much real food in his cabinets when I was over last weekend. And I could understand. Sometimes, after spending all day with my hands in the dirt, the last thing I wanted to do was trim my own bush—so to speak.

"Here we are," I murmured when I arrived outside the thrift store. "Right?"

I double-checked the doors. Definitely only one door with peeling paint in between Fringe, which promised great haircuts for stylish men, and Treasure Aisle, the thrift store.

I carefully set down my bags so I didn't drop them. There was the buzzer, a metal button next to the door. When I tried to hit it, I managed to jam my thumb into the wood underneath. I rubbed it and cursed under my breath, then tried again.

"Oh, hey!"

I squeaked and turned on my heel, leaning on the door so I didn't lose my balance. It took me a moment, but I recognized Kev. He was in the same loose friendship circle as me, since we hung out at the same places a lot. He was closer to Adam than Billy, though.

"Hi," I answered with a casual wave. "What's going on?"

Kev held up his plastic bag. "Picked up a few new cups. I just got a new kintsugi kit and I wanted an excuse to use it. This place is great, isn't it?"

"Sure is!" A distinctive clatter didn't even give me time to grab hold of anything before Ricky yanked the door open, removing my source of support.

I fell into Ricky's arms. He caught me before I was even halfway to the ground, hauling me back upright and holding on tight. "Sorry, sorry! Sorry! Oh, shit. Hey, Kev."

Kev looked at us like we were crazy but he laughed, covering his mouth. "Jesus. You okay?"

"Fine, fine," I told him, staggering back upright. I wanted to kiss Ricky for saving me, but now was not the moment. That left me with an awkward pause as I tried to figure out what to say instead.

"Now I've seen everything," Kev said with a wink, breaking the silence. "A man swooning into Enrique's arms."

Ricky laughed a little too loudly. Like a storefront at night, I could see the iron curtain slide down across his eyes. I internally sighed.

It was gonna take him a few minutes to open up again when we were alone.

"I better get going," Kev added, raising his bag. "Work calls. See you around."

"Bye," I managed, well aware that both of us were suspiciously silent as we watched him walk away and waited for him to be out of earshot before talking.

"Sorry—" we both started at once, and then chuckled.

"No, no," I broke the stalemate, flapping a hand. "Let's get upstairs, huh?"

"Yup!" Ricky bent over and grabbed the bags. He was forcing the cheer, which was what he did when he didn't want people to over-hear this.

I followed him up the staircase. He'd left open the inside door so there was light spilling across the staircase, and the small window above the door provided some light, at least.

"There we go." Ricky led the way inside and then closed the door behind us, setting down the bags on the floor. "Are you okay? Shit, I'm sorry I threw you off-balance."

"And I'm sorry Kev surprised us both." I laughed, putting a hand on his arm. "What a pair we are today. And every day, it feels like. Get used to me being a clumsy asshole, though."

"Doesn't make you an asshole," Ricky told me, like he had before. He turned his back and headed for the kitchen with an armful of bags. "Anything need to go to the fridge? Oooh, avocado."

I smiled to myself and shook my head. Well-meaning, far more able-bodied people liked to say that. Especially those that didn't know my history.

Still, uncertainty stirred in my chest. I'd had a couple guys get freaked out when I brought up those big words—*cerebral palsy*. One had thought it was a progressive, fatal thing. The other had just said some nasty things about a crippled relative of his, and I'd walked out on him.

I sure could pick 'em.

But I couldn't hide it from Ricky if this was a long-term thing—and I didn't want to. First, though, the name thing. We could transition into that conversation.

"Most of the cold stuff is in that blue bag. So, you go by Enrique at work? And Ricky on Grindr?"

Ricky let out a startled laugh and plucked out the milk and cheese for his fridge. "Yeah. You could say that. Just keeps the lives separate, you know?"

"Mm." That didn't sound healthy to me, but Ricky at least seemed aware of that.

When I sidled up beside him and tried to slide the yogurt into the gap in the door, I missed the first time but managed to get it in the second try, my hand shaking.

Ricky caught his breath and held my hand instead, stopping the tremor. "You okay? Did I rattle you? Or is it your hand? That burn still looks bad."

I sighed and shook my head. "It's healing, that's why it looks worse," I told him. "You know that."

"Yeah. But…" Ricky trailed off. We both jumped when the fridge beeped. "Oh, it's mad I have the door open."

I stepped out of the way so Ricky could close it, and then sighed. "I'm getting hungry. Mind if I grab a snack?"

"I can make you something!" Ricky rummaged through a couple bags before stopping, his eyes wide. "I mean, if you don't mind."

I grinned at how eager he'd been. "No. Knock yourself out." It was kind of nice to be spoiled like this.

"You relax and I'll figure something out. No allergies, right? Or preferences?"

"Other than a dislike of limp bacon?" I smirked at him. "No."

"Cheeky," Ricky scolded as I grabbed a chair from the mismatched dining room set and dragged it over so I could have a seat. "So, are you that nervous to see me? I mean, I'm hot stuff, but…"

I laughed and shook my head. No point in hiding it. "I have cerebral palsy. Ataxic. Least common form. That's why I'm so skinny. Makes me a little unbalanced, and gives me intention tremor. My hands shake when I try to work precisely," I explained. It was the explanation I'd given hundreds of times, including once explaining to cops that I wasn't drunk in public just because I'd knocked over everything in sight.

"Oh." Ricky looked startled and then apologetic. "Shit. I had no idea. Sorry."

I smiled at him. "Nah. Most people don't, it's okay." The usual platitude I gave people, but this time, it was true. He hadn't meant to make fun of me.

"But don't most people have, like… wheelchairs?" Ricky winced. "Sorry," he said again. "I should Google this."

"I don't mind, as long as you're not being a dick," I told him.

Ricky laughed. "I'm pretty often a dick. More than I think. I should stop while I'm ahead."

"Luckily, I like a dick sometimes," I told him straight-faced.

"Do you?" Ricky tried not to grin, but it was impossible. "I see you distracting me…"

"I'd never do that," I played coy, batting my lashes. I sobered up then, trying not to scare him off with the explanations while anticipating his questions. "I had physical therapy as a kid, and some injections. Speech therapy too. I was born with this. The other forms of cerebral palsy are much more common—mine is rare." I shrugged. "It's a brain thing. I've had it from birth."

"Oh. Huh." Ricky was already washing and chopping veggies, and for a moment, I envied how damn quickly and precisely his hands moved. It was graceful to watch him chop peppers into even slices —weirdly like a moving work of art. "So that's why… the culinary school thing."

I nodded, folding my arms and resting each hand on the crook of the other elbow. It was a move I'd used a lot as a kid to keep my hands steady. "It was really disappointing, but it was a dumb idea. My parents didn't say so in so many words, but they've always been big on letting me make my own mistakes."

"I don't think it's dumb. If you were careful and you had someone preparing ingredients for you, you could learn a lot," Ricky told me, putting down the knife and turning to me. "And maybe handling the hot stuff, huh?"

I ruefully smiled. "Yeah. But I left that dream behind and headed to the source instead. You guys need people to grow things for you."

"We sure do." Ricky resumed chopping, working fast but not letting me see much of it. It was like he was trying not to show off, which was the opposite of what I'd expected from anyone.

Was that a sweet side of him I was glimpsing, or was I projecting my own hopes onto him?

"Some guys get weird about it," I added. "Or think it's progressive, and… I dunno. I can understand being scared of what that means, but it hurts, too."

Ricky grabbed a pan from the cart sitting next to the counter and made a noise of sympathy. "Yeah. That sucks. Thank you for telling me. Doesn't worry me at all."

"You say that, but I've never tried to playfully grab your dick out of the blue," I said with a grin. "For good reason."

"Do you end up with the nipple instead?"

I laughed. "Or I grab 'em by the balls."

"Best way to handle men," Ricky said with a serious nod, and then snorted. "So I've heard, anyway. Not that I'd know. I guess that's my big insecurity, if we're sharing."

He seemed to talk easier when he was cooking, keeping his hands distracted or maybe calming his worries about coming off too emotional. I liked this side of him. "Yeah?" I asked, trying to encourage him to talk more.

"I relax when I'm around you, but I've always been afraid that I'm… you know, gonna screw up with a guy."

He'd said as much before, but I nodded. It had to be bothering him, then. "So what does that mean for us?"

"Us? Like *us*-us?" Ricky paused as oil glugged from the bottle into the pan, then flourished and flipped it right-side up again. "I've been kinda taking it steady, not rushing into anything…"

I smiled at him. "Yeah, but people are gonna notice. Kev, for one."

Ricky hummed and looked over at me. "Yeah. I'm ready to let my worlds collide, I think."

I sat up a little straighter and beamed. "Really?"

"Yeah." Ricky focused intently on the pan, his voice dropping. I had to lean in to hear. "I guess I just... found someone worth busting all that down for."

Who's that? It actually took me a second to realize he meant me, especially because he wasn't looking at me. But there was a blush creeping up his neck, and he finally cast a really quick sideways glance as he shook the pan over the flame.

"O-Oh." I cleared my throat. "You'd come out if we took this any further?"

"You said you don't date closeted guys," Ricky murmured. "It makes sense. And I don't want to hide you. That seems rude. I just have to get over disappointing other people."

Hmm. Less than ideal, but he was making a lot of progress in a week. I wasn't going to push him. "I really appreciate that you're willing to do that." It spoke highly of him that he was listening to my needs and planning this huge, life-changing stuff.

Actually, it spoke highly of his intentions about me. I blushed as I realized just how serious he must be, and it was my turn to duck my head.

"You're worth it," Ricky told me in that supremely confident tone of his. Like the world could fuck off if they disagreed.

Tears pricked the corners of my eyes, but I refused to let them fall. I'd spent enough time crying on his shoulder this week. Tonight, I wanted more from Ricky.

I cleared my throat and looked up. "Just for that, you get a blowjob tonight."

That had the desired effect—Ricky froze for a moment over the stove, his jaw dropping as he stared at the food and then over at me. "Uhh. Ohmmnh." The funny noise sounded agreeable, and I noticed the boner starting to form.

Well, that was easy. Not even a finger on him yet and he was ready for me. I grinned at him and cocked my head. "What?"

"You just—that's not fair." Ricky laughed, rummaging in my bags again to pull out green onions. A pot of water went on the stove, and he pulled out the rice noodles I'd picked up.

I recognized the dish now. "Pad Thai? From scratch?"

"I have the sauce already. You've got the rest."

"Mmm. Can't wait to taste your sauce," I moaned. "I bet it's great."

Ricky made a strangled whimpering noise as he fiddled with the burner controls. Then he strode over to me and straddled the chair, settling his weight carefully on my lap.

My every sense was engaged now—I could see his eyes, dark and wide with arousal, smell his shampoo, feel the warmth of his skin on mine, hear his rasping breath… fuck, I could practically taste him already.

"You," he whispered, poking my chest with a finger, "are trying to turn me on."

"I don't have to try," I answered, channeling a bit of that cockiness as I grinned at him. "I just do."

Ricky moaned and shifted his weight until his boner pressed into my thigh. His lips brushed against my neck, making me gasp and roll my head to the side as pleasurable nerves lit up throughout my whole body. "Too damn right."

"How much time have we got?" I whispered.

He pulled back to look at me with a grin. "Until the pot boils."

I fumbled for Ricky's zipper, slid it down, and licked my lips.

"Dry. Until the pot boils dry."

I laughed as I zeroed in on his button and finally popped it. "I'm flattered, but my jaw might break by that point. Stand up."

"Oh, yes, sir." Ricky grinned cheekily and hauled himself up, grabbing the back of my chair.

"You know, if you want…" My heart raced. "We don't have to use any, like, relationship label… but I could be with just you."

Ricky stared at me in such surprise for a moment that I wondered if I'd screwed up. "With just me? You'd do that?"

"Um. I mean, yeah," I laughed. "You're hot as fuck, and I like this."

Ricky grinned. "Yeah. Sure."

"I still want us to get tested together before we ditch the condoms," I told him, but my eye was drawn to that sexy bulge. "I might be willing to skip it this time, though…"

"Negative all the way down," Ricky told me. "Got tested after Madison dumped me, and… oh, God. Do I have to say it?" When I blinked at him, he scowled and added, "And I haven't had sex in six months."

I gasped quietly. Nathan had dumped me around the same time, if not a few months earlier, but I certainly hadn't been starved of sex since then. When Ricky talked about being awkward around guys, no wonder he'd sounded so desperate to try them out. "Aside from me? Oh, shit. Let's fix that."

"Does oral count as sex?" Ricky squinted. "I never thought so."

"Told you: I say it does." I pulled his pants down and grinned. "Watch me prove it."

He was fucking delicious. From the moment my tongue made contact with the velvety underside of his cock, I was in heaven. There was nothing like the power that came with giving head—someone else's pleasure entirely in your hands and mouth.

Making him feel good made *me* feel good, but I was too busy stroking him and cupping his balls to pull myself out yet. I could wait until later, I convinced myself. Barely.

Then he moaned, and I whimpered at how fucking hot it was to hear him vocalizing in pleasure.

"You're so good," Ricky gasped. "Man, it's been so long..."

I knew what he was trying to say. He was swollen and needy now, his hips pushing forward insistently every time I bobbed my head down. He was getting close to the edge, but he didn't want it to be over yet.

Just round one, I thought. If I stayed the night, we could totally do it again.

I moaned and grabbed his hips, pulling him forward into me.

"Got it," Ricky breathed out, pulling one hand away from the back of the chair and grabbing the back of my head instead. He thrust into my mouth in quick, shallow motions as I ran my tongue around the head and tried to sneak glances at his expression.

Why was he so damn hot I wanted to cream my own pants? It wasn't like I was starved for sex, but when we did it, it was like a circuit in my body was completed. A little bit of him in the right spot—apparently my mouth—and I was on fire.

"Yes!" Ricky whimpered. "Babe, I'm seriously nearly there—oh my God, are you going to swallow?"

I tried not to laugh at the excitement in his voice. I just kept my mouth around the tip of his cock, sucking hard and running my tongue along it as I stroked the rest of his shaft hard and fast.

Boom, it was over like that. Thick liquid hit the back of my throat and I swallowed. It was a relief to find out that he didn't taste bad. Essential boyfriend requirements: nice semen.

"Oh my God, Cedar," Ricky breathed out, his knees buckling as he grabbed the chair again. He still gave a few shuddery thrusts of his hips as his body rode out the rest of the orgasm. Finally, he pulled out and grinned at me, flopping down on my lap again. "You're amazing."

"Is that the orgasm talking?" I teased, running my hands through his hair and walking my fingers down his back. "I bet it is."

"It's all me," Ricky whispered, and then he grinned at me. "But you're right. It's been so long since I've had a blowjob at all—let alone one that good. Jesus."

"Compliment accepted. Want me to get the rice noodles?"

"You bet." He grinned at me and scampered to the bathroom to clean up, still wearing a mile-wide grin.

God, how was he so adorable *and* so hot? It wasn't fair.

I worked carefully as I tore open the noodle package, then dumped them into the boiling water. I couldn't see a timer on his stove, so I pulled out my phone to watch the time.

When Ricky rejoined me, he shooed me away and took over again, assembling the meals into two bowls. "I feel bad making you wait."

"For what? Supper?" I laughed. "It's amazing having someone cook."

"No, duh. For your turn." He flicked out his tongue at me and then winked as he grabbed forks. "Come on."

Oh, I like the sound of this. I bit my lip and followed, hot on his heels.

I'd never liked foods that required precision eating, but I'd learned strategies to help control my utensils. Now, pretty much all I had to avoid was soup. I knew how lucky that made me, and it was another weird layer of confusing guilt. Too disabled for some people, not disabled enough to feel like I could complain about it.

Even when I'd had to give up my own dreams.

"I'm glad you can cook so well. I could live vicariously through that," I told him with a smile when our bowls were empty.

Ricky hummed and collected the dishes. "Yeah? I'd teach you some more, if you want. I'll prep things for you. If you're still passionate about it, I want to share this with you."

God, he was sweet. I smiled and shrugged. "Yeah, maybe. We'll see."

"But first," Ricky pointed, "you. Bed. Now."

I nearly tripped over my own feet as I headed for his bed, ducking around the screen and crawling up it.

I was barely on my back before Ricky was hovering over me, kissing me hard. "Your turn... or my turn," he whispered. "Depends how you look at it."

"You don't have to, like, feel obligated." I licked my lips with the half-hearted protest.

"You want me to suck you off?"

I nodded breathlessly.

"Then shut up and let me suck you off," Ricky said with a grin at me, cupping my cheek fondly. "You deserve nice things."

Fuck. Just like that, I was blushing.

He smiled, kissing me a few more times for good measure before he pulled up my shirt. "Let's ditch this."

Although Ricky tried his best at foreplay, sucking my nipples and rubbing my cock through my jeans, he had me naked within five minutes. The eagerness was actually hot in itself, and I was long past ready to go by the time he kissed his way down my body.

He took a deep breath and I stroked his forearm, my eyes straying to the tiny marks of grease spot burns along the smooth skin.

"I want to taste you so bad," Ricky admitted. "Just… just let me know if it feels good, all right?"

"You're already doing fine," I assured him with a grin, rubbing both his shoulders now.

Ricky's grip on my shaft was tentative at first. He wrapped his fingers around it awkwardly and stroked a few times, then adjusted. Within moments, he'd found a comfortable pace and rhythm.

Then he licked around the head, just tasting me and licking his lips. That in itself was the hottest thing anyone had done to me in ages.

"And what does the cook think, now that he's tasted it?" I teased.

"So fucking good," Ricky moaned. He wrapped his lips around the tip and pushed his head down, and the warm heat that enveloped me made me tingle with pleasure.

Oh, yeah. I could get used to this.

Though his movements were tentative at first, Ricky was a

quick learner. He listened to my moans, letting them be his guide as he tried out different pressures, suction, and tongue motions.

He had the knack before long, and I was seriously starting to go out of my mind with pleasure. I didn't usually have a guy pay me this much attention before pulling back and fucking me. Just lying back and letting him treat me was fucking mind-blowing.

"Fuck, Ricky," I panted, my body tense and breath short. "Suck a little harder, and rub your palms—yes!"

There went my capacity for speech. Now that I'd taught him that trick, he leaned into it and set to work shattering my nerves.

"That's the best thing ever… oh my God," I mumbled, covering my face. "I'm gonna come so quick. I'm sorry."

Ricky mumbled something, and even the sound of my cock stifling his speech was too damn hot. It was my turn to grab the back of his head, but I was gentle as I fucked his mouth. Just watching my cock disappear between those pretty lips was almost too hot to handle.

"Okay," I breathed out with a shaky laugh. "You don't have to swallow." It was all I could do to form sentences, I was so close to coming.

Ricky just determinedly pushed his head down and redoubled his pace, taking me in almost to the root.

I came hard, my inhibitions and caution shattering into a thousand pieces as I grabbed his shoulders and pushed my cock into his mouth hard and fast. "Yes, yes, yes!"

When I finally collapsed on the bed again, Ricky grinned at me, wiggling up the bed to flop next to me. "Okay?"

"More than okay!" I laughed, resting a hand on his side as I tried to catch my breath. "God, if that was your first time, you're starting from a mile ahead of where I did."

Ricky smirked. "I've been reading articles online."

That was the most adorable thing. I stifled the urge to tell him that, though, because I felt like it might make him defensive. Instead, I grinned. "Well, it's working." As I went soft, I pressed against him, squishing our bodies together and wriggling against him in some attempt to share the joy and bliss that radiated through me.

Ricky chuckled gently. "You got work today?"

I shook my head. With the gardens mostly shut down for the late fall and winter, no educational events, and minimal admin work… winter was a long, open stretch of days for me.

"Stick around here, then." He winked. "We could spend a lot of days like this."

"Yes, please." I snuggled into him and closed my eyes, letting my body thrum contentedly at the bare, warm skin against mine. Naked and stripped of all our defenses, not just our clothes, was my favorite place to be with him.

"Tell me about your last couple days," Ricky encouraged me, running his fingers through my hair. I glowed at the attention and obliged him with the more interesting details.

This year, I wasn't going to spend the winter chasing someone who never let me be right and never wanted my thoughts.

Ricky was already one of the most sincere people I'd talked to, under those layers of self-consciousness and performance anxiety. When I could get through to him—which was just about every time we saw each other—he talked to me like a peer, not like I should be grateful he was fucking me.

The only open question was whether this would really be enough to get him to let down the wall between his lives. He'd said so, but I'd learned not to trust what people said.

It didn't matter what people said. Only their actions spoke the truth.

15

RICKY

"Heyyy. Ricky."

And my Saturday had been going so well, too. I looked up from the grill only to find an annoyingly familiar face lingering in the doorway of the kitchen. That was becoming way too common an experience.

But this time, it wasn't Madison. It was Nathan, the neighbor—and, I knew now, ex-boyfriend—of my not-boyfriend-but-exclusive-sex-buddy. I was gonna need a shorter acronym for that.

More importantly, what the hell was he doing here? Wait. I'd seen him around here before, now that I thought about it. If he hung out at Friction, that made sense. It was a shockingly small borough sometimes.

"Hi," I greeted tersely. "Enrique."

"Ricky, Enrique, same difference. Didn't hear Cedar shouting either name through the wall the other night, if you get what I mean." Nathan winked. "I'm just saying, if he's all frosty…" He was fluttering his lashes as he looked me up and down. "Not everyone around here is."

I narrowed my eyes at him. The idea that I might want him instead of Cedar? This was some sick power play or revenge he was trying to enact, and I wasn't going to let myself be a pawn in his game.

"Get out."

"What's the matter, baby boy? You look like you saw a ghost." Nathan pouted and ran his finger across his lips. "I thought we were getting along great."

"Not interested."

"Cedar gets all the good stuff." Nathan sighed, rolling his head back before he snapped it around to look at me with a hard stare. "Like my dad paying his rent." He let that one hang in the air between us and didn't look away.

It took me a few moments to realize what he was saying. Then my gut and jaw dropped at the same moment.

"You gotta be fucking kidding me."

Nathan held up his hands. "What? It's just the facts."

If he thinks he can blackmail me into sleeping with him so Cedar doesn't lose his apartment, he can think again. My job came first: I shut off the grill, plated the hangover specials, and shoved them under the heat lamps.

Then I stomped over to him and grabbed him by the front of his shirt, hauling him in close. "If you ever try to blackmail me, you'd better fucking know what you're doing." I'd break his face before I let him exploit me like that—or worse, hurt Cedar through me.

"What, is he your boyfriend?" Nathan smiled at me, gripping and twisting my wrist to break the hold I had on his shirt. He didn't take the chance to step away, though. He just got up in my face, dialing up the obviously fake charm. "How sweet. You don't have to take on a charity case, you know. I already did." He leaned in even further, his breath hot on my ear as he whispered, "The handjobs are extra-great, but don't let him finger you."

I saw red. I ripped off my apron and batted past his hands to grab his shirt in one hand again, the fabric nearly tearing as he stumbled backward to try to yank himself away from me. Before I could wheel back and punch him, Billy was there—and so was Jared. They forced us apart, Billy getting up in Nathan's face while Jared stood between me and the asshole I wanted nothing more than to rip apart.

"Guys? Oh, my God. Oh, my God! What the hell?" That was Cedar, standing dumbfounded and frozen just behind the group of us.

What was he doing here? Shit. He'd probably come to eat with Nathan, and now... well, this didn't look great. I couldn't possibly tell him what Nathan had said. The guy had a damn key to his apartment; he was clearly a friend, even if he annoyed Cedar sometimes.

I panicked. "Shit. Um... I definitely wasn't about to punch your ex." Jared was still holding me back by one arm, which sort of undermined my defense. I wanted to get loose, but I didn't trust myself yet.

"Your boyfriend's crazy," Nathan breathed out, shaking his head. He was feigning fear now, and he was doing a damn good job of it. "Get off me, Billy."

The restaurant went quiet for a moment, all eyes turning to me. I could *hear* people's lips silently moving: *boyfriend?*

"I've never liked you, Nathan," Billy informed him, dropping his hold on him and staying between us. His back was to me, but I could see that his arms were folded. "I didn't like what you did to Cedar, and I don't like you even more now that you're doing this to Ricky."

"Doing what?" Nathan widened his eyes.

I nearly spat on the floor. If Jared wouldn't have immediately fired me for health code violations, I would have. I just growled instead and moved forward a pace, but it did nothing to alleviate the feeling of helplessness.

I was backed into a corner, and nobody but me could get me out of it. "Outing me," I hissed, all too aware that the restaurant was silent and everyone nearby was trying to listen in. "Thanks a lot, asshole. Choke on a dick, why don't you? Sure as hell won't be mine, *or* Cedar's."

"Like that's your choice," Nathan commented, his voice strangely bland and calm.

"What—" Jared started to ask a question and then cut himself off, shaking his head and scoffing. "Never mind. Enough of this bullshit. Nathan, you get out of here and you don't come back until you apologize for trying to start a fight with my staff. And you better kiss a lot of ass, too. You sure as shit don't get to out anybody on my turf." He looked as pissed as I'd ever seen him.

"I didn't realize he wasn't out," Nathan scoffed. "All I did was talk to him! It's his own fault if he's hiding it. From what, a bunch of fellow gays?" He gestured at all of us. "Man, he's got issues, Cee."

I started forward before stopping myself, and Jared blocked my way with an arm across my chest.

"Guys," Cedar moaned. "Come on, please. Act like adults here."

Nathan drew a breath and let it out as he looked at Cedar, and then Jared and Billy, and finally at me. "You're right," he told Cedar. "We had a misunderstanding, that's all."

Jared looked at me, his arm still in place.

Oh, now he's setting himself up to look good. I bared my teeth for a second. "It wasn't a misunderstanding. Jared told you to fuck off. I second him."

"Shit," Cedar whispered, looking around at us all. "I'm sorry. I didn't realize you guys weren't… Nathan, don't be mad. Ricky, you neither."

"Why's everyone calling him Ricky all of a sudden?" Jared complained to nobody in particular. "Did I not get the memo?"

Nathan managed to look wounded. "It's fine," he told Cedar. "I don't need everyone to like me." I could hear him manipulating him with just a few words, and I decided I'd earned myself a deathbed enemy.

Continuing the fight with Nathan was only going to look worse, though. Had to let him win this battle and concentrate on the war. It took all my self-control not to respond, but I turned and stormed into the kitchen so I didn't have to see him make a pity-grabbing exit.

Jared was hot on my heels. "What the hell, Ricky?" he whispered.

"Yeah, I'm gay," I hissed, turning back to him and folding my arms. "So what?"

"That's not what I'm pissed about," Jared told me with a roll of his eyes and a gentle smack upside the head. "I mean, why are you letting some prick get to you? You usually laugh this shit off."

"He told me…" I broke off, looking over Jared's shoulder.

Cedar was hovering there, chewing his nails while Billy tried to tug him back to the table.

"Hold on. I gotta talk to him," I muttered. And it had to be right there, in full view of the restaurant.

But at least I didn't have anything to hide now. I wanted to laugh and cry at the same time. Maybe Nathan had done me a favor by ripping the Band-Aid off. Billy backed away and headed for the table with an anxious glance over his shoulder, and Jared held back to give us some space.

"I'm sorry," I whispered and opened my arms. Everything had happened so fast that I wasn't really sure who was at fault, so I didn't blame him if he was confused about it, too.

Cedar shook his head. He looked as sick as I felt. "No," he muttered. "I'm sorry for you. I should have told him you weren't out. I didn't expect him to..." he trailed off, casting a stricken glance outside and then back at me. He leaned into me and hugged me tightly.

That touch made all the difference in the world. The stress was still eating away at me, but it gave me a lifeline to hold onto: *Cedar isn't pissed beyond repair.*

"I have a bunch of stuff to do now, and I have to try not to get fired, and..." I trailed off. Daisy was lurking on the other side of the central counter, looking positively delighted. *And tell Mama, then. Madison's gonna know in thirty seconds.* "And stuff. Oh, God. I wish technology didn't exist."

Cedar winced and nodded, pulling away from the hug at last and resting a hand on my shoulder. "Text me, yeah? As soon as you can?"

He doesn't hate me? Probably? "Are you pissed at me?" I whispered. "Cause I can pick up more flowers."

Cedar gave me a distracted little smile and not the laugh I'd expected. Shit. That wasn't a good sign. "No. Yeah. A little. I don't know—I have to go calm Nathan down. Ugh." He rubbed his face. "Look, just… text me so I know you're okay?"

"Yeah," I murmured, though I had no such intentions. I had a whole lot of shit to process on my own and no time to do it in. "I'll cover your check. You do what you need to do."

As he headed after Nathan, I regretted the moment I'd ever thought that asshole was charming. Manipulative little snake was more like it. *Maybe he and Madison should be besties.*

Oh, man. My hands were shaking, and I couldn't breathe. As I headed back into the kitchen, Jared grabbed me by the arm and towed me into the office.

The door swung shut, and I tried to form an apology, but my throat was too tight. Apparently, none was needed, though. Jared just took a moment to look me over and then grabbed me for a quiet hug.

I let a long breath out and relaxed when I realized he wasn't about to fire me on the spot. "I shouldn't have started a fight in the kitchen. Fuck. I'm sorry, boss."

Jared shook his head and let go of me, then sat on a pile of paperwork on his desk. "I'm not worried about that. I'm worried about you. I had an inkling, but… this is a horrible way to get outed for anyone. I can talk to Daisy and—"

"Don't bother," I snorted and offered him a half-smile. "You think she'd stay quiet about anything, even if you paid her? Fat chance."

"Especially not to Madison," Jared murmured, folding his arms. He was still watching me closely, like he expected me to faint at any moment.

I *did* feel sick and dizzy and I could barely feel my toes, but that was beside the point. It was the adrenaline surge, that was all. I'd been so damn close to punching Nathan in his smug little face.

"I can't believe he turned on me that fast," I breathed out. "Oh, Jesus. He told me his dad pays Cedar's rent. If Cedar sides with me…"

"I know who I'd side with," Jared scoffed. "If Cedar has any sense, it's you. Outing someone without their say-so is never, ever right. Even to other people like yourself, and even by a friend, and even with good intentions… there's never an excuse. It's the lowest of the low when one of our own, and an enemy of yours, does it because they're mad at you. That's gutter-snipe behavior."

"Maybe he really did think…" I trailed off and then shook my head. Those mind-games were how he'd gotten such a hold on Cedar. I wasn't going to let his *oh, I didn't know you weren't out* work on me.

I nodded dumbly. Nathan *was* someone like me, because I was gay, and so was he, and now Jared knew it, and he was gay, too… I found myself sitting on Jared's office chair a few moments later. "Oh, God. I'm gay and now they all know it."

"Deep breaths, kid," Jared told me, his steadying hands on my shoulders. "We've all had a moment or two like this. You're gonna get through it. Who have you told?"

"Nobody," I mumbled, putting my face in my hands. "Well, no. Billy and Cedar." At least Billy had realized what was going on in time to help, and it meant a lot to me that he'd stood up for me, too, not just Cedar.

"Cedar's the twinky little blond guy, isn't he? The one you were… uh…"

I sighed and sat up straight, letting the chair ground me. "Yeah. And he's not my boyfriend."

"I didn't say he was," Jared assured me. He chuckled quietly. "But you two are cute together."

"You think?" I finally looked at him, and he was wearing a hint of a teasing smile. "Aw, fuck off." It made my chest swell anyway to hear that, even if I tried to pretend I didn't like it.

"It's true," Jared protested, grinning as he sat on the desk again. Then the smile faded and he leaned in. "So your family don't know?"

I shook my head. "Kept thinking I should tell Mama these last six months, but… here we are." I laughed shortly. "Madison has her number, and Daisy has *her* number…"

Jared held up a finger. "Wait right here."

I took the chance to get a hold of my breathing, which helped the dizziness fade, at least. Next came the shaking—I reminded myself that I was safe, and that I knew where Jared's stash of Snickers were.

I was just shoving the last bite of the bar in my mouth when Jared walked back in and raised his eyebrows.

"Sugar," I mumbled, pushing the chocolate drawer closed. "For shock."

He laughed and flicked my ear. "Brat," he said, but I could hear the affection in his voice. "So, I told Daisy not to tell Madison on pain of awful shift scheduling. That should shut her up for a day or two and buy you some time."

I could have hugged him. I popped the last bite of chocolate into my mouth and tossed the wrapper in the trash. I tried mumbling around it, then swallowed and tried again. "Shitty still."

"Sure is." Jared clapped my shoulder. "Take off early. You're almost done here anyway, and you're off tomorrow. I got this."

I let out my breath and nodded, half-hugging him on the way out. He held on for a few long moments, and I drew strength from his presence. I could be like him one day—solid as a rock, able to help others like he was helping me.

I wasn't going to be this fragile mess forever. If I had the guts, I was about to take a huge step forward.

I practically sprinted for the restaurant door. I usually headed out to the street since it was quicker to get to my place, but today, I used the back entrance to get out of the kitchen and into the shady little alley behind our diner and the club.

No need to do the walk of shame through the place. That might just be the last straw, my nerves as frayed as they were. I was sure my mama would still love me, but the *just in case* voice whispered that I could find myself an orphan in a few short words.

But no, Mama wasn't that kind of person. She wouldn't see me as a disappointment to the family name, or scold me for being any less of a man.

And my heart was finally telling me one thing loud and clear: no matter how it ended, I had to be honest. That started at home, with the only person—well, nearly the only person—whose opinion mattered to me.

Mama deserved to know the truth about me, and she was going to find out today.

16

CEDAR

Three unread texts and a call that went straight to voicemail, all within this last crazy hour and a half—I knew how Ricky had felt when I vanished in the depths of the subway station.

"Nope," I muttered as I tried for the fifth time to press the buzzer next to Ricky's door. I'd been walking back and forth between the salon and the thrift store. I kept looking up at the window above the door—an ornate stained-glass piece too far off the ground to have been taken out by vandals in the last few decades.

On the one hand, I could help Ricky. His private life had been made public in front of his coworkers and his boss, and I knew how much he'd wanted to tell his family first.

On the other hand, I was kind of responsible for this. Nathan might not have known he wasn't out, but if I hadn't been so fucking clumsy, making me late, making the two of them meet…

Ricky might just tell me to fuck off, and I wasn't sure I'd have the heart to stand firm today and tell him I wouldn't. I might scamper back to my apartment like a scared little mouse, like always.

A stylist with a thick Jersey accent and a lilting voice stuck his head out the salon door. "Looking for a cut? Wet shave? Don't be nervous, I can give you a deal." He was cute—flippy blond hair, in his mid-twenties, a thumb hooked into the loop of his jeans.

"No, thanks." I managed a weak smile at him. "I just need a sign."

"That you're doing the right thing? Or a street sign? They've changed them so they're a lot harder to steal. They're about forty bucks online though, and you don't risk the petty larceny on your record."

I was only half paying attention to him, still staring at the buzzer to Ricky's apartment. "A sign that—wait, what?" I wasn't sure if he was serious.

He grinned and patted down his pockets. "Aw, goddamn it. I'd offer you a smoke for your nerves, but I'm all out. I'm on the patch now. Filthy habit, you know?" He flopped in the rickety wooden chair in front of the salon and folded his arms. "All right. The counselor is in. Spill your problems."

Wait. My head snapped around to the window. "There it is!" I breathed out.

There was a light in the window now, which meant the interior door was open. As quickly as that, it vanished. Had he heard me through the window? He must be on his way down the stairs.

One way or another, it was too late to run. I had to do this and hope it didn't go south.

"Your sign? Oh, is there a cutie on the other side of that door? Awww, you go, pal!" cheered my new stylist friend as I rang the buzzer. He leaned forward eagerly to watch, lacing his fingers on his lap.

"Ricky," I breathed out when the door opened. I only had a second to assess his emotional state.

Not great. His lips were tight, his expression closed-off, and he was breathing quickly. That could be exertion from trotting down those hellish stairs, but I didn't think so.

He was wearing shoes, too, unlike the last time he'd let me in. Which meant he was planning on going out, right?

"What are you… huh?" Ricky blinked like he wasn't expecting to see me here. He looked around and then back at me.

"We need to talk." I glanced over my shoulder at the stylist who grinned and gave me a big thumbs-up. No way would we get privacy out here. "Inside."

"I—okay." Ricky backed up and I let the door swing shut behind us in the little vestibule. In the gloom, it was hard to make out his expression.

"Upstairs in your place?" I questioned when he didn't move for the stairs.

"I was literally about to leave." Ricky's breath was hot on my face. "I've only got a minute or I'll miss my bus. Here. Sit down, at least." He gripped my shoulders and guided me down to sit on the steps.

As my eyes adjusted to the scant light pouring through the top of the window, I could at least make out the outline of his face now.

"Okay," I breathed out, refocusing. I didn't need to see him, if I could feel and hear him. And he might be more comfortable with that anyway. "Are you okay?"

Ricky gave a short, sharp laugh.

"No, that was a stupid question," I mumbled. I groped until I found his shoulder and his chest, and then rubbed his back and looped my other arm around his shoulder. "I'm sorry, Ricky. That all went down horribly."

"I need to go talk to Mama." Ricky drew a shaky breath. "That's where I'm taking the bus. She lives with my aunt. I was planning to see 'em today anyway."

I'd never heard him so rattled, and I felt awfully guilty about the role I'd played in it. I should never have let Nathan out of my sight —but he'd never conflicted with anyone I'd hooked up with, either.

I leaned in and hugged Ricky tightly, rocking him gently. For the first few seconds, Ricky resisted. Then, at last, I felt his stress melt away as he leaned into me and squeezed me so tightly my spine protested.

"I know she loves me." Ricky's tone was still frantic, like he was trying to convince himself of that fact, and my heart went out to him. "And if she doesn't get grandkids, that's okay."

"Of course she does, baby," I murmured back. "And she'll be proud of you for telling her first." If nothing else, even if she took it badly, I was sure she'd be glad to learn from him and not some other gossiping asshole. "I bet she's a hell of a woman, if she raised a smart, kind, gorgeous guy like you." Ricky blushed, but I didn't give him a chance to brush off the compliment yet. "And she *could* get grandkids. Same-sex couples have some options these days."

Ricky blinked at me a few times, but he finally nodded. "Yeah. You're right. I could still have a family."

"You will, if it's what you want," I told him firmly.

"Would you..." Ricky trailed off, then cleared his throat. He mumbled to himself, "You're probably busy doing things."

"I'm free if you need me," I told him, tightening my hold for a second. He wasn't getting away that easy. "What do you need?"

Ricky's voice was tentative. "Come with me to my mama's?"

Whoa. He wanted *me* there? Wouldn't I just make the situation worse? Hadn't I caused enough bullshit in his life? I caught my breath and pulled away from him. I could see just enough now to make out the frown on his lips.

"Are you sure?" I asked, groping my way up from his shoulder to his face. My hand shook, but I managed to catch his cheek without poking him in the eye. "I—I don't wanna mess this up for you. I feel like I screwed up the situation at Bubbles. God, I'm sorry."

"It wasn't your fault," Ricky said automatically. "And I don't wanna scare you off," he added with a breathy laugh. "I'm sorry I wasn't answering my phone. I was so wrapped up in the what-ifs… and I wasn't sure if you hated me now."

"Me too," I mumbled, resting my head on his shoulder now and rocking him again. The dust in here was getting to me, but I tried to resist the sneeze. "I don't hate you. And I'd love to come with you."

It would be an honor, really. His mama would no doubt assume we were together, hearing the news and meeting me at the same time, and Ricky had to know that.

He'd barely said enough words to me to make me believe he liked me, but all the other signs were there. Maybe I just needed to read between the lines. Asking me to come meet his parents—or his mom, at least—was a big sign.

"Does this mean you're serious about me?"

I heard Ricky gulp before he answered. "Enough that it scares me.

I don't want to make you choose sides to be with me, though. If you owe Nathan anything, I don't want to put you in the middle."

"Oh, honey." I nearly crushed him with my hug. I was gonna kill Nathan later for making Ricky think he came second to my ex. "I've already chosen sides by showing up here."

I'd only known Ricky for a week, but he'd come such a long way and so quickly. Now, he was being forced to evolve even faster than before, and he wasn't running away from it.

He was a good guy. My heart told me as much.

And it had long ago told me that Nathan wasn't—at the very least, he was an inconsiderate jerk. And maybe he *had* deliberately outed Ricky, which would make him a total scumbag in my eyes.

But then he'd seemed so confused and vulnerable. I knew what it was like to feel like people hated you, and when he'd left the diner, he'd had that look in his eye.

I hadn't been able to catch him before he locked himself in his apartment, and all I could do was trust that he was okay. I knew him when he shut down—if I pushed, he'd only turn on me and insult me.

No matter what was going on with him, my gut instinct had told me to come to Ricky, and I hadn't been wrong. Ricky was the one who needed me right now, not my ex. And Ricky was the one who I saw my future with; sure as hell not Nathan.

Ricky hadn't turned on me for showing up, though. He'd resisted for a few moments, but those walls had crumbled as soon as I hugged him. I was only just realizing how much I was programmed to be Nathan's counterpart—including thinking anyone I tried to comfort would snap at me.

"Nathan's always been good to me, but sometimes he's been cruel at the same time." I rested my cheek on Ricky's shoulder. "I trust you not to be."

"I'm glad you can trust me. I trust you, too." Ricky rubbed my back. "The first thing is to make sure Mama knows, so I can tell other people, because I *don't* want to hide you away. Not that there's many people to tell who don't already know now," he laughed with just a touch of bitterness.

I couldn't imagine losing that control over my own identity, having people speculate or gossip behind my back. I'd come out so long ago that it had almost been a non-issue. Sure, I had to come out again in new situations, but it wasn't the same.

This wasn't just stepping out of the closet, it was having a bomb dropped on it.

"I can't imagine," I admitted again. "I mean, when I came out it was practically boring."

"And I can't imagine that," Ricky countered. His sigh turned into a quiet hum. "Okay. If you're coming with me, let's run for the bus."

"Shit, I don't want to make you late. Yeah. Let's go."

He grabbed my hand and opened the door again, leading us out—blinking and dazed—into the street.

I could barely see the stylist in the sudden bright light, but I could hear him. "Aww, are the lovebirds reconciled? That's the sweetest."

"You have a good day," I told him, fighting back a smile as the world came back into focus. He was still perched on the chair, his phone in hand, beaming up at us.

Ricky snorted and pulled me along to the bus stop, but I noticed him slowing his pace. Especially when I ran, my feet were a little wider apart, so I couldn't keep up with others. Track and field day in school had always been horrible.

He's noticing the little stuff. Stuff Nathan had never even thought of, and I'd always silently adjusted my behavior so I wouldn't inconvenience him. Okay, I knew I needed to stop comparing them, but it seemed impossible.

It was like having the world's worst fast food and then a rich, gourmet, home-cooked feast. I could barely get over the difference, and it seemed too good to be true.

"Okay," Ricky panted. "Who's your friend?"

"I just met him a minute ago." I grinned up at him. "And he's not my type, so don't be jealous."

"I'm not—I wasn't..." Ricky trailed off and then made a distinct *harrumph* sound. "Fine. I like you, and I don't want other guys to notice you." His hold tightened on my hand. "But I don't wanna be an asshole about it like Nathan."

Oh, now we were getting to it. Ricky hadn't breathed a word of what their discussion had been about. By the time I'd arrived, they'd just been in a full-fledged testosterone war.

"Is he being a dick? I really didn't expect that," I admitted. "We've been working so well together."

I could tell Ricky didn't want to answer the question, but his grip on my hand was tight as he glanced over at me a few times. Finally, he sighed. "Yeah. I don't want to stick my nose in it, but he said some pretty horrible stuff."

"Oh," I murmured, gazing across the street at the fried chicken place. If Nathan was trying to be possessive, did that mean he still wanted me? Was that why he kept trying to get me involved in his parties? I had no doubt there was sex and drugs involved, from the glimpses I'd gotten of guys stumbling away on a Sunday afternoon afterward.

But I didn't ask questions and he didn't tell me.

Maybe I should ask more questions, but if I did in other areas of life, Nathan shut me down.

Fuck. Ricky was right. Nathan *was* a jerk, and he always had been. I was probably just his grunt labor for the charity because he'd never liked getting his nails dirty.

It was a harsh realization, and every fiber of me wanted to reject it. But I also trusted Ricky implicitly, and I'd sworn to myself I wouldn't turn on him, however harsh the truth.

I scuffed my shoes on the sidewalk as we lingered around the bus stop, neither of us speaking right now. Ricky was giving me time to think through everything.

Billy and the other guys at the diner had been on Ricky's side, not Nathan's. That was a sign, too. Strangers loved Nathan, but nobody close to me liked him. Another red flag.

"Thank you for telling me," I murmured at last, as the bus pulled up. "Now, how far away is your mama?"

I had to turn my attention to getting ready to impress Ricky's family. If I was going to take sides and help them accept Ricky, I needed them to like me.

If they turned on him, I needed to be ready to shelter him as best I could and tell him that he was gorgeous and perfect the way he was. Even if he blushed and tried to stop me, I needed to be ready to tell him how I felt about him.

Because that was the one and only thing I didn't doubt: that the right place to be was by his side.

17

RICKY

"Pleasure to meet you, Mrs. Rosa." I could tell that Cedar was nervous because he was standing stiffly, but his shyness just made him more lovable.

Just as I'd expected, Mama ignored his handshake and hugged him, kissing both cheeks. "Oh, you're a skinny thing! We'll have to fix that," she told him, and then gripped my arms to look at me.

I couldn't hide my stress and worry from her, but I tried for a sunny smile anyway. "Hi, Mama. Looking gorgeous."

"Oh, come in, you charmer." She kissed my cheeks and then ushered us both inside.

She and my aunt shared an apartment with two bedrooms and a cozy living room. Most importantly, the kitchen counters and cabinets stood up to the weight of all her cooking equipment.

Cedar peeked in the kitchen on the way by and then gasped. "I see where you got it from."

"My boy's cooking talent?" Mama pinched my cheek. I suspected she was going to spend this visit trying to embarrass me. "Oh, that's all from me. When he was four, I had him up on a kitchen stool making tamales."

We settled in the living room with iced tea while Cedar chuckled. "That's a mental image." He was clutching his glass close to his chest, not sipping from it yet.

"When we moved here, he painted the place himself. Such a handyman, too." Mama was in proud mama hen mode, and there was no interrupting her.

I hadn't grown up in this place—we'd moved here after my dad died. I'd only been here for two years before I moved out and my aunt took my old bedroom, helping Mama with the rent.

She'd held onto this place since then. The landlords loved her and the rent didn't go up too much every year. I didn't have to support her as much financially now as I had the first couple years, so I could afford luxuries like name-brand groceries.

I needed a quick trip to the bathroom to compose myself. I didn't want to ditch Cedar alone with her, but I knew she'd like him. He was safe enough there. My mama was too busy interrogating him about his job and where he lived to notice my absence.

When I made it to the familiar old bathroom, I stared at myself in the mirror, taking a deep breath as I rearranged my hair. I splashed cold water on my face and it helped ground me for a moment before the nervous anticipation built again.

I felt kind of sick, but I had to remind myself that this was nothing like having Nathan attack me in public. Coming out wasn't supposed to be like that. It was supposed to be a good thing, wasn't it?

I could do this. I *had* to do this. If I didn't, Madison would do it for me, and I'd always remember that I was too much of a coward to tell my mom my biggest secret myself.

"Mama!" I called. "The light bulb in the hall is out again. I'll fix that."

"Thanks, baby!"

It gave me another minute to do something useful and delay the inevitable conversation. The ladder was in its usual place in the closet, and when I'd scrambled up, I was just tall enough to reach the bulb.

One out, one in. Any more handiwork that needed done? I'd have to ask her. *No, dumbass,* I told myself, shaking my head as I put the ladder away. *Get your ass in there and do the job you came here to do.*

The terror of rejection had never been easy for me to deal with, but when it was my own mom? Mama's respect was more important to me than anyone else's. I'd spent years pushing myself into a corner to live up to what she wanted for me.

Sure, she wanted a good woman by my side and kids in my future. If I was going to marry a prince and ride into the sunset, that didn't mean the rest of the plan had to change. She cared about me more than the rest of that stuff.

Time to steel my nerves and be the man I tried so hard to be at every turn.

I walked into the living room just in time to hear her ask, "How did you boys meet?"

"Um, at the diner. I've seen him around, but we got to talking." I fought back a smile—that was a wildly inaccurate portrayal of the first meeting, but I thanked Cedar mentally. Mama would have killed me if she'd heard I'd been such a dumbass.

"He meets everyone at that place!" She beamed at me. "Girlfriends, guy friends… I'm so glad he got the job there. I wasn't sure at first." She'd come by a few times early on and Jared had lavished her with attention, so she liked the place now. My boss was kind of the best. "You tell Jared hi from me," she winked.

"I will. And his boyfriend too," I added, straight-faced.

My heart raced. She knew he was gay, and so was most of the neighborhood, which was probably why she hadn't been sure about me working there at first. But I hadn't told her that Jared was dating a man since the relationship started in, what, January? It had been nearly a year and Jared showed no signs of losing interest in Shay.

It was also the perfect testing ground for the conversation we were about to have.

"Oh, he's finally got himself a man?" She clicked her tongue. "About time."

That was it? I was almost dizzy with relief. This was going to go okay.

It was different for family, though. She didn't have expectations of my boss like she did of me. I'd grown up hearing how it was my job to take care of the family, especially as the only child. And taking care of the family meant having a good, stable marriage and kids of my own, and everything that came with that.

A steady job was about all I had so far. The rest of my life was like a row of dominoes. Every time I thought I could arrange it just right, I knocked it all over again. But what was I expecting, trying to build it on the shaky sands of a lie?

My palms were sweating, but I put it off by asking her for family news, and then we got to chatting about the holidays we cele-brated. That spun off into a tangent about traditional foods, and I just couldn't bring myself to interrupt the conversation.

Especially because Cedar was holding up the majority of the

conversation with Mama, and she seemed to be liking him more and more. As she told Cedar how she'd learned English from watching CSI and he talked about which of the cities had the best CSI, I rehearsed my speech in my head.

"And what's eating you up?" Mama looked straight at me, nearly jarring me out of my skin. "I know you aren't here just to talk about TV and change my light bulbs."

I flashed her a smile and wiped my hands on my palms, then grabbed my iced tea for a casual sip as I shrugged. "Not much," I mumbled, swishing around the liquid in my glass.

"Oh, I don't have all day. Spit it out," Mama insisted.

I leaned forward and set it down again. Was everyone else here feeling the tension in here, thick as frosting? "So… you remember Madison? Has she called lately?" If Mama already knew, that was one big weight off my mind.

Mama shook her head, a knowing gleam in her eye. "Is this about that wedding of her cousin's? I told you, if you go, you might win big." She glanced at Cedar. "Atlantic City! I've only seen it on TV."

"Win big by winning back a girlfriend?" I added, half-smiling. I could see what game she was playing.

Mama grinned at me. "I want grandbabies while I'm young enough to run after them in the park."

"About that…" I drew a breath and shook my head. I couldn't just drop the bombshell like this. I had to start slowly. "Madison has been practically blackmailing me for months now. She's angry at me because I lied to her—and everyone else."

I heard the sharp inhalation from Cedar, and I didn't blame him. It kinda sounded like I was about to dodge the big purpose of the visit.

"Did you?" Mama's expression hardened. "I thought she sounded a little too nice to be true. But you were head over heels for her, honey. What lies did you tell?"

My heart jumped into my throat. My palms were slick, and my head spun. This was the moment, and even now, I couldn't quite put it into words. "It wasn't just everyone else... I was lying to myself, too."

Mama just nodded slowly. "What are you trying to tell me, Enrique?"

"I'm gay."

The words dropped from my lips in a fraction of a second. So quick, and yet they fit like a glove after so many years of running from them.

My words tumbled out of my mouth as I kept talking, barely aware of anything I was saying. "I tried dating girls for so long, but it's never going to work. I'm sorry." This time, at least I was in charge. It was my choice to come out.

Not fully, but enough that I felt more confident than I had at Bubbles. This was my mama, after all. She had my back, and she always had.

Mama just looked at me for what felt like a long minute, and then she got up and sat next to me. Cedar scooted over to make more room, his glass trembling against his chest.

When I looked at my mom, I wasn't sure how to interpret her expression, but I knew without a doubt there was love there.

"You be you, baby. I only supported you because you said you always wanted kids and a fairytale wedding. You never told me it was to a man."

I opened and closed my mouth a few times. She was right—I'd

carefully avoided saying that part of it, hoping that if I tried and tried enough, I could change it. And back when I was ten and chasing after girls' pigtails on the playground, the idea of two men raising kids together had been so far out of left field that I hadn't even thought I'd be *allowed*.

Now, though? Things were a little different.

"I'm sorry, Mama." I put my head on her shoulder and wrapped my arms around her. She smelled like safety, and home, and unconditional love. "I didn't want to disappoint you."

"It's breaking my heart that you thought you had to love a woman for me to love you. Didn't I raise you better than to think that of me?"

I bit my lip and shook my head. Her hand rested on my back, gently cuddling me close as she had when I was a kid. "I knew—I hoped I knew—that you'd be on my side. But then…"

"You started doubting yourself." Mama pulled back and wiped her eyes, then took my hands and gave me a shaky smile. "You always have. If there was one thing I wished I could give you… oh, your dad would be so proud of you." She finally looked over at Cedar. "Did he tell you? His dad died when he was sixteen. He took it on himself to be the man of the house, and I always thought he believed in himself from then on."

I ducked my head, my cheeks heating up. "Mama." I didn't need Cedar feeling pity for me now, of all times.

"He'd be proud of you for finally trusting yourself," Mama told me, squeezing my hands again. "I love you, baby. Just the way you are."

The touch made it all sink in: she *loved* me still, no matter what.

"Oh, thank God," I whispered. I wiped my eyes a few times,

blushing fiercely as Cedar handed us both tissues. "I'm sorry I waited so long."

"You waited until you were ready." Mama dabbed her eyes. "And I can't pretend it's not a surprise, but... then... I think I always knew, too."

"You did?" God, how long had I been pushing the truth so far away from myself that I thought it was invisible to everyone else? And how long had they been biting their tongues, waiting for me to let it in?

Mama just gave me a warm smile and hugged me again as I melted into her arms, the stress finally fading. I was still home. *She* was still home.

Once we'd all stopped sniffling—Cedar was trying not to show it, but I heard him blow his nose—Mama folded her arms. "So, how much does Cedar have to do with this new Ricky?" I could tell she was teasing, but she looked serious.

Cedar's hands jolted and he spilled iced tea in his lap, then tried to cover it up by brushing at his legs and crossing them. "Uh..." His eyes flickered between us like he wasn't sure what to say.

I laughed and took the glass from him, putting it on the coffee table before taking his hand. "A lot. More than he thinks."

"That's my biggest fear dealt with." She touched my shoulder. "I just want you to be loved. That's all any parent wants, isn't it?"

I let out a shaky breath and smiled as I glanced at Cedar. "Well, we're not dating, exactly... but we'll see."

Neither Mama nor I missed the hopeful expression that Cedar quickly cleared his throat and smoothed away. As much as I doubted that Cedar would want to date me, I couldn't deny the truth when it was written there on his face.

And *I* was the one who'd looked right at him when she'd mentioned love, so… here I was, blushing again.

"I hope you're going to be happy. That's all I want." She smiled and winked, sniffling again. "That and grandbabies."

"Surrogacy is an option," I murmured, folding my hands. "If I date someone who wants kids, too. Or adoption, or fostering."

"You'll find a way." She cleared her throat and dabbed at her eyes again. "You always have. All right. This calls for cookies. Excuse me a minute."

I glanced anxiously after Mama as she headed for the kitchen, but I gave her the space she needed to come to terms with this. It was probably a shock, however coolly she'd handled it.

Cedar rubbed my arm immediately and scooted over to sit right next to me. "You okay?" he murmured. "Is she okay? Do you need to talk to her?"

"She's fine. She just needs a minute to process this," I told him, biting my lip and trying not to let the worries creep back in. *Is she upset about me lying to her for years? Or that I made myself miserable lying to her? Is she blaming herself for me not telling her?* But I gave him a great big smile despite everything inside my head. "It's done."

Cedar's perceptive look pierced the bubble. "You don't fool me," he told me and gave me a light smile. "But yeah, it's done. You should be proud of yourself."

"And you should prepare for the interrogation," I leaned in and warned him with a grin. "Mama's gonna want to know what you eat for Christmas dinner."

"Uhh…"

"I hope you don't have plans for Christmas," Mama called out as she came back in with a plate of cookies. That was my mama—right on cue. "Or if you do, we can steal you for Christmas Eve, or Christmas Adam. That's the day before Christmas Eve."

Cedar cracked a grin. "I'm sure I could persuade my parents to let me sneak away for a day." He cast me an excited little glance. "I'd be honored."

Okay, this is sounding more and more like we're dating. I gave him a giddy smile in return. Mama had always invited my girlfriends over, and most of them had said yes. It had usually been pretty awkward, and I hadn't even been able to reward them with great sex when we finally stumbled back home, full and drunk and happy.

Cedar, though? No problem.

It was gonna be the best Christmas ever. As long as Nathan kept his fat nose out of it, and I didn't believe for a second that he was capable of that much respect.

Oh, well. I had to celebrate the victories and the moment of peace that descended before the next battle. If there was one thing I'd learned, it was that there was always a fight just around the corner. You could never let your guard down.

18

CEDAR

"Finally getting home, huh? Feel like bothering to do some work?" Nathan's drawl outside my door was unmistakable.

I had the choice of letting him in or letting him shout about my business to all our neighbors. Only now was I seeing that he'd trained me to expect that choice, like either option was okay.

God, Ricky was so right about him. But Nathan was still going to play this like Ricky had suddenly snapped on him and turned into some psycho. And I was going to be right in the middle of that.

I kicked my shoes off before I yanked open my door. Pretty much all my shoes were slip-ons, which meant Uggs this time of year. Nathan always made fun of them. "What?"

"This drag lunch. What kind of waste of time is that?" Nathan laughed. "Or is it an excuse to get to see your pretty boy in drag?"

I tried to grab the door when I saw him moving to come in, but I didn't get it in time. Nathan brushed by my arm and strode past me, waving papers in my face.

"Wait," I hissed, and then sighed and threw up my hands, kicking the door shut and turning around. "It's not a waste of time," I told him, raising my voice. Two could play that game.

"I've got papers for you to sign, now that you've bothered talking to me." Nathan didn't even look at me. He wandered around, flicking the leaves of my plants and eyeing the apartment as if checking to see that Ricky wasn't lurking in a corner somewhere.

"Stop touching the plants," I said, irritation building in my chest. Even though I knew he enjoyed getting a rise out of me, I still rose to the bait. It pissed me off—more at myself than him. "What the hell's gotten into you?"

"I could ask the same thing. You were out all night again," he said, finally turning to me and folding his arms. "I'm hurt that you took his side, but whatever. We don't have to be friends. We're just coworkers. If you'd rather suck dick than stick by a friend, that's up to you."

Ouch. There went the *staying friends with my ex* thing. Even if Ricky had been a real jerk to him—and I was doubting that more and more—when the going got a bit tough, Nathan was willing to ditch it? Yeah, I'd definitely made the right call.

"What did he say to you?"

Nathan shrugged. "Threatened me. Grabbed me by the shirt and tried to punch me. Standard jealousy stuff. You should be careful of him."

"He's not storming in here calling me a slut," I snapped back at him, making my slow way toward him.

"I never called you that. You know what you are," Nathan added with the world's least mature smirk. "Guilty conscience, huh? I heard about you and the bouncer. Really? The dude's like, the opposite of your type."

As pissed as I was that he was taking my words and using them against me, I refused to apologize for anything right now. "Yes, I was out. I don't see a voicemail from you." I wasn't going to address the *side-taking* thing, like we were in kindergarten. Or the *he's not even your type* jealousy over some frankly lousy sex.

We ought to be able to fight like adults, and I was going to do so, even if he didn't.

"I didn't bother calling you. Obviously you're ignoring me," Nathan snorted. "What do you think we'll make from this fundraiser? Two hundred bucks? You expect me to care about that?"

"That can go a hell of a long way," I retorted.

Nathan sneered. "Sure. Around here, it can just about buy a day's groceries for some *needy* person."

Whoa. I really didn't like his tone there. It sounded like he didn't give a shit about the people we were supposed to be serving. Given that he never got his hands dirty in the garden, harvesting, or even giving educational workshops... it shouldn't be a surprise.

But I was only now seeing that all his "admin" work was pretty hollow. Where did he go when he was doing it? Right back to his place.

Maybe when I was spending long summer days out in the gardens and he was doing *admin,* he was...

No. Suspicion wasn't going to breed a happy, productive working relationship. And I didn't care what he was doing, as long as the other half of the charity—the paperwork and money side—was running smoothly. It wasn't a tit-for-tat thing where I expected him to work exactly as hard as me.

But two hundred bucks wasn't worth scoffing at.

I fired back, "The needy people we help access fresh, healthy produce? It'll feed a hell of a lot more than one. You know how much seeds cost for the uptown site?"

Nathan worked his jaw around but didn't say anything. We both knew he had no idea what things actually cost.

"How much it costs for the soil mix for the rooftop place?"

"None of my business. I just pay the receipts you give me." Nathan eyed me. "Maybe that's a mistake. Anyway."

I reeled. "A mistake? Wow," I muttered. Way to pull the stops out. Was he implying that he didn't trust me to submit the right receipts? Or worse—that I was defrauding the charity? Still worse was the next thought I had.

A guilty conscience shouted the loudest.

"Speaking of mistakes, you don't know shit about what's going on at the meeting Tuesday. Just sign the damn papers, let me handle it, and go handle your dumb… *drag* thing." Nathan's condescension couldn't be clearer. "I mean, I can always forge your signature, nobody will be able to tell the difference."

My jaw dropped. He'd never made fun of my handwriting before, which *was* shit. It was a form of precision movement hell for me, and the fact that I could get it legible at all was down to years of physical therapy.

Not that Nathan had any idea or appreciation of work that went on behind the scenes. He never did.

I still didn't say anything, though. As much as I wanted to explode, it wouldn't help smooth things between us if I told him that he was being an ableist asshole right now. There was so much he took for granted, and I'd never gotten on his back about it. But he sure as hell hadn't held back on making fun of everything I couldn't do, or did a bit differently.

It hit me like that: no wonder I felt so bad about my disability. Outside of kids making fun of me at recess and when we had to read each other's handwritten notes, I'd never really had a lot of people make me feel bad. My parents had tried to make sure I did everything that the "normal" kids did, so I felt normal, too.

Nathan was the one making me feel like I wasn't normal.

"Hah, I bet if I let you sign, it'll look like it's been forged anyway." Nathan laughed harshly. "I can do it for you." He waved the bundle of papers at me and then threw them on the bistro table that served as my dining table.

"Is this because I have a boyfriend and you don't?" I kept my voice as calm as I could, walking toward him.

He didn't let me corner him in the living room, though. He wandered around the apartment, forcing me to turn unsteadily on the spot to follow him with my gaze. "No," he snorted as he wandered, running his hand along the walls. "I don't give a shit if you're boning some random fast food loser."

Oh, man. If I could punch him, I might be tempted. If he'd been saying stuff half this mean to Ricky, no wonder he'd lashed out.

"This isn't you," I said instead, shaking my head. I had no idea why he was so damn cranky, except... I squinted at him and folded my arms. "Are you in withdrawal? Coming down from something?"

"What?" Nathan yelped, turning on his heel. His cheeks were flaming red. "How dare you?"

That's a yes. I sighed and rubbed my face. Bingo. Everything made more sense now. "Whatever. I don't give a shit what *you* do, either. But if you go unhinged and rant at my—at my friends, I'm gonna have a problem. If that's drugs talking, you better get out of my life until it's *you* talking again."

"Wow. Big man," Nathan taunted, wandering up to me. He was a couple inches taller, and it forced me to tip my chin back and look up at him—which made my balance unsteady, and he knew it.

I braced myself on the chair behind me and said nothing. I wasn't going to provoke him any further. I'd made my line in the sand clear, and it was time for him to respect that. Right? My heart pounded, my palms sweaty.

Nathan kept approaching me, getting his face nice and close. "I'm the people person, not you. If it's my word against yours…"

"They won't give a shit what you do, either," I hissed back, trying not to shrink back and stumble into the chair. "But I'm telling you, this week you haven't been yourself. Whatever the hell you're on, it's gonna wreck you and everyone around you."

"Don't know what you mean. You should mind your own business."

I laughed—I couldn't help myself—at the idea of him telling me to mind my own business when he'd gone and gotten into Ricky's head, and then outed him to his work life and family.

"What?" Nathan spat, and I did stumble this time, landing in the chair.

"Jesus. Nathan, listen to yourself!" He'd never been physically intimidating before, but his very presence looming over me was scary as shit now. I didn't stand up, but I also didn't look away. I trusted him not to cross that line, but he sure as hell wasn't respecting any other lines right now. "I'm not gonna listen to a word you say until you're back to yourself. Go back to your place and sleep."

"Why?" Nathan stretched and backed up, then flopped onto my bed, lacing his hands behind his head. "I could just hang out here until you give me what I want." He fluffed up my pillows and settled himself down again.

My heart flip-flopped. It was the first time I hadn't felt safe in my apartment, and I didn't know where this was coming from. I looked at the papers he'd thrown down on the table. Some kind of agreement about signatures.

"What is this?"

"You're waiving your right to sign on the accounts. Complicated legal stuff you wouldn't understand," Nathan waved a hand. "Basically, I can meet Jacob without you sitting there being an awkward dweeb, and finish getting last year's accounts ready to submit. Our fiscal year being what it is… oh, never mind."

This smelled rotten. I wasn't an idiot, whatever Nathan thought. But as clear as day, I heard myself think: *This is the moment.*

Either I was going to find out that my suspicions about Nathan's lifestyle were true, or he'd uphold the faith and trust I placed in him. Or maybe the support that our supporters and clients placed in us. Other people's opinions always meant more to him than mine.

If I gave him this power, I gave him power over me, but also the choice. I couldn't resist the chance to see what he was really made of. One way or another, pretending I didn't understand what he was doing would fix this.

"Fine," I sighed. Anything to get him out of my face. "If you get out of here and give me back my key. No more pushing into my life whenever you want." I had to get something out of this, too.

Now that Nathan was invading my personal space—none more personal than my own bed, which he didn't seem keen to get off any time soon—it was time to take back what was mine.

And I could never get further in a new relationship until the old one was properly dealt with. That wouldn't be fair to Ricky. I wanted so badly to have more to offer him, and this was all I could do: some guarantee of privacy when he was over here.

"That's harsh." Still, Nathan stood up. "Deal."

I wasn't sure which of us was the grass and which was the parasitic weed choking its roots, but we were about to find out.

I grabbed the pen he handed me and signed the papers where he pointed, my vision a little blurry. Signing without reading might have been stupid, but I knew damn well my records were clean.

Could he say the same?

"Good." Nathan snatched the papers the moment I was done signing and grabbed the pen, too. "See you whenever."

I let out a long breath as he stomped out and slammed the door. I didn't get up or move yet, just listening. Not more than a minute had passed before the lock rattled. Nathan opened the door, tossed the spare keys inside, and slammed it again.

I slowly pushed myself to my feet and headed over to the floor in front of my door, bending over to pick up the spare keys he'd thrown down. I balanced them in my palm and looked over at the wall that separated our places.

Before I could stop myself, I did the same thing—found my spare key of his, opened his door just enough to toss them inside, and let it click shut. I stood for a moment, looking at the door. Had I ever used that key? I couldn't remember.

The hallway was cold. Standing here catching pneumonia while I rummaged through useless old memories helped nobody. I shivered as I trotted, barefoot, back to the cozy rugs that lined my hardwood floor.

The gulf between us only seemed to be growing, and running this thing with him was only going to get worse if he didn't have to talk to me on a regular basis. I mean, how would he even know how much money to hold back every year for supplies without asking me? He had no idea what a plant pot cost, much less everything else we needed.

Maybe all wasn't lost, though. Just because I was keeping my home and hearth conflict-free didn't mean I had to bend over and take it from Nathan anymore. He was clearly trying to intimidate me now, and I didn't care about that—but he wasn't stopping at me.

I might have done that all summer, but I wasn't going to let him hurt Ricky any more than he already had. Nathan had managed to find a sore point at last—sore enough that I was willing to be a pain in his ass.

Ricky was worth standing up for, whatever he thought of himself.

What could I do? If I was backing down and letting him handle all the "complicated" stuff that my delicate brain apparently couldn't handle, well… what was the point in partnering to do this at all? I was just his employee.

I could probably argue that I had an equal say or no say at all. Hell, quitting the charity and finding a new place to live was starting to sound appealing. I didn't want to be the kind of emotionally abused victim one read about in the newspapers. Finding my own way had to be better than letting him trample all over me for years to come.

I'd been so confident as a kid. "Despite my disability," many adults had said. I didn't see their point, and I didn't let either my cerebral palsy or adults' ideas of what I could do hold me back. I had to give my parents credit—once I'd tuned out the teasing from kids and they realized they couldn't get a rise from me and gave up, that was it. I'd never really seen my own body as a limitation to overcome.

Not until I'd met Nathan, fresh out of my failed semester at school. He'd offered me some purpose in my life, and if it happened to work out well for him… he could have found anyone else to make that offer. You'd be crazy to turn down free rent in Brooklyn and a small salary just for playing in the dirt every day.

No. I was done being used and abused. Nathan's behavior *was* abuse, even if it wasn't physical. Emotional and verbal abuse could still break a man down over the course of months and years, one water droplet at a time.

For a moment, I'd thought of myself as too stupid to understand that agreement he'd handed me. For months now, I'd been thinking of myself as "just the manual labor."

I knew what Ricky would say if he could hear that: *fuck that, and fuck them*. And he'd be right.

Time to find my own way out of this mess.

The next meeting with Jacob, the accountant, was at ten on Tuesday morning. Nathan was never early for anything. I could show up early, like at nine, and grab Jacob for a chat. He wasn't a lawyer, but he knew his stuff. If there was a way to split up the charity, or force Nathan out, or else step away myself…

Whatever I ended up doing, I couldn't keep letting him run my life. Whatever the consequences, I had to stand up for myself, too.

Or I was going to keep getting people hurt when Nathan felt petty and vindictive? That thought was perhaps the only thing that could get me to willingly cause an explosion between me and Nathan.

I was worth it, too. Right?

19

RICKY

The shrill buzz of the doorbell didn't even surprise me anymore. I already knew it was Cedar, since I'd told him when I got off work. It was the day after my big outing, and I wanted to do something to thank him for having helped me so much.

Dinner was ready, and I was pretty proud of myself. I'd even cleaned the place up, did laundry, and set my table with a romantic place setting for two. Jared had been extra-nice and hadn't teased me *that* much when I asked him where the hell to find a tablecloth nearby on my way out from work.

I quickly arranged a tea towel over my arm and took off down the stairs to meet Cedar.

"Good evening, sir. Reservation for two?" I greeted, giving him a dazzling grin. "I believe one Enrique Rosa has arranged a date."

Cedar stepped inside and grinned at me. "Ricky Rosa. I see why you go by Enrique at work. It sounds kind of like a wrestler's name."

I snorted with laughter and then cleared my throat, trying to stay in my persona. "Right this way, sir." I ushered for him to lead the way.

"There's light in here!" Cedar didn't pass me by until he'd cupped my cheeks carefully and kissed me.

I smiled and kissed him back, then patted his ass to get him moving. "There is. I changed the lightbulb today."

"Oh my God, but it's like umpteen feet up."

I blushed. "So my mom broke her arm a few years ago and had one of those reacher-grabber things…"

"Yeah, you took that home and pinched my ass with it," Cedar reminded me, grinning.

"I'm sure I did no such thing," I laughed. "Perhaps Mr. Rosa did, though, sir."

I loved seeing Cedar laugh and roll his eyes at me. He climbed the stairs carefully and I kept my pace slow and steady. As we climbed, I admitted, "I used the grabber arm and stood on a chair. I still broke two lightbulbs before I got it right. I flung one all the way down the stairs."

Cedar burst out laughing. As he reached the top landing, he shook his head and headed inside. "I'm glad you're not the accident-prone one of us two. Now you know what it feels like not to trust your hands, huh?"

"Those things are horrible!" I agreed, glaring at the plastic arm in the corner. It had been embarrassing not to be able to trust my own grip—like my body was betraying me. "Press a little too hard and you crush the bulb… all over your head…"

Cedar gasped and ruffled through my hair. "Did you get all the glass out? Oh my God."

Oh, that felt good. I closed my eyes and smiled as he fussed over me. "Eventually, yeah. You can give me a scalp massage anytime. Now, I'm sure Mr. Rosa will be jealous of all this attention. May I offer you a seat?"

Cedar laughed and grabbed my hips for one more kiss. All this closeness wasn't unlike him, but there was still something else not quite right that I couldn't put my finger on. I kissed him back and looked him over.

"Hm?" Cedar frowned when he saw me inspecting him.

"Are you stressed out?"

Cedar shrugged, but I knew I'd got it in one. "A bit. We'll talk after dinner. I'd hate to ruin Mr. Rosa's careful planning. And the chef's, for that matter."

"Oh, wait until you hear my chef voice." I adopted a horrible French accent. "Mais oui, good sir! Dees beef was mar-ee-nated in the finest—"

"No," Cedar groaned and covered his ears. "Please."

I grinned and pulled out his chair, ushering him into it before sliding him forward. The chair legs caught and I nearly sent him into the table, but managed to steady it just in time. "I keep telling the owner we need to fix this floor, good sir."

Cedar laughed. "I didn't realize a whole cast was going to be entertaining me tonight."

"Oh, you got lucky." I winked. "I'm pulling out all the stops."

"I got really lucky," Cedar agreed with a soft smile that made me go red right down to my toes.

I rushed to the kitchen to get the warmed plates loaded up with food. Fancier food than I'd cooked in a long time, but I'd really enjoyed the task. Leeks and pork medallions with creamy mushroom sauce. Fresh thyme on top, too.

"Leeks. Seasonal," Cedar approved with a grin as soon as I delivered the food. "Wow. That's plated so beautifully."

I tried not to beam at him and immediately failed. "Thank you."

"I liked it when you called me sir. You can keep that up." Cedar winked as I gasped at him.

"Oh, you *are* cheeky tonight," I told him approvingly. Apparently, introducing him to my family had been the way to his heart. It had sure been the way to mine. Without that fear of being outed to my mama by some vindictive asshole, I was free to do whatever the hell made me happy.

Why had I waited so long, anyway?

"Oh my God, this is amazing." Cedar looked around at the place, and then down at the plate of food as he took his first few bites.

"Also what you're going to say in bed later." I gave him one of my signature cocky grins when he stared at me. "See if it isn't true."

Even I had to admit my cooking was downright awesome. It was comfort food to the max—rich and creamy and totally worth an extra half-hour on my feet after a long shift. I really should cook for myself more often.

"I'm coming here for my three square meals a day," Cedar joked. At least, I thought it was a joke.

I grinned at him. "That might not be so bad. I put a lot more effort in when I cook for someone else."

"Me too." Cedar smiled slightly, and there it was again—the anxiety and sadness of whatever was chewing him up inside. He quickly busied himself eating and I tried not to worry too much about it until he was ready to talk.

It was a surprisingly nice, relaxing meal, even with my internal voice counting up the reasons he had to say no to the question I was about to ask.

When I finally couldn't take any more suspense, after I cleared away the dishes, I cleared my throat and sat opposite him. "So, I remember we were talking about where we were going…"

"As in, relationship-wise? Or for dinner? Because I'm glad you made us a reservation right here," Cedar teased.

I grinned. "The both of us. I like being exclusive, but now that I'm out… hell, I don't know how long you're supposed to wait before you do this, but I'd like you to be my boyfriend."

Oh, my God. I did it. I asked him. The thought that he might say no had me sweating bullets. As cool as I tried to play it, I couldn't contain my grin as Cedar practically leapt to his feet. "Really?" he exclaimed. It wasn't in a horribly offended tone. Phew.

"Yeah," I laughed and took his hands in mine. "That's why I wanted to come out so fast. I was already thinking about it before Nathan… well." The last thing I wanted to bring up during *this* conversation was *that* motherfucker. "Anyway, it sped me along. But I feel better asking now that I wouldn't be, like, hiding you—"

"Yes."

It was my turn to blink and stare at him. "Really?"

"I reserve the right to set the terms later," Cedar said with a wink. He leaned in. "They might include more of this delicious cooking."

I laughed and swept him off his feet to spin him around once. "My pleasure."

"Whoa!" Cedar grabbed my shoulder and missed, nearly punching me in the jaw. "Oops!"

I laughed and set him down, keeping a hold of him for a minute to make sure he had his balance. "Sorry. Couldn't help myself there. Come on, lie down with me. I can even carry you…"

"Oh, no." Cedar laughed, but I was determined now.

"My bad for making you lose your balance. I have to make up for it!" I declared and swept him off his feet into my arms properly this time. I carried him, bridal-style, to the bed.

"I was going to say you're acting weird, but, well… you look really happy now," he murmured, scooting up from the foot of the bed as I followed.

"So do you. You looked pretty stressed out earlier." I settled on my side and ran my hand up his arm. "Want to talk?"

Cedar let out his breath and nodded, closing his eyes for a moment. He busied himself arranging pillows behind his head rather than looking at me. "Nathan came over and he was kind of a dick about charity stuff. Anyway, I think he's getting into some bad shit, and… I'm not gonna stick around and watch that going down. He never listened to me, anyway. He sure as hell won't now."

I scooped him into my arms, regardless of how perfect the pillow nest behind him was.

Cedar put his head on my shoulder and rubbed my chest, his breathing hitching. "I'm just so disappointed. I thought we were friends."

"He's an asshole," I murmured. "It's not your fault. Sometimes good people get used."

"Sometimes we let ourselves be used. It's my fault for not seeing it sooner."

I gently shook him until he looked at me. "Hey. No. None of that," I told him firmly. "I'm not bluffing. You're not gonna blame yourself for *his* actions, or he wins yet again."

"Oh." Cedar gazed off for a moment and then smiled, looking back at me. "I like having a boyfriend who's smart as hell."

I scoffed and dusted off his shirt. "Nah. I just know a thing or two about fucked-up relationships. Trial and error, right?"

"If at first you don't succeed… you will sooner or later," Cedar told me with a smile. "And I plan to make that happen this time."

I smiled at him and ran my hand through his hair. "I love your optimism." It felt like a solid foundation for my own overblown, usually fake, self-confidence. When I had his firm conviction, I could tell myself we were gonna be just fine and actually believe it.

Cedar hummed. Despite his obvious pleasure, I could tell his mind was still on Nathan. I had two choices: let him talk it out or distract him with mind-blowing celebratory sex.

How about both? That works. I started with the talking. Better out than in… or out, then in.

"He made me sign this agreement to waive my signing privileges at the bank and accountants' and so on. At least, that's what I think it said. I didn't read it all very well." Cedar bit his lip and looked up at me. "It makes me feel like I don't have any power at all in this."

"You don't, because he's taken it away." I rubbed his back and tried to think of more practical solutions than taking Nathan out back for a good thrashing. "It doesn't sound legal."

Cedar sighed and shook his head. "It's not just that. It hurts that he doesn't trust me. He pretty much said I was too dumb to understand what's going on at the accountant's office."

Nothing would surprise me after hearing Nathan make the worst kind of fun of Cedar's disability. There was no way I was going to tell Cedar what he'd said—it would only hurt him unnecessarily—but I wasn't going to let him spend a minute more with Nathan than he had to.

God, wasn't punching him an option? Even just once?

"But I arranged this drag lunch on my own," Cedar murmured. My heart broke when his voice wavered. "I'm… I'm good with people. At least, good enough. It's Nathan that's been telling me I'm awkward, and I trusted him, so I believed it."

I kissed his forehead and nose and stayed quiet, letting him vent his pain and rage at the betrayal. If only I didn't feel so damn guilty that I was one of the causes of it. If I hadn't lost it at Nathan, he would have kept treating Cedar decently.

And then there was the threat—of him losing his home.

It wasn't my fault, I reminded myself, using words I'd just used to reassure Cedar. The slightest bit of independence from Cedar and Nathan seemed to be losing his shit. We were all dealing with the consequences.

"Look, I know you were joking about moving in with me for the food," I said with a weak chuckle. "But if he ever makes you feel unsafe, you come right over here, okay?"

Cedar let out a long breath, relaxing against me. "Thank you," he murmured quietly.

The fact that he hadn't brushed it off or politely thanked me and turned me down made my brain kick into overdrive.

He *was* feeling unsafe.

Okay, first things first: get his mind off it, and take a moment to celebrate *us* in the middle of all this bullshit. I grinned and walked my fingers up his side. "Living with me would come with extra pokes... er, perks."

Cedar giggled softly and turned onto his side to face me. "Oh, really?"

"Uh huh." I slid my finger back down the center of his body toward his jeans.

"If you want anal, we can do that," Cedar told me with a little smile. "But we have to use condoms until we get tested," he reminded me.

"Of course, baby." I grinned at him. "But I was thinking something else. I keep thinking about you saying that sex isn't just..." I imitated his finger movements, making him laugh. "And I guess it's right. That's not all I want from you for being your boyfriend."

Cedar's sparkling smile had returned again. "Really?"

"Really. What I want is *this*." I rubbed his side. "Just getting to hold you sometimes, and talk to you. You can visit me at work. We can go do little errands and dumb stuff together. That's what relation-ships are supposed to be made of, not..." I poked his perky little ass, which made him jump and laugh.

"You're such a jerk," he laughed, rolling away from me and swat-ting my hand.

I scooted up behind him, spooning him and locking my arm around his chest. "Gotcha," I whispered, kissing the back of his neck.

God, he felt perfect fitting against me.

"I can't believe I struggled against this for so long," I whispered. It was kind of hard to say embarrassing stuff like this out loud, but he never once judged me. He leveled with me instead, and that meant the world.

Cedar ran his hand along my arm gently. "I'm glad you've stopped resisting it. What will be will be, right?"

"Mmhmm."

Cedar had to know what he was doing as he wriggled back against me, squeezing us even more tightly together and also rubbing his ass along my cock. It was very interested in what was going on.

"Nnh. Honey…" I couldn't let myself give in, but I didn't want to ruin the mood. Cedar deserved more than a guy who was just interested in sex.

Really interested right now. And not allowed until we got tested. I was going to do that ASAP.

"Shh," Cedar whispered, turning enough that I could see him grinning at me. "There's lots more we can do together."

But he didn't turn to face me, and if he didn't plan to let me fuck him… what else were we trying? I just had to wait to see what he had planned.

I ran my hand up Cedar's chest and kissed behind his ear. The advantage of this position was how many sensitive spots on his neck I was suddenly locating.

"Oh, God." I grinned to myself, letting myself dwell in this happy place for a bit longer. "This is so much better than sex ever has been." No longer was I freaking out about staying hard for one specific sex act with people I wasn't really into, in order to… what? Buy a picture-perfect life with sexual favors? That was really what I'd been trying to do, and it made me feel fucking cheap.

Oh, man. I've been used, too. I hadn't wanted to admit it, but there we were.

Madison was the worst, but not the only. However much I'd apologized, I'd also been trying my hardest to find love, and commitment, and something meaningful.

The girls I'd dated hadn't wanted that. They'd wanted my dick, not my love. They'd told me *something's wrong with you* and *men always want it.* Like I had no right to be anything but grateful for the attention. The moment sex was off the table, they were out of there. I'd been letting them try to get it on with me when I knew it wouldn't work, and why? Trying to prove to myself that I deserved a shot at normalcy?

This was normal, too. The better kind of normal—the kind that made my toes curl and my lips curve into a smile before I even realized I was thinking about Cedar. My life before now had been a mess of bad ideas.

Cedar was completely different, and not just because he was a guy and my sex drive went crazy the moment I caught a whiff of him or brushed my bare skin along his. He'd gently held me back from trying to prove myself, and God, I was glad now that he had. It would mean a lot more when we did finally make love.

"What's this idea you've got?" I whispered.

"You'll need to get me naked first," Cedar told me, squirming out of his shirt. It didn't take me long to strip him down, and he laughed. "What's the hurry?"

"I want to make you feel good right now, not in a year's time."

Cedar snorted and grabbed my hand to kiss the back of it. "You can make me wait sometimes, you know. It'll feel better in the end."

Ohhh. The exact same principle I'd just been thinking about. I nodded and craned over him to kiss his lips. "Gotcha," I murmured.

"Now you," Cedar whispered.

"I gotta get naked too?" What was he planning? Body-to-body massage?

"Well, no, but I want you to be."

That was all it took to get me fighting my clothes off and throwing them aside. My jeans hit the folding screen that separated the bed in the corner from the rest of the room so hard it toppled and nearly fell, but we both gasped and laughed when it stayed upright.

"Much better," Cedar approved, rubbing his bare ass against my cock and lacing fingers with mine to keep my arm tightly around him. With his other hand, he guided my cock between his thighs.

For a moment, I wondered if he was going for penetration after all, and then my hardening cock slid between his thighs as he squeezed tight.

"Oh!" I groaned. Sure, I'd done this now and then as a prelude to sex, or plenty of times when I was trying to get hard enough for it, but this was different. With Cedar's scent in my nose, my lips on his neck, it was impossible *not* to get hard.

And with every thrust of my hips, my cock slid between his thighs, which were the perfect tight, warm pressure.

"Good, huh?" Cedar whispered. He wriggled until my cock was thoroughly trapped between his thighs, the head brushing against his balls.

It was his turn to shiver and lose control for a moment, his breath catching.

I did it again, thrusting hard as my cock made contact with the base of his and slid up along his shaft. Just as thrilling as frot, but in a very different way. The extra pressure all the way to the base of my shaft was divine. I was so hard it hurt.

I couldn't go too hard with Cedar without risking friction burn, but this slow pace was actually… dare I admit it… kind of nice. Maybe there was something to be said for taking my time to build up the pleasure.

I got to hear him whimper and moan every time my cock brushed along the base of his, and his own erection was looking pretty needy before long.

"You feel so good," I whispered, kissing his neck as I gazed down his body at his quivering, thick shaft. "You must be getting horny already."

"With you against my ass? God, yes," Cedar whispered, laughing hoarsely. "Oh, my God. I need you in me soon, baby."

"Soon," I promised, and then I grinned. "But I'll keep you waiting."

His answering noise was some kind of mix of animal frustration and pleasure.

"It's okay, baby," I laughed. "It'll feel all the better. I'm sure you said that. How are you feeling?"

"Frustrated, horny, can't stop imagining you fucking me. You better hurry up and make me come," Cedar told me, so I slid my arm down his chest to run my palm across his throbbing cock instead. "Oh, God!"

That was a much better answer. I ran my fingers gently up his shaft and then circled them tightly around his head, sliding them down the wet skin. Within a few jerks, I'd found a nice rhythm—thrusting into him as I let him fuck my fist.

It wasn't as tight as being inside him, but it was the next-best thing—and those thighs were so fucking smooth. He was so hot I couldn't stop myself. "Oh, my God, you were right. This *is* good." I paused for long enough to rub my tip around that sexy, tight hole. "I can't wait to be inside here. But for now…" Cedar groaned and I squeezed his cock. "I gotcha, baby."

"Not yet. Roll me over," Cedar whispered.

I grinned and obeyed, gently pulling his cock down against the bed as I rolled him over, face-down into the pillows. I could still reach between his thighs and stroke him, if a little awkwardly, and I had that gorgeous ass to admire. In fact…

Cedar gasped when I kissed one round cheek. "Ricky?"

"Tell me if you object," I told him, kissing his other cheek and then his inner thighs.

"N-No objection. None at all. The opposite of object. Subject? No, approve." His rambling was breathy and frantic, and he squirmed against the bed as I ran my tongue gently along the crack from his balls to his sensitive little hole.

Cedar gasped and arched his back, then pressed himself flat into the bed again, spreading his legs even more. "Fuck. It's been *ages* since I felt that," he whispered.

Well, I was going to make sure he had a good time, then. It couldn't be that much different from going down on anyone else, right? Find the nerve endings, tease them until he lost his mind with pleasure, leave him sticky in my mess…

"Yes, yes, yes," Cedar panted as I explored with my tongue, licking small circles and then pressing kisses against his desperate little hole. I loved the idea that I was keeping him waiting for me. First, I planned to reward him with everything every other loser ex should have given him.

Great rimjobs were just the start.

"Can't take much more," Cedar finally whimpered. "Please!"

He pushed up onto his hands and knees and I reached around him, pressing my torso along his back so I could kiss his neck again and blanket him with my weight. I jerked him off with a practiced hand, wrapping my other arm around his chest to hold him tight. "Come for me, baby. And then I'm gonna come all over that sexy little ass of yours."

That did it for him—he gasped and squirmed against me, and then he threw his head back and cried out beautifully.

I grinned like an idiot as I kept stroking, slowly gentling my grip around him until he was done. "That... was cool."

"I think you've got something left to do, though," Cedar whispered, flopping down flat on the bed again. He wiggled his ass. "Get to it."

He twisted to watch over his shoulder as I knelt back, rubbing my cock along those sexy cheeks before stroking myself hard and fast.

When I came and left my passion streaked across him, my cheeks hurt from grinning.

It felt too damn good to share this moment of release with someone. Somehow, orgasm was so much better when sharing it with someone else.

No more furtive jerking off and then apologizing to my now-exes that I hadn't left stamina for sex. No more embarrassing moments being made fun of, or outright jeered at. None of that shit in my bedroom anymore.

Just playful, loving banter, and all kinds of sex I'd never considered before.

Cedar was so perfect. I grabbed tissues to wipe us off and help clean up the bed, grinning to myself. Totally worth doing laundry again.

"How was that?" I murmured.

"Great."

"Close enough." I winked at him. I hadn't forgotten my promise from earlier, and I grinned at him. "What happened to *amazing*?"

Cedar's laugh was rich and long when it clicked. He rolled over and rubbed my chest, putting his head down on my shoulder. "My bad. I should have said, amazing."

"Damn straight."

"No. Not at all straight, and I love it." Cedar grinned up at me. "And I'm really proud of you, baby."

"Damn gay." I kissed his forehead and closed my eyes. "I'm proud of you, too. And even prouder to call myself your boyfriend. I've got my first boyfriend," I added in a sing-song voice. "And he's the sexiest man in Brooklyn."

Cedar made a happy little sound and snuggled into me, and I wrapped my arms around him. I immediately vowed to keep him safe no matter what. If I was going to be his other half, I was going to do it right.

Whatever else happened—whoever else tried to fuck with us—we were together. At least we had each other, and nobody could get between us.

20

CEDAR

Breathing almost hurt again today. I shoved my hands further in my pockets, regretting that I'd ever loaned my gloves to Nathan last winter, along with my self-respect.

It was a few minutes before nine, and I stomped back and forth to keep my toes warm as I waited for the receptionist to unlock the door. Veronica seemed surprised to see me, shading her eyes as she twisted the lock and pushed open the door.

"Oh, right on time. Come on in out of the cold."

"I know, I—wait, what?" I glanced at my watch and mentally confirmed that we weren't switching to Daylight Savings time or anything. It was so grim and gray in the mornings now that I'd do anything to buy more daylight.

"I think Jacob was expecting you at ten, though, and Nathan first. Is that right?"

I stepped into the lobby, shading my eyes against the fluorescent lights for a moment. "Um..."

"Maybe you should talk to Jacob. Go on ahead," Veronica hastily added, gesturing for me to head in.

"Thanks." I had no idea what that was about. If anything, since I signed those papers, Jacob ought to not be expecting me at all.

"Oh. This is a surprise." Jacob closed the file folders he'd had open and waved me into the office, but he didn't stand up to greet me. His lips were pressed together in a thin line.

I knew when I wasn't welcome, but I had to proceed anyway. It was too late to turn around.

"Morning," I greeted. "I know Nathan's here in an hour for a meeting."

Jacob checked his wristwatch and made a noncommittal humming sound. "What can I do for you?"

"Well, I…" I had to fight every instinct not to lose my nerve. I took the chair opposite his desk and leaned forward. "I wanted to talk about options for dissolving or changing the ownership structure."

"Mmhmm." Jacob looked apologetic. "I'm sure you'll understand I can't help with that under the current circumstances."

Oh. Well, that was a clear no. I bit my lip, cursing myself for being dumb enough to think Jacob could be neutral. He was Nathan's dad's friend, after all.

"I believe Nathan's on his way to talk about something similar, actually."

"Huh? We're supposed to be here at ten, only I signed his stupid papers so I wouldn't even have to come." I rubbed my forehead.

"Excuse me," Jacob said as his phone went off and he picked it up. "Mm. Yes. Send him in, thanks."

Before I could ask what was going on, Nathan entered. He was less than pleased to see me, judging by the way his nostrils flared and his eyes narrowed.

"Well, this is a surprise." Nathan sneered at me.

I rolled my eyes and stayed seated, forcing him to take the other chair and scoot it closer to the desk if he wanted to join the conversation. "I'm full of them today, apparently."

"I guess it's good you're here." Nathan said it like he didn't really care either way, and he dropped into the chair opposite Jacob. "I want to shut down the charity. When everything pending is settled, of course. I'm done working with him," he gestured in my direction without even looking.

"Of course." Jacob couldn't do enough for Nathan. He leaned back and laced his hands behind his head, immediately warmer than he had been since I set foot in the office. "We can go over your options."

Confusion set in. "Wait, I wanted to and you just said we couldn't." Unless the rules were different for Nathan. Of course they were. Jacob didn't owe me a thing, but Nathan was his best friend's son.

I was just the leech hanging onto him. The glance Jacob cast me told me that much.

"Not until everything is settled," Nathan said, emphasizing every syllable like I might understand better that way. "Obviously."

"And depending on the outcomes, well... we can't do much yet," Jacob said.

It was like they were talking in a whole new language, but one thing was sinking in: Nathan wanted to break up the charity and the partnership as much as I did.

"Let's skip that and look at the implications going ahead, though,"

Jacob said, waving off the conversation Nathan had been about to start. "Probably most pertinent to Cedar's concerns." He riffled through papers. "I understand via Nathan's father's lawyer that, effective immediately upon dissolution, he will no longer be held responsible for the rent on either of your apartments. You'll need to set up separate rental agreements with your landlord…"

I felt dizzy for a moment. Okay, this was really happening. I was no longer getting a pay check, however small, from the charity. "Effective when?"

Jacob looked at Nathan, and Nathan's lips curled into an all-too-pleased smile as he looked over at me. "He sent notice Monday morning."

Yesterday, then. It had already been decided without me. "And you couldn't *bother* to tell me—" I cut myself off. No, he was not going to make me sound like the bad guy here, in front of Jacob. "Fine." I rose to my feet. I needed to get out of there and try to clear my head.

Everything was about to change. God only knew how long Nathan would have waited to tell me if I hadn't tried to beat him to the punch today. Just that thought made me sick.

"Notify me in writing when my lease is coming up," I told Nathan and headed for the door.

"Fine," Nathan echoed. "We signed on the twenty-fifth, so… the twenty-fourth."

I whirled on my heel. That wasn't just cold, that was downright spiteful. How long had he been planning this? He had to have given notice… to get *me* out early. On Christmas Eve.

Nathan fluttered his fingers. "You got a couple weeks to house-hunt. No need to stick around."

Somehow, a small piece of me had always known it would come down to this. I couldn't keep getting a free ride forever, and Nathan's dad had always thought I was the expendable one in the partnership.

"Unless you wanted to work out some arrangement," Nathan added when I didn't move.

I wasn't about to stay here and grovel for his forgiveness when I'd done nothing wrong except trust him. And Jacob was clearly on Nathan's side, though he wasn't saying anything. It was obvious from his body language.

It wasn't exactly my life passion, but I was going to lose something important to me just because Nathan couldn't be a grownup. Served me right for trusting anyone. All people were assholes. They just took their sweet time showing it sometimes.

"Suck a dick," I told him and stormed out of the office. I even slammed the door on my way out, even if it made me almost sick with nerves to do so.

"Oh, goodness—" Veronica broke off when she saw my face, rising to her feet.

I'd planned on not even stopping to say goodbye to Veronica, but it wasn't her fault all of this was happening. "Bye, Veronica. Sorry for the trouble," I told her with as much of a smile as I could manage.

I was striding for the subway station moments later. It took me a minute to register the cold air on my face and hands, I was so hot with rage at Nathan's underhanded trickery.

Okay, Nathan had used me, and I was a damn fool for not spotting it sooner. All I could do was make the best of my situation now.

Two and a half weeks to find a new apartment and move, and then I wouldn't share a wall with my ex anymore.

Also, the same time frame to find a job that would cover the rent on that place.

Shit.

And what about the drag show this weekend? Maybe I could raise funds for *Cedar House*. I fought back a laugh. It wasn't funny, but hey, that was life.

No, it wasn't fair to take that away from Neil's hotline, LGBTalk, when they still needed the funding. It was only a morning and afternoon of my time, and Jared had been advertising the drag brunch for the last few days.

The show must go on, even if my life might never look the same behind the scenes.

In a moment like this, there was one person I knew I needed to see.

It took several trains, a bus, and an Uber before I fumbled with the statue on my parents' front porch. The spare key was hidden underneath, and I'd never found it easy to get the compartment open.

When I finally shook it free, I unlocked the door and let myself in, and my stress finally melted away.

Well, it didn't vanish, but at least I wasn't stewing in it like a well-marinated roast chicken. I *had* just jumped into the fire, but everything was back in perspective—Nathan was some asshole hopped up on power who wanted to hurt me, and I wasn't going to let him.

"Honey?" Mom came around the corner and lit up at the sight of me. "Oh, Cedar!"

That was it—hugs, a mug of coffee, and a blanket around my shoulders as she ushered me to the living room to sit with her.

I think she'd get along with Mrs. Rosa. I tried to shoo away the thought, but I was already smiling.

"What news do you have?" She wrapped her hands around her mug and smiled at me. "Before I bore you with tales of the cold frame your dad is building."

"Oh, I'd love to hear," I started, and then my smile crumpled. Right. Like a smack in the face, a reminder that I was about to lose my job—and all the sites I'd carefully cultivated, and everything I'd built with blood, sweat, and tears.

"Honey," Mom murmured, putting aside her mug and scooting closer. She folded me in one of those hugs that made me feel like she could fix it all.

But she couldn't. Only I could.

"Nathan's breaking up the charity, and his dad is stopping paying my rent. I need a job and a house, and I'm scared I won't find them this month." I knew I was welcome at home, but I couldn't just leave behind my life in Brooklyn. Even an hour north, it was a whole different world. To my New York friends, I might as well live on Mars.

She sucked a breath in. "I knew that cowardly slimeball was going to—oh, hon. Why? What happened?"

"I have a boyfriend, and he got jealous. By the way…"

"Oh!" She lit up and pulled away, holding me by the shoulders as she looked me over. "I thought you looked different. Love suits you. When do I get to meet him?"

I laughed. "Well, I met his mama last weekend, so... maybe soon? I'm sure I can finagle that. Oh, God. He told me to ask if I want to move in with him, but... I can't ask that. We've only known each other for a couple weeks."

"Well, you sometimes don't meet roommates until you move in with them," Mom said. She had her practical, problem-solving face on. "That's a bit different, but perhaps it isn't disastrous. Do you trust him?"

"Yeah," I breathed out. "But I trusted Nathan..."

She squeezed my hand and then pressed my mug into my hands again, helping steady my hands until I had a grip on it. Just that little gesture made me smile.

"No," she murmured. "You can't judge one man by another's actions. What's this mysterious man's name, anyway?"

"Ricky," I told her, and there I was—smiling.

She smiled back at me. "Ricky," she repeated. "So, if you don't want to move in with him—you know there's always a place here..."

I shook my head. "Thanks, Mom. But you know I can't."

"It's nothing to be ashamed of. Mrs. Brook down the street has both Adam *and* Angela back home now. Millennials and Gen Z don't have it easy. Your dad will be happy to have you around, you know that."

"No," I said again, straightening up. "I've just got to adapt."

"If there's one thing you're good at, it's that," Mom told me and patted my knee. "I'm very sorry to hear that you're losing the charity, but let's take this chance to think of other opportunities this opens up."

"I couldn't do anything besides charity work," I agreed, nodding slowly. I wasn't physically strong or agile enough for other kinds of outdoor landscaping work, or I'd ask Adam for connections. "But I can try to find another career path."

"And if you don't get hired right away, ask your friends for help. If you're staying in Brooklyn to be around them, they'd better be the kind of friends who'd want to help."

"They would," I agreed, immediately thinking of Ricky. If I *did* move in with him and split rent, it would be a lot cheaper to live… and I'd have company.

No more long, lonely evenings listening to partying and sex sounds—sometimes both at once—from my neighbor.

"Stay for the night," my mom urged me. "I'll make up the spare room."

I set aside my mug again and hugged her. "Thanks," I murmured. "But I think I should go to Ricky."

A smile bloomed over her face. "If you've found the kind of man you want to go to when everything's going wrong, I'm very happy for you. Hold onto him."

Yeah. I planned to. As long as moving in didn't scare him out of his mind, which it probably should if he wasn't crazy.

But he was just a little bit crazy, and I loved that about him.

"Did you feel like Dad just… fit in your life?" I asked, a blush heating up my cheeks. "When you started dating?"

She gave me a knowing smile. "Yes, hon. I've always said it was like finding my other half. You just know when someone's your match."

My match—I liked that. Not just my support, and not way out of my league like Nathan pretended to be. Just my equal. "Do you think it's too soon?"

Mom chuckled. "Only time will tell. But the fact you're asking that about Ricky but you never did about Nathan tells you everything you need to know."

I'd tried so damn hard not to let myself get excited over this, in case my heart was on the line too soon. But I couldn't stop the excitement that vibrated through me now.

"I think I'd better find out when he gets off work," I told her, nervous excitement building deep inside. "And I'll ask him if I can move in with him temporarily. If things work out… we'll see."

I couldn't imagine sharing space with him all of a sudden, but at the same time, I wanted nothing more. Every night apart these last two weeks, I'd fallen asleep thinking about him, and I'd woken up disappointed that I couldn't snuggle into him.

Maybe I was falling head over heels, but for once in my life, that was a good thing.

21

RICKY

I knew something was wrong the second I got the text message asking what time I was getting off work.

Sure, I wasn't really supposed to keep my phone on me in the kitchen, but Jared hadn't said a word about it. He could be a pretty decent guy a lot of the time.

He'd checked on me when I got back to work, and though I'd blown him off, it meant a lot that someone actually gave a shit about me. I was grateful to have him in my corner.

All I could hope was that, in turn, Cedar would let me be in *his* corner. That text was a good start.

I sent a quick response. *4 today. I'll be home ASAP but you can stop by to grab the key if you need to.*

The answer came a few minutes later, as I was sliding plates through the window to Jess. My phone chirped obnoxiously, making sure I didn't miss the message, and neither did anyone else.

Jess raised her eyebrow and looked at the counter where my phone sat, then at me.

"Shut up," I grumbled, turning my back to hunch over my phone and read his answer.

OK I'll be there at 3 and wait for you to finish. Might be late if traffic's bad.

Traffic? Where was he, Manhattan?

Sounds good babe xox. I grinned as I sent back the response, wondering how he'd handle the cuteness.

I got a single *xxx* in response almost immediately.

I like xxx even more, I texted back.

Perv!

You love me for it. GTG, I added. I pocketed my phone hastily as Jared dropped off an order and I tried my best to look innocent.

It was all I could do to focus on work today as the hours dragged by. The post-lunchtime slowdown didn't help, either.

Though she'd once been overly friendly—no doubt trying to find gossip to pass on to Madison—Daisy wasn't talking to me these days. I finally grabbed Jess near the end of the afternoon when she was on break. "What the hell's going on with her?"

"Oh, I might have told her a few things," Jess answered, keeping her voice down and grinning. "Like that I know she's a homo-phobic asshole, but me and my girlfriend will kick her ass if she's a dick to you."

I blushed. I didn't need anyone defending me, but once again, it meant a lot that someone wanted to.

What was it with everyone who seemed to like me all of a sudden?

I'd felt like nobody did for ages, but when push came to shove, they seemed to be showing their true colors. And there was a lot less steely gray than I'd expected.

"Thanks," I brought myself to say. "I'm more worried about Cedar than me."

"Are you two officially…" Jess leaned in. "Dating?"

I let out a long sigh and flopped in the break room chair, keeping an ear out for the bell on the door or Daisy dropping an order off. "Yeah. I came out to my mom at last, so I felt better asking him out."

"Oh my God! Congratulations," Jess exclaimed and slapped my shoulder. "About time!"

"Yeah, well." I scoffed. "Apparently it's all a lot easier than I thought it would be. I always figured I'd be the family disappointment."

"Oh, I'm working hard on being the family disappointment, sexuality completely aside," Jess told me. She grinned. "My mom found out about my belly button piercing."

"They don't care about you and your girlfriend?"

"As long as we're happy," Jess shrugged. "That's what most parents want."

"Where were you a month ago—three months ago—six months ago—when I was freaking out about this?" I laughed, burying my face in my hands for a moment. "I mean, I knew Mom loved me, but…"

"I was right here. So was Jared, and all the regulars, and… a lot of people. You weren't ready to share," Jess told me, touching my shoulder. "Don't beat yourself up."

Yeah, she was right. It had taken me a long time to be ready to set out on this journey. Maybe I was a late bloomer, but I was making up for lost time. "Boyfriends. This is so cool."

"Order up!" That was Daisy's barked voice.

Jess and I rolled eyes at each other as I got up. "On my way!" I hollered, then muttered to Jess, "I'm gonna make a point of making out with Cedar today, just for her."

She snorted with laughter and gave me a thumbs-up behind her bowl of soup.

I kept peeking out at the dining room as the time marched on, but even though I was expecting him, it was still a surprise when I spotted Cedar's blond hair in the small group gathered around the regulars' corner booth.

One quickly fried plate of bacon later, I headed out. "Special delivery for Cedar," I told him, winking as I slid the plate across to him.

Cedar's face cracked into a big, beautiful grin as he looked up at me. "Looks perfect," he approved.

"So do you." As I said it, I cringed.

Billy was there, and Charlie must be off work early. Shay was the last member of the group right now, but I expected after work hours, Kev and maybe even Adam or Darren would be by, along with a few of the hangers-on.

"Ohhh," everyone else exclaimed and elbowed each other.

Billy grinned at me, folding his arms and looking every inch a proud mama hen.

"Okay, shut up, everyone," I told them and slid in next to Cedar, putting my arm around him.

Charlie mimed zipping his lips, and everyone suddenly got busy looking elsewhere.

"Do me a favor and wait til Daisy looks at you, then kiss me," I murmured, leaning in to whisper into Cedar's ear.

Cedar grabbed both my cheeks and hauled me in for a hard kiss, bending me backward. I just about saw stars, grabbing his shoulders and holding on tight as he pushed against me.

The other guys couldn't pretend not to see that. They cat-called, even as I flipped them off. As much as I loved the aggressive, forthright attitude, this wasn't the Cedar I knew. Another warning bell went off in my head.

"Good? She looks like I slapped her with a fish," Cedar murmured, looping his arm around my neck.

"Uh. Yeah. Um." My thoughts were definitely not on Daisy anymore. I just really hoped Cedar was sticking around to go home with me. Why did it have to be another hour away?

"Work going good?" Cedar's voice was still a little too high.

"Yeah. What's up?" I frowned.

Cedar shook his head slightly and crunched my bacon, not looking at me. I got the hint—wait until later.

Probably Nathan being an asshole again. Why couldn't he just leave Cedar alone for good? I wanted to put my arms around Cedar and keep him safe from Nathan forever. If only he'd let me.

"Okay. Well, I better get back to work before Jared yells at me." I pecked Cedar's lips, waved at the other guys, and took off for another hour of imagining what else could be going in Cedar's life, and how I could fix it.

He'd been there for me when I needed it—even when I hadn't

know I needed it—and I'd give anything to help him in return. So long as he let me.

"So I've lost everything at once."

I hated hearing the misery in Cedar's voice. It was even more tempting to risk the legal threats from Nathan and give him a good thrashing. He seemed like the kind of spoiled rich kid who'd never had one.

"Not everything, baby," I murmured, pulling him into me as we cuddled on the rickety couch in my apartment. All I could do was wrap my arms around him and try to make him feel safe, if only for tonight.

The fact that he'd come to me had to be a good sign. He wasn't running and hiding away his problems, as I'd done for so long.

"Not you?" Cedar looked up at me with a sad little smile. "Thank God."

"Never me," I promised in a whisper. I kissed his forehead and hugged him so tightly he yelped.

But was I really worth trading everything else in his life for? I couldn't even summon up a cocky response that would sound like I believed it. Without me around, no doubt he'd still be coasting by, not aware that Nathan thought so little of him.

Was that a fate any better?

"I can't believe his parents aren't ashamed of him," I muttered. "Mama would be hitting me around the ear if I ever tried that."

Cedar chuckled. "Yeah. I can see that. I went to see my mom

earlier, by the way. Dad was at work, but her office was closed today. Anyway, she… made me feel better about it all."

Thank God he had parents like mine, then. I'd never doubted that Mama or Dad loved me, no matter what.

"I'm sorry about your dad, by the way," Cedar started, hesitating. We hadn't talked about it after visiting Mama, but she was proud of my dad and his fight. She'd never seen reason to hold back on talking about it just because others were uncomfortable with death.

I'd come around to her way of thinking. Dad had been a damn fighter, and I'd grown up at least ten years just watching the way he handled the indignity and inhumanity he'd faced.

I shook my head and scoffed. "Cancer can go fuck itself. It's nobody's fault. It just made me appreciate what I have."

I'd hurt for years afterward, and yeah, a decade later, part of me still wasn't fully over it. But that seemed like part of life: losing people too soon.

"So do I." Cedar swallowed hard. "I'm scared, but I have to hold on to the people around me, Mom told me."

"Smart lady." I rubbed his back. "Especially me. You can hold onto me however you like—" *Oh God, don't think of Nathan's awful words,* "—whenever, baby."

Cedar grinned at me for a moment, and then his expression grew taut. "Actually, uh… okay." He let out a shaky breath. "You mentioned moving in with you if I needed to?"

"Yeah." *Wait, he's taking me up on that?* I sat up a little straighter and caught my breath. "I haven't lived with anyone in a couple years, but I'd love to have you here. If you want."

"Starting tomorrow, I'm working on finding a job first," Cedar told me. "But I have to be out by…" He paused, and rolled his head against my shoulder.

"By?" I wanted to know how much time we'd have to prepare.

"Christmas Eve."

"You're fucking shitting me." I wanted to march over there and kick Nathan's door in. "You don't have a spare key for him, do you?"

"No." Cedar laughed shakily. "I gave it back when he gave me mine back. It's been a hell of a week and it's barely started."

I rubbed his shoulder. "Okay. Well, we'll figure it out. You'll be out in plenty of time," I assured him. "And you're spending Christmas with me, no ifs, ands, or buts. And the rest? We'll figure it out, baby. Get a job first, and then if you want to find your own place, you can do that. Or if we haven't started passive-aggressively leaving notes on the fridge, maybe this can be long-term."

Cedar laughed, rubbing his forehead against my shoulder before he raised his head for a firm kiss. "Thank you. I feel a little less crappy. You're so kind to people. I like that about you."

"Of course," I whispered, my cheeks heating up. "You shouldn't feel bad about doing what you gotta do, man."

Cedar smiled—a faint, sad ghost of his usual bright sunbeam. I wished I could scoop him up and wipe all those clouds away. "I've spent months trying to pour myself into that damn charity, because… I don't know. I felt obligated. But I really felt obligated to Nathan, I guess."

I seethed inside, but I kept my touch on him gentle. "Because of his dad paying the rent?"

"Yeah," Cedar's response came in a quiet breath, the tension draining from his body.

"Well, screw that." I shook my head. "You were burned out for ages, weren't you?" When Cedar nodded, I kissed his cheek. "You don't have to do it all. Making yourself miserable won't help anyone. Charity starts at home, they say."

Cedar nodded. His smile was a little bit brighter, at least. "Yeah. I know. I can find something else that helps people without wrecking myself. Or keeping that jerk around."

We lapsed into silence for a little while, and I let Cedar gaze off in thought. When I started to worry he might be mired in self-doubt, though, I rubbed his shoulder. "Hey. You're incredible, you know."

Cedar blushed and squirmed against me, his gaze suddenly on my lap. Apparently a few little words were all it took to get him shy. "Really? I just… work hard at whatever I do."

I smiled. "Yeah. Even when the going gets tough, you stick around. That's a good trait to have."

Cedar blinked rapidly and then kissed me—this time, harder. "How the hell did I get lucky enough to stumble into you?"

"Anything I can do to help. I mean that."

"Well…" Cedar's suggestive expression was less than subtle. He peeked up at me through his lashes and tilted his head a certain way.

I grinned at him and walked my fingers along his thigh toward his cock. "Does the mighty cedar need… help to harden up?"

Cedar squinted at me, genuine concern written over his face. "I'm not sure if that's sexy or not."

"Take it as sexy," I advised him with a grin, squeezing his crotch playfully. "What did you have in mind?" We'd already done a lot together that I'd loved. My opinion on what "counted" as sex had done a one-eighty.

"Would you make love with me?" Cedar ran his hand up my chest and rested it on my shoulder, kissing my cheek. "I trust you. I want you."

Those words were the aphrodisiac I'd never known I was missing. I could even overlook the cheesiness of that phrase I'd never fully believed in. With Cedar, *making love* was exactly right.

"Of course," I whispered. I laced my fingers with his and pulled him to his feet to lead him over to the bed, nearly bouncing on my toes as I walked.

"See? Waiting is even better for you, too," Cedar teased. He scooted up the bed on his back, using his elbows to help himself up, and I followed. There wasn't room for my bed to fit sideways behind the screen in this corner, but he'd never complained.

It gave me time to pursue him on hands and knees until I managed to tackle him, and he dissolved into giggles. "Oh, no!"

"Oh, yes!" I tickled him until he begged for mercy, and then grinned as I kissed him. "I'm sorry. I just love how you laugh."

"If I love how you cry out in bed, should I step on your foot?" Cedar retorted, out of breath, his hair all messed up. He was grinning at me.

I tilted my head at him and then laughed. "Fair point. Truce. I'll make you laugh with my incredibly witty words."

"Come here." Cedar rolled onto his side and pulled me alongside him, then hugged me and kissed nice and slow. I expected it to last just a few seconds before we hurried along, but—of course not.

I lost track of how long we made out. I wasn't paying attention, because I was enjoying myself way too much.

When Cedar ground up against me, I ran my hands down his

sides to grab his hips. That way I could push back and tease him with my bulge.

"You're getting way too good at teasing me. Should I be worried?"

"I'll always please you in the end," I promised, kissing him again. "But maybe I want you to beg for it."

"Oh, I'll beg all night," Cedar whispered, his gaze clear and sincere. "You're worth it."

For a moment, I was speechless. I cleared my throat and shook my head, then kissed him. "You make me speechless. Very rude of you."

"Sorry, not sorry." Cedar was already wriggling out of his clothes.

"Hey, did I say you could do that?" I pretended to gasp.

Cedar smirked. "Say, who's the *sir* around here?"

"Oh!" I laughed, enjoying the sight of Cedar peeling himself out of his clothes. It was so much better to get to see every inch of him that I wasn't about to protest any further.

When he yanked off his underwear, Cedar ran his hands up his own thighs and rolled onto his back.

I straddled him to kneel between his legs, and when he wrapped them around my waist, a part of me felt complete that I'd never felt before. Like this was just the right place to be.

Well, *almost* the right place.

"I've got condoms, hold on…" I mumbled. I had to roll with him to get them, laughing all the way. "You're strong."

"Surprisingly, yes." Cedar held on with both arms and legs, and I loved the feeling of him tightly around me. Like he'd never, ever let go.

And I sure as hell wouldn't let him go, either. He was mine, however much Nathan wanted to keep his claws in him. I was going to take care of him, however he needed it, however long he wanted me to.

Cedar had a beautiful heart and I was going to keep it safe.

"You're smiling like the cat who got the cream," Cedar whispered.

I grinned as I tore the condom open. "I did. And now you're gonna get mine, baby."

"Ew," Cedar laughed. "Can we not call it cream? That makes me wonder about your pork medallions."

"Is that another name for my nuts?" I smirked. "Would you rather my jizz?"

"You're the worst!" Cedar laughed, covering his face. "I can't believe I'm dating you."

"The best worst, thanks very much." I stroked myself as I rolled the condom on.

"Or just the best," Cedar told me, his laugh finally tailing off. "I'm so excited." He grabbed the lube, biting his lip as he flipped the lid open. It took him a few moments to get his fingers lined up with the opening so he could squirt the lube over his fingers.

"Do you want me to do that?" I asked.

Cedar winked. "You can finger me some other time. I might just blow my load that way if I let you do that right now."

"We wouldn't want that." I stroked myself slowly, my eyes on the fingers disappearing into his tight hole.

God, how I wanted that to be me.

"Okay, babe." Cedar grinned. "Come on, kiss me."

Rather than jumping right on my dick, he pulled me down and kissed me until I barely remembered what we were doing. Cedar's hand in my hair and his other hand squeezing my ass were far too distracting.

"Wow," I breathed out, closing my eyes to enjoy the way he sucked my lower lip until my cock twitched. "Okay, before *I* blow my load early... a phrase that I've never said before," I laughed. I wasn't used to having to hold myself back—only push myself forward to get it over with as quickly as possible.

Now, I wanted it to last.

When I pressed my tip against him, Cedar hitched his legs further up my waist and held on tight.

I tried to slide inside as slowly and gently as I could, but I choked back a moan at how good the rings of tightness felt giving way to my arousal. My nails dug into his shoulders, and I couldn't stop staring at the taut expression on his face.

Cedar took his time adjusting, and I wasn't going to rush it. I felt it when he was ready. He relaxed just a little more, his breathing steadying as his eyes flickered open to meet mine. "Finally," he whispered, his hands flattening on my back rather than gripping me so tightly.

I knew what he meant. It felt like we'd been waiting forever to do this, and finally being so deep inside him felt like the most intimacy I'd ever experienced.

"You're perfect," I whispered. I wouldn't have kept the awe from my voice even if I'd been able to hear it.

His expression softened and glowed. "Yeah?"

"Feels amazing, baby. You're so beautiful, and sweet, and smart, and I can't believe..." *You're letting me do this?* It didn't seem like the right thing to say, exactly. "You're mine," I finally realized what I wanted to say.

Cedar grinned at me. "I am. I'm yours to fuck. Get that pretty little ass to work." He slapped my ass, startling me into pushing into him.

"Oof! Demanding," I teased. "Yes, sir. At your service."

I really was, though. I pushed into him in a slow, steady pace, reveling in how fucking good it felt to be wrapped in his warmth. I wanted to stay locked together with him like this forever.

"Yes," Cedar panted, his moans and groans encouraging me to go harder. It seemed like he was ready before me, and much more practiced—but he didn't make me feel bad for my inexperience.

This wasn't too different after all, except that I felt more comfortable by far. I didn't have any direct comparison to make since I'd never tried anal before—it felt like asking too much.

I could have been having great sex like this all along? I thought before I caught myself about to heap more guilt on myself. Like I needed that.

No, I couldn't. I hadn't met Cedar yet, and most of what made this amazing was knowing the man I was balls-deep inside.

And wanting him to feel so good, not because I felt like I owed him out of a sense of obligation or guilt. But because he was the sexiest thing alive, and when I thrust just right and his lips parted, I wanted to kiss them until we lost our senses.

Cedar's breathing became quick and raspy and his little pants of *yes* grew more and more frequent as I fucked him hard and fast, sparing the mattress no strain.

"I'm gonna come," Cedar finally whispered, one hand in between our stomachs and stroking himself. "With you inside me."

I grinned at him. There was something about those words that no man could resist. "Yeah, baby. I promised I'd make you feel so good."

"You do," Cedar managed. "Oh, yes!"

He arched toward me, his feet flat on the bed now as he let go of me and grabbed the sheets by his hip. His grip was so tight I wondered if he'd tear the fabric for a moment. As I pounded into him hard and fast, his stroking motions grew ever more erratic.

"Let me," I begged him a moment later, resting my hand on his.

Though he gave a protesting moan, he relented and let go, grabbing the sheets on the other side too. "Hard, please, baby."

"Hard as you want," I promised, matching the pace he'd been setting a moment ago. It was so hard not to just lose control myself, my body so tight and tingling with warmth. A fire of need burned so deep in me that it couldn't be ignored.

The rest of the world was gone, my world narrowing to Cedar. I was seconds away unless I slowed down, but I wasn't going to do that. It was Cedar's turn, and nothing would stop me from making him feel exactly as good as he deserved to feel.

Cedar cried my name as he arched off the bed, and the sudden extra squeezing pressure around me was more than I could hold out for. I gritted my teeth and grunted, nearly collapsing over him as my body finally let go of all that tension.

We rode out our orgasms with, around, and inside each other. I pressed close to him, burying my face in Cedar's neck so he was all I could smell or taste as pleasure shuddered and jolted through me, centered perfectly on my erection deep inside him.

It took a long minute before I slid out, still gasping for breath.

God, when had we both become so sweaty? I hadn't even noticed the exertion, I'd been so desperate for release.

Cedar giggled and hugged me, rolling onto his side away from me to make me spoon him. It was kind of adorable, and I obliged him easily, pulling him against my chest.

We lay like that for a long minute before Cedar finally groaned and rolled onto his back again. "Better clean this up."

"I'm all taken care of," I told him, easing the condom off with a smirk. "Shoulda come prepared. Haha, come prepared. Get it?"

Cedar's voice was so fond it almost hurt when he murmured, "You're awful."

"I know." I stretched out and closed my eyes when I was done, feeling him shift about beside me.

Finally, he settled down by my side and hummed quietly. "You know, when I move in, we can do this a lot more often." When I opened my eyes, Cedar was beaming at me.

I chuckled gently and cupped his face. "Perfect. That'll keep me in shape. Everyone wins." I ran my hand down his side. "And maybe sometime, you could show me how to bottom, too."

"I'd love to," Cedar promised me. He kissed the back of my hand, and I turned my hand over to catch his and inspect the healing burn. It looked just about back to normal. Thank God it hadn't been worse, then.

Cedar chuckled. "You're too sweet. But you'll have to stop worrying about me. I hurt myself a lot. That'll be a fact of life."

I shook my head. "Not if I can help it. I'll try to help and stop that. And I'll always worry about you."

"As long as I get to worry about you, too." Cedar stroked my chest gently, closing his eyes as he leaned into me. "And maybe cook for you sometimes. I don't want people doing everything for me. I value my independence."

I could understand that. He was fighting harder than anything right now for that independence, after all. And he'd done so for longer than I'd appreciated until just now. "Fine, if you insist on spoiling me, I guess you can twist my arm…"

"Good," Cedar said with a smile. He pecked my lips and closed his eyes, then shook his head. "I can't thank you enough. You're really rescuing me here. My hero."

I squeezed him against me, barely conscious that I was holding my breath as if it would keep the emotions inside my chest. My eyes were wet and warm, though. "It's my pleasure to help."

I wasn't the hero in this story—Cedar was. But if I could help, hell yeah, I'd do it.

Even if he broke my heart, it would be worth it.

22

CEDAR

"Do you wanna hang out here while I'm at work?" Ricky sounded almost shy as he asked me, like he didn't quite believe this was really happening. "I mean, you can go home whenever you need to… I don't want to kick you out just yet."

"I'd love that." I nodded awkwardly and offered him a smile. "Thank you."

He trusted me alone in his place—hell, I was moving in here. Even that meant the world to me. I'd had Nathan's spare key, but I'd never had the sense I was allowed to use it, let alone *encouraged*.

And there I went, comparing Ricky to my ex. Damn it, I needed to stop doing that. Ricky deserved better than that. He wasn't just "better than Nathan," the lowest bar known to mankind.

He was the sweetest guy I'd known, and he'd stolen my heart before I even knew it was available for stealing.

"I'll leave you the spare key, then," Ricky told me. I then had an amusing minute watching him rummaging in every kitchen drawer before he exclaimed. "Got it! Oh, wait. It's stuck in here."

"Stuck…?" The sticky sound of the key pulling away from the drawer was audible even from over here in bed. "Oh, God!" I exclaimed and wrinkled my nose.

Ricky squinted at his drawer. "I think that was a Coke explosion. Anyway, I'll leave it on the counter. Can't stay, gotta get to work!" Ricky grinned and pulled his shoes on, then came over to the bed and bent over. "Come here, you."

I grinned and pushed the covers down so I could scoot to the end of the bed and kiss him back. That little goodbye kiss—and the three or four that followed—made me feel all kinds of warm and tingly.

I couldn't believe I was lucky enough to have a boyfriend who gave me goodbye kisses on the way to work. I'd definitely never experienced this before, either.

"Have a good day at work," I murmured when he finally pulled back. I hoped he wasn't feeling too much fallout from the horrible outing, but he hadn't mentioned anything yet. He'd brushed it off when I'd asked, so I assumed Jared was protecting him.

"You take care," Ricky told me with a smile. "Don't head over to your place if you're not sure about it, huh? Wait for me and I'll go with you."

The offer of extra protection made me smile even more at him. "I'll be fine, but thank you. See you later." I was pretty sure Nathan wasn't going to get physical or obnoxious if he caught me moving out. After all, he knew it was coming.

Sure, he might try to make fun of me for jumping from being reliant on one guy to another, but it was different. At least, I tried to convince myself of that. Ricky wasn't using me the same way Nathan had—he was freely offering to help, and I was accepting it only for as long as I needed it.

Ricky kissed me again and sprinted for the door. I listened for the sound of the front door closing and then flopped back in bed, pulling the covers over my head again.

Since I wasn't about to be interrupted by loud music or sex sounds, I might as well take the chance to catch up on my sleep.

Dozing off in Ricky's bed, enjoying the smell of him and the very presence I felt by all his stuff around me, I felt safe.

Maybe I could rebuild my life with this man by my side.

I ignored the first knock on Ricky's door. I didn't want to be the awkward guy opening his boyfriend's door to, like, a relative or friend I didn't know.

But the hammering hadn't stopped, and I couldn't resist the curiosity. If it was the mail guy or something, I didn't want Ricky to have to trudge to some far-off post office to pick up a package.

I managed to get one of the windows by the bed open, and craned my head out to see who was at the door.

Oh, God. It was a cop—the uniform instantly recognizable—and some guy in a suit.

The cop looked up and spotted me, then held out a badge. "NYPD. Open up!"

Neither of them were Nathan, and Nathan wouldn't benefit from calling the cops on me anyway, would he? It didn't seem like a trick. But what the hell was going on?

Oh, God. Didn't cops come to the door when someone had been hurt—or died? The squeak of fear that came from me was embarrassingly loud.

I nodded and pulled back, swaying for a moment as I shut the window again, nearly jamming my finger in it.

Maybe it wasn't Ricky. Maybe Nathan had finally done something too stupid. Regret that flashed through me, followed by annoyance. Why did I even care what happened to him when he'd been so awful to me?

Wait, I was only half-dressed at best. Clothes first. I yanked on jeans and a t-shirt, running a hand through my hair before heading for the interior door.

Even though it was easier to grab them, it was harder to handle knobs than handles. Both the doors were, unfortunately, fiddly old doorknobs.

"Hurry up!" I groaned at myself. It took me longer than I would have like to finally get downstairs. "Cold, cold, cold!" I moaned with each slap of my foot on bare stairs.

Finally, I shivered as I pulled the exterior door open. Barefoot and in a t-shirt, December was forcing its way inside.

"Yes?" I said breathlessly, clutching the knob like it could save me from whatever the hell this was. It better not be bad news. I couldn't handle any more bad news right now.

"Hal Jones, and this is Detective Kennedy," the guy in the suit introduced himself. "Are you Cedar?"

"Yeah. Why?"

"I'm from the attorney-general's office, Charities Bureau. Can we come in?"

Well, I was going to die of pneumonia if I tried to have this conversation in the hallway, so I jerked my head in a nod and turned around to pad back upstairs. I couldn't feel my toes already.

At least Ricky wasn't dead or horribly injured somewhere. It was just something to do with the charity. Like it wasn't giving me enough headaches lately.

It made my progress upstairs slow and clunky, and the self-consciousness was hard to work through. I kept my hand on the rail and thanked God I'd left the interior door open. One fewer thing to mess up.

When we were inside, I winced at the state of the place. I could see them looking over the place, registering last night's takeout containers and an unmade bed.

"Sorry for the mess. Sit down," I offered, gesturing at the couch. "Watch the left side."

"Why—ah." The suit-clad man, Hal Jones, sat so delicately it seemed like he was worried a cockroach would crawl up his butt. "We're here because you're one of the co-founders of Plant for the Future."

"Yeah." Was this a random inspection? Why was a cop here? I stayed standing, preferring not to sit next to them and try to avoid the spring poking through the couch cushion. "Why?"

"We're investigating suspected fraud."

Oh, God. As usual when I was under stress, I kind of blocked out the details. My hearing went all funny as my heart squeezed tight. I couldn't feel my fingers.

Was this because he had sole signature powers now? I'd laid the trap for Nathan, but I hadn't in a million years expected him to *actually* take advantage of it. Much less within practically three seconds, like he'd been waiting for an excuse. Planning this. Was Jacob in on it?

Surely he didn't want to send me to prison so he could keep spending money on booze and drugs and God knew what else.

A chill ran down my spine. *That's exactly what he wants.* Tears welled up, and I choked them back. No way was I breaking down around a couple strangers.

Focus, Cedar.

"Wh-What kind of fraud did you say?"

"That's what we're trying to track down." Hal had a grim expression. "Normally we don't investigate charities that are this small," he glanced down at his notepad, "but we've had a direct, substantiated allegation that there's misappropriation of funds."

"Shit." I looked between him and the cop. "You're not, like, arresting me, are you?" My voice climbed up an octave. I would never survive prison. What the hell had my life turned into? Why was that even on the table?

"Not just yet, sir." Hal leaned in. "We have some questions to ask you."

"Of—of course," I stuttered. "I haven't done anything wrong. I'll answer whatever you need me to. I might be able to help clear this up."

They explained that there were a couple types of suspected fraud going on—skimming cash before it was counted and deposited, and withdrawing more for expenses than were actually going to the charity.

"The public counts on us to investigate every case of fraudulent activities at nonprofits with equal gravitas," Hal told me. "The consequences are no less severe than if you were skimming money from the Red Cross or the WWF. In fact, when small, community-based charities are operating illegally, it has even more of an impact on the public's trust."

The tears that had pricked at my eyes returned. "Nathan's been doing it. I'm sure. I think I can prove it," I told them. "Why do you think it was me?"

They exchanged glances. "Well, for a start… your lack of attendance at important meetings with your accountant to go over the books when these irregularities were spotted. You gave up your signatory rights to the bank account. Nathan told us it was because you'd been caught. He checked with friends of friends and found this address where you might be."

The asshole! I resisted the urge to dig my nails into my palms. For half a crazy second, I wondered if maybe I'd accidentally done exactly what they'd said. Maybe I'd put cash in my pocket, and…

No! Fuck. I gritted my teeth. *That's Nathan at work again, making me doubt everything I thought was true.*

I knew the truth, and he could never take that away from me.

"I'm not *doing a runner,*" I hissed, fury making it difficult to form sentences. I was going to throttle Nathan. "He's my ex-boyfriend —Nathan. He pretty much bullied me into signing those papers by telling me I was too stupid to understand what was going on at the meetings. I knew it would give him this kind of power, but I didn't think… he'd use it."

Hal was taking notes as I talked. He handed over a sheet of paper. "We understand there are a lot of missing receipts—and money. And you ran the cash box at these events, right?"

I skimmed down the list of events without really seeing them and nodded. "He was at all of them, too. But I didn't see anything go missing."

"Do you have logs of individual donations to back up your story?"

Tears pricked my eyes and I rubbed them with the side of my hand as I shook my head. Thank God my hand had healed, because I didn't need a sudden burst of pain to tip me over the edge to tears in front of strangers—worse, strangers who thought I was guilty. "I can't believe this," I whispered.

"You said Nathan's your ex-boyfriend?" They exchanged a look as Hal wrote down a few more notes.

"Yes. We founded this charity together, but we broke up six months ago." I tried to keep breathing despite the dizzy, sickening, overwhelming fear that was seeping into my bones.

What if I couldn't prove anything? What if Nathan pinned it all on me? Was it even Nathan? It had to be! Especially now that he was the only one with access to the bank account.

"I'm not overcharging for receipts. I handed them all over to Nathan, who took them to the accountant."

"Physical copies?"

"Yeah, of course." I wasn't a total idiot, whatever everyone seemed to think.

They exchanged looks but didn't let me in on whatever that meant. "All right," Hal said. "That gives us some lines to follow up. Don't skip town."

"Of course not," I muttered and then sighed. "I'm moving… maybe here, maybe back with Mom, I don't know."

"Why?" Hal seized on that like a shark to fresh blood.

"Nathan's dad paid my rent—both of our rent." I rubbed my eyes, my hands having trouble reaching them. It was such a familiar sensation that it took me time to realize that adrenaline and fear were making my hands shake. "Now that the charity's shutting down…"

"And you're not taking over the lease?"

I snorted bitterly. "How can I?" I shook my head. "I need another job to guarantee the rent."

I saw a glimpse of Hal's notepad as he stood up and moved past me: *financial troubles, check past.*

Shit. That was really, really bad, wasn't it? It made it look like I might just be desperate enough to steal from a charity to make ends meet. Why the hell had I told them that?

"So whose place is this?" The cop spoke up for the first time as he gestured around. "He gave this address as somewhere we might find you."

"My boyfriend, Ricky."

"Got a last name?"

I hesitated and frowned at the two of them for a moment. The last thing I wanted to do was drag him into it. "He doesn't know anything about the charity."

The cop just scratched his head, sounding bored as he answered. "That's a mouthful."

I sighed at the sarcastic response, my cheeks flushing. I knew I was being a coward again, giving in rather than cause conflict, but I didn't have the fight in me right now. "Rosa. He works at Bubbles."

"Great." Hal offered a handshake. "Thanks for your time."

It took me a few moments to get my fingers in the right place, and by then the moment had passed. He just grabbed my fingers and shook them in the least satisfying handshake ever, then strode for the door.

"Bye," I weakly managed as they let themselves out.

When they were gone, I sank back onto the couch and rubbed my face, letting the anguish set in for real.

Nathan must have been using me all this time as his cover, fiddling with the books. Was Jacob in on it? I had no idea, and I couldn't trust this bureau to find the truth, if this meeting was any indication.

If I'd felt stupid and naive before, it was ten times stronger now. I couldn't believe I'd been such an idiot as to trust Nathan and think he was giving me something for nothing.

Or something in exchange for *friendship*.

Or that he was my friend at all.

I had no idea what to do. Nobody could help me out here except myself, and I was way too late to do anything to protect myself.

God, I was stupid. I should have known better than to think I could outsmart him. I was pissed at Nathan for rising to every suspicious thought I'd had about him, and at myself for having given him the chance.

I should have kept log books. I would have spent less time fiddling with my phone and feeling invisible at accountant meetings. Surely my bank records or something would prove my innocence, right?

Nathan was going to have the last laugh when I went to jail for his reckless spending. How had I ever had the nerve to think I could go off and live my own best life?

I couldn't even feel stupid without then feeling guilty that I was letting him get to me this way. Over the last two years, Nathan's bullying—taunts disguised as jokes—had made me feel stupid for the first time in my life.

It wasn't my fault, I told myself, but the voice was thin and reedy compared to the echoing boom of guilt that thundered in the back of my head:

You should have known better, idiot. Just give in and let him have his way.

As always.

Too many emotions to keep track of boiled down to one awful conclusion: I was a hot mess, and I didn't deserve to drag Ricky into this.

I buried my face in my hands and gave in to the sobs that were already shaking my shoulders. Every time I thought I'd hit rock bottom, I just bounced off a ledge and plunged further down.

When the hell would it be over, and how many more people's lives would I wreck first?

2 3

RICKY

Unlike a normal Friday when I was happy to stick around and pull a double for the extra tips from drunk Friction patrons, tonight, I couldn't finish up work fast enough.

"Everything all right?" Jared asked, catching me on my way out of the diner.

I glanced past him at the exit door, then scanned the restaurant again. There'd been no sign of Cedar today, for the third day in a row. "Yeah, fine."

Jared gave me a look that said he didn't believe me, but as always, he didn't push me to talk. "Okay. Let me know. See you Saturday, right?"

"Yep," I said, my mind not at all on what was going on. I had some vague inkling that it was the drag brunch tomorrow, and we were fundraising. The only important part about it was that Cedar was supposed to be there.

"I've got everyone else lined up." He patted my shoulder. "Thanks for helping out again. Good night."

"You too." I barely even glanced back as I took off for the door, filing that conversation in the *process it later* bucket. I had one huge question on my mind to deal with first.

I pushed my way out the front door to the street and made a beeline for my apartment.

Cedar hadn't been at my place on Wednesday when I'd come home. I had to admit I was disappointed—more so than I'd expected. My only shred of hope was that he'd taken my spare key from the counter.

"Out of my way," I muttered, dodging around some lookie-loo tourists. I had places to be, and gaping at Brooklyn architecture was not going to improve my mood.

Stupid traffic. Stupid people. Stupid smog. I hated everything about the city right now, but I'd admit it was probably channeling how useless I felt—and how scared.

It was probably a bad sign when your boyfriend dropped off the radar right after you started dating, right?

I pulled out my phone again to scroll through messages as I walked, praying that something had come in that I'd missed. Nope. Like the last hundred times I'd checked, there was nothing.

My message to him on Wednesday night had asked if he was coming back that evening or not. I hadn't gotten an answer until an hour later, and then it had been a simple, *No, good night babe.*

No texts at all on Thursday, even when I'd sent both good morning and good night texts, plus one in between to check on him.

This morning, still no greeting.

The most damning piece of evidence was that he'd been reading my texts, just not replying. It wasn't that he'd suddenly disappeared or anything. That was my only consolation.

Something was wrong, and I was going to find out what.

It was supposed to be my Saturday off tomorrow, but I was still going into work for his drag event. But according to Jared, he hadn't heard back from Cedar on the final plan. If I waited until tomorrow, Cedar might still be a no-show.

I cursed under my breath. *I've already waited too long*, I thought, rounding the corner to my place. I should have searched more for him on Thursday or something. Today was the day, then. I wouldn't let another day slip away without getting answers.

I'd stopped by his apartment four times now between Wednesday, Thursday, and this morning—all at different times of day—but no answer every time I tried. Nathan hadn't even come to check out what was going on.

"I've gotta do it," I breathed out, arriving outside the front door. I drew a breath, hoping beyond anything to see a light coming from the window onto the street.

But there was nothing, and I had the awful feeling he wasn't just sitting there in the dark. So he wasn't here, for the third day in a row, when I came home from work.

Sure, he had a couple weeks left before he had to move out of his apartment, but vanishing from text messaging, too? Not even stopping by? After our last couple weeks of seeing each other as often as possible, I was missing him like crazy.

That wasn't helping matters. I needed to see him again—needed to hold him and touch his skin and smell his hair, and… goddamn, I was so into him it hurt. Maybe it was infatuation, but it consumed every inch of me and made it impossible to think straight.

Whatever was going on, Cedar was trying to deal with it himself, and I wasn't going to let him do that. Or Nathan had turned on him and gotten into his head, and that wasn't gonna fly, either.

"Ugh," I whispered when I cracked the door and saw the mail scattered across the landing. If he'd been here, he would have picked it up off the stairs for sure. No footprints on top of it.

I shut the door again and glared up at my apartment. I didn't even want to change or shower before I headed over to his place. I wouldn't be able to relax until I'd heard *something* back, at least. After this many unanswered texts, I was entitled to go search in person again.

"Hey, buddy. You looking for the cute little twink who was here the other day?"

That was the guy in front of the hair salon. He sat in the chair outside, fiddling with his phone again, hunched into his coat. No cigarette in hand, despite the only people being outside in late afternoon as winter approached being smokers.

Wait, he was outside a lot. He might have seen something. My heart leapt with hope.

I flushed with embarrassment but nodded. "Have you seen him?" It was a lead, at least. It felt like this was a missing persons case, and I'd been seriously considering calling the cops, just in case.

"A couple days ago I saw a cop show up at the door with some suit." The guy shrugged at me. "That's it. I had an appointment, so I didn't see anything else after that."

A cop? What the fuck was Nathan up to? I had no doubt that asshole was behind this, and I hadn't been around to protect Cedar. For whatever reason, Cedar didn't want to ask me for help.

He was trying to deal with this himself, then. If he wasn't in jail for some stupid, made-up reason.

"Fuck. Fucking fuck," I cursed under my breath and then tried to get myself back to normal enough for a conversation. "Okay. Thanks."

"Good luck!" the guy called after me as I took off at a sprint in the direction of Cedar's apartment. "Hope you find your sweetheart!"

By the time I got to the dull gray complex, my lungs burned. Showing up like this made it look like I'd been outrunning a bear.

I had to lean against the outside of the building for a couple minutes until I cooled off, but that gave my brain plenty of time to go over the possibilities. Just as the sweat chilled me, I headed up the stairs to the apartment door.

Time to do this.

I rapped loudly on the door. "Cedar. I know you're in there, and I'm going to keep bugging you until you let me in."

When I leaned in to listen, there was no sound, but there was also no way he'd been away for days. If so, there was some serious crap kicking off.

I stood back and eyed the door. How pissed would he be at me for kicking it in?

Okay, wait. Save the damage deposit and go with a smarter first plan: see what Nathan knew. I narrowed my eyes as I listened again, pulling back. There was no noise from this apartment, but there was definitely music coming from somewhere.

That had to be Nathan's place. At least one of them was here.

"Gotcha," I whispered and knocked.

A couple moments later, the door opened. Nathan stood there, considerably more disheveled than I'd seen him before. His collared shirt was opened to the first few buttons, and he was leaning on the doorframe like he needed to hold it up.

"Oh." He seemed surprised to see me. He blinked at me a few times. "What?"

Meanwhile, I got a chance to look over his shoulder—there were a handful of guys in the living room, but nobody who looked like Cedar. "Cedar?" I called out, just in case.

"He's not here," Nathan snapped and moved into the hall, shoving my chest so he had room to step out. He jutted out his jaw like he thought that was going to intimidate me at all.

"Whoa." I put my hands up but glared at him, taking a step back. I was ready to hit back if I had to. I wouldn't put it past him. "Hands off the goods. If he's not here, why so touchy?"

Nathan left the door just barely cracked and folded his arms. "What do you want, dick?" He looked me up and down and sneered.

I wasn't entirely sure which way he meant it—calling me a dick, or asking if I was looking for dick. With his words in the argument at Bubbles...

"Look, I'm putting behind what you did at Bubbles," I hissed. Damn, it was hard to sound pissed off when you said *bubbles*. "I just want to talk."

"Talk, then." He feigned a yawn. "I don't have all day."

Well, he had nerve. I resisted the urge to call him a fuckhead. I needed information, after all. Instead, I drew a breath and folded my hands behind my back. "I wanna know where Cedar is." If I could stay polite for a couple minutes, I'd catch more flies with honey than vinegar.

"Not here. Haven't seen him." Nathan shrugged. "Not in a couple days. Why? Is loverboy missing?" A grin spread across his face. "Oh, shit. Did he *dump* you? Told you you should have picked the good one." He gestured up and down himself with a finger.

"Ew," I snorted. "Not a chance. I'm looking for my boyfriend, not whatever guy throws himself at me."

That was it—if Nathan was trying to push my buttons by saying Cedar had dumped me, I was going to strike out that possibility in my head. Whatever he was trying to cover up, if Cedar had gotten uncomfortable, he would have said so.

Because unlike Nathan, he was a fucking adult.

"I dunno. You look like you could use some stress relief." Nathan jerked his thumb toward the apartment. "Cedar can tell you how much stress this would take off you."

Okay, that was it. Cedar was *not* showing up at some freaky sex party, or whatever Nathan had going on here. Nathan was grinning as he saw that he'd gotten to me.

"No more fucking around." I grabbed Nathan by the front of his shirt and hauled him in. "I'm going to find Cedar," I hissed at him. "And if I find out you know anything you're not telling me, I'm going to kick the crap out of you when you least expect it. Watch your back, *Nathan*."

For a moment, he looked genuinely afraid. Then he put on that mask again—the cocky, overconfident expression I recognized all too well. Fuck. The old saying was true—what I hated most about him was what I recognized in myself.

"You better let me go, or the cops will be in touch with you, too."

"*Too?*" I hissed. He'd slipped there. Unless he was involved, he shouldn't know that detail. "How do you know about that?"

Guilt flashed across Nathan's expression before he tossed his head. "Doesn't matter. I'll call the cops and tell them you're harassing me. Won't look good on your employment record, pretty boy."

I didn't let go of him. "You sure you want the cops showing up?" I reached past him with my other hand to push the door further open. Just as I'd thought, his eyes widened and he tried to yank it shut again.

Two could fight dirty. If he was gonna blackmail me, I'd do exactly the same.

"I bet they'd be interested in adding this to their investigation," I said, taking a chance that there was some kind of active investigation that had spooked Cedar.

"Fine," Nathan spat. "He's been home at night. No idea what he's doing in the daytime. The cops have figured out he's stolen money. That it?"

"What time?"

"I dunno, suppertime?" So, about now, then.

Footsteps sounded from behind me, and I let him go, spinning around for a look at the staircase. "Cee—"

But it wasn't Cedar this time. And for my pains, I got a shove in my back that made me stumble a few paces forward. At least I hadn't gotten sucker-punched—it was a stupid move to turn my back to that asshole, and I knew it.

"Fuck off and never talk to me again," Nathan told me, then waved at the other guy who had stopped at the top of the staircase to stare at us. "Over here, man."

I rounded on him and hissed, "This isn't over." Then I stomped past Cedar's door and past Nathan's friend to head downstairs and back to the street.

Whatever was going on in Nathan's place, as long as Cedar wasn't there, I didn't care. My mission was to find Cedar, and I was going to do it one way or another.

Stolen money? I didn't believe that of Cedar for a second. Nathan was trying to get in my head, and I wasn't going to let him do it.

Cedar hadn't left me alone when I'd been outed, desperately in need of people but not sure how to ask for help. I wasn't going to ditch him now. I'd put a red alert out at Bubbles to let me know if he showed up there.

Feeling like there was something I could do made me a little calmer by the time I got to the street. "Asshole," I muttered before trying to let it go. Instead, I pulled out my phone and sent Cedar a text.

I've just been to your apartment and talked to Nathan. I'll come by again tonight if you don't talk to me.

It took a few minutes, but by the time I was halfway home, I got a response. I nearly dropped my phone with my excitement to hear from him—and my fear at what he might be saying.

Sorry, babe. I don't want to drag you into this.

I cracked a grim smile. *Like it or not, I'm a part of it now. So tell me what's going on.*

Cedar seemed hesitant to respond, but finally I got my answer. *I'll come by your place tonight? I'm sorry I took the key btw.*

I bit my lip. Whatever Nathan had done to get in his head, I hated him for. *I wanted you to have that key. Let yourself in any time if needed, but I should be there tonight.*

OK. See you tonight. Thank you.

Of course. I took a deep breath and let it out. At least Cedar was finally talking to me. Whatever he was doing, and whatever the cops wanted with him, and whatever this stolen money was about, I'd find out.

Like Mama said, if you weren't in jail, dead, or in the hospital, you could fix anything else. It was never too late in life. As long as we were together, we could fix this… right?

24

———

CEDAR

I was cool, calm, and collected on my way to Ricky's place. Sure, my life was melting down around my ears, but I was going to *own* it and not ask anyone for an ounce of help.

I didn't mean to start sobbing the moment I got to the top of the stairs and Ricky pulled the door open and hugged me. It just… happened.

"I'm sorry I dropped off the radar," I mumbled into his shoulder, my voice thick with emotion and my arms tight around his waist. No way in hell was I letting him go right now.

Ricky shook his head. "I'm just glad you're okay. Come here." I found myself sitting on his couch with his arms around me a minute later.

Moving around a little helped break my focus on the fact that I felt like I was about to drag him into a cesspit of my own making. "It's all bullshit. Everything is shit right now, and I… it's embarrassing how much I feel like I need you."

Ricky took my hands and squeezed them, then let go to grab

263

tissues and hand them to me. "Here, baby. Deep breaths. We'll figure it out, okay?"

I blew my nose and pocketed the tissues, then buried my face in my hands. I could barely make myself say the words.

"Nathan stole a bunch of money from the charity, and now the authorities are after me because I look like I'm guilty and I don't know how to prove I'm not." It all rushed out in a sentence, even though I'd meant to explain it.

Oh, God. Please don't let him think *I* stole the money. If he'd talked to Nathan, I had no doubt Nathan had tried to sell him that story.

I was way too emotional to try to get into the details—a cop had been here, in Ricky's place! And some investigator! And then they'd gotten in touch again yesterday on the phone to ask me questions about some specific soil purchase last year...

Shit, I was crying again, and it was the kind of ugly-sobbing that nobody wanted to show anyone else—least of all their brand-new boyfriend.

But Ricky drew me into him with one strong arm and stroked my hair with the other, just rocking me gently until I managed to get a hold of myself.

"God, I'm sorry," I mumbled. "I just feel like he's won. He didn't tell you I'm the thief, did he?"

Ricky's voice was fierce and immediate. "He hasn't won. Not by a long shot. He did tell me that, and I didn't believe it for a second. He also tried to come on to me, and hell, he said some other nasty shit I wasn't gonna tell you about. He's a drama llama, just like my ex."

I moaned and pressed my face into his shoulder. He'd probably told all my friends, too. I wouldn't put it past him for a second. "He's won with the charity at least. He gets to shut it down before *I* can shut it down. Should I even do the drag brunch tomorrow?" I wiped at my eyes. I'd put so much work into it, and I'd gotten so far outside my comfort zone to do it all.

"He didn't want you to do it, did he? Don't let him win. Keep going with it," Ricky urged me. He kissed my forehead. "It's your idea, and you're gonna see it through. Even if the charity's shutting down, you were splitting the funds with another charity, weren't you? There's no better way to prove you're innocent than to keep raising funds for a good cause like LGBTalk."

"What if they think I'm stealing, too?"

Ricky pulled back for a look at me and then frowned. "Well, we can go over cash handling protocols. Someone will have more training and know how to keep you safe. Oh, bingo!" He clapped his hands together. "We'll get Jared to handle the cash."

I couldn't possibly drag him into this. No way.

But before I could protest, Ricky laid a finger on my lips. "He's not under investigation. If anyone tries to start shit with him, you know he'll slam-dunk them."

I managed a little smile. Jared was a tough cookie. "Yeah," I murmured. "Do you think he would help?"

"Honey, if you ask for help, people will give it." Ricky gave a rueful chuckle. "I'm just learning that lesson now."

"If anyone even wants to talk to me." I felt useless, stupid, and worse than either of those emotions: ashamed. Now I was under investigation, and God only knew who else they'd talked to in the last few days.

People were going to think it was me. After all, if you hadn't done anything wrong, why would people be asking about you?

Mortification twisted my gut. I'd been living in this emotional place for the past few days, and I was so unused to it. I'd never felt ashamed of my body, or my sexuality, or my behavior. But somehow here I was, afraid to show my face in the streets.

"They know you," Ricky murmured and clapped my shoulder. "And you're doing this for a good cause. You're helping out the community, even when it doesn't benefit you. Who wouldn't support that?"

It was hard to be miserable with him here shooting holes in my logic. I drew a long sigh and wiped my face. "God. I've been hiding from everyone. They definitely think I'm guilty. Nathan will have told them."

"Okay, deep breaths, blow your nose, and up you get," Ricky told me. He hauled me up when I was ready, and brushed me off. "It's Friday night; some of the guys will be there. You're gonna see your friends."

I caught my breath in fear for a moment. Did he understand how convinced I was that they were going to hate me?

Yeah, he did. His smile was soft and sympathetic, and he was firmly holding my hands, glancing down at the once-injured hand. "This is doing good now, right? Doesn't hurt for me to do this?"

"Yeah." I knew he was trying to distract me. I let out a breath and shook my head. Just as he'd helped me in the kitchen when he barely knew me, Ricky was trying to help me challenge my fear head-on.

I gulped hard and nodded. I owed him this one after keeping him worrying for two days.

"Good man," Ricky approved with a small smile, kissing me. "Freshen up and let's walk over there. We'll let someone else cook for a change."

With my face washed and shirt tucked in, I felt a little more put-together. Adding my coat and shoes gave me just a tiny extra bit of confidence, like armor.

By the time we hit the street together, I was clutching his hand tightly but ready to try this.

"Hey. You found your lovebird." It was the hairdresser from before, and he was grinning at us. "I like a happy ending."

"It's not over yet," I said with a grim little smile. It could still go south. A cop could show up and arrest me for something I hadn't even done, and I could lose the very little employability I'd ever had.

Ricky just squeezed my hand. "No, it isn't." He meant it in a very different way than me, I could tell from the uptick in his voice. There was that cocky grin again when I looked over at him.

"Keep me posted." The guy was sucking on a candy, staring at us in fascination like we were the subject of a reality TV show. "You go, boys!"

Ricky grinned and waved as we headed by him and straight to Bubbles. He didn't let me pause outside and have another attack of nerves, either. He headed straight in, holding the door for me and following me right in to steer me to the regulars' booth.

"Hey!" Billy stood up and waved as he spotted us. "Are you going out? Where you been, stranger?"

I blushed and shrugged. "Life." I hadn't exactly lived here—ever, or lately—but ever since he'd met Nathan and me, Billy had been extra-nice to me. It was nice to feel like I had a friend, but even nicer to realize he really had missed me.

"I'm curious too," Ricky murmured, taking my hand again as we headed over there. "But you can tell me later."

"Job-hunting," I told him and then shook my head. I might as well tell everyone at once.

Once the customary hugs and kisses were over and we'd tucked into one side of the booth, I looked around at everyone. It was a full night tonight: Kev and Charlie, Shay and Jared, Adam and Darren —taking a break from renovating their old house for a night… Billy was there, and a couple other single guys that sometimes joined us.

But for the first time, I was here as part of a couple and it felt *good*. What would it be like to go out dancing with him? I wanted to know. "We could stay out tonight…"

Ricky grinned at me. "That's the spirit."

"Have you been into Friction?"

"Who hasn't?" Ricky wanted to know and rolled his eyes, then grinned. "Never kissed a guy in there, though. I feel like that's a milestone."

"No, a milestone is a bathroom blowjob," Billy told him.

Ricky groaned and elbowed him. "Gross." He put his arm around me. "Unless you don't think so."

"We can wait to get home, I think," I told him, my lips quivering with amusement as I glanced around.

No doubt everyone had heard about my exploits a few weeks ago, but they were discreet for once in their lives. I saw several of them fighting back grins.

Billy leaned in. "What's going on? I saw some guys coming in here earlier, asking to talk to Ricky Rosa. I'm guessing that's you... you go by Enrique or Ricky?"

"Enrique, Ricky, don't matter," Ricky shrugged. When Billy persisted in staring at him and awaiting an answer, he laughed. "Ricky, I guess."

"Ricky it is." Jared grinned at him. "So what's that about?"

"It's probably to do with me." I felt miserable as I said it, but I couldn't hide it from people—he was right. I needed support to get through this.

Like a tennis match, Charlie looked over at me now. "How so?"

I squeezed Ricky's hand under the table, trying to think how to phrase it. "Well... it started with the cops coming to my door."

It didn't take long to explain the situation. I felt a little bit better that at least, looking around the table, everyone looked horrified and not disdainful. How deep in my head had Nathan gotten, that I expected them to judge me for being dumb instead of him for exploiting me?

"So he's been stealing money all the time, making me feel like an idiot so I didn't look too closely or question him..." I trailed off, sighing. "And now he's framed me for it. Did he come talk to you guys, or...?"

Jared's lip curled. "Did he, like hell. If he walked in here, I'd toss him out on his ass. He knows that."

"That's a load of bullshit," Shay burst out with, reaching over the table to take my other hand. Everyone else joined in with him to agree, touching me or reaching over the table to hug me.

My lips wobbled as I tried for a smile, but I ended up burying my face into Ricky's shoulder for a moment as he hugged me. "It's okay," Ricky murmured. "See? We all wanna help you."

"It's my fault for dating that piece of shit." I groaned and shook my head, finally peeling myself away from Ricky for long enough to look around at them. "You all knew Nathan was an asshole, didn't you?"

Nobody said anything for a moment, but from their expressions, I could guess the answer. Sympathetic, just a little bit guilty, but not wanting to make me feel any worse.

"Yeah," I sighed. "But I wasn't ready to hear it." I'd thought the world of Nathan for some damn reason. He'd never earned it—in fact, he'd humiliated me from our very first date when I'd spilled a glass of beer everywhere at Friction, and he'd started a round of applause from everyone nearby.

Since then, I'd told most of these guys that I had a condition, and in drunken conversations with some of them, what exactly it was. Nobody else had made fun of me like that. But Nathan? I'd thought joking around meant he was openminded, but he'd just been looking for a punching bag.

Ricky, though? It was strange being respected for the first time in years. I didn't need to ask these guys what they thought of him. From the moment he'd sat down tonight, they'd made him welcome.

Not like Nathan, who they'd always sort of left on the periphery of the group. No wonder he'd hated me going out with these guys where he wasn't the center of attention. Instead, like a dweeb, I'd gone out alone with him, forcing me to watch him pick up guys.

"God, I'm a dumbass," I mumbled. Every time I thought about it, I saw another toxic pattern that I could have noticed months earlier.

"No." Ricky wasn't the only one who said it, but he was the loudest and closest to me. "You think I'm a dumbass for Madison leeching onto me like a… like a leech?"

I sighed and shook my head. "That's different."

"Not really. She latched onto another insecurity. It's a little different… but same underlying bullshit."

"Neither of you deserved them—or should I say, neither of *them* deserved you," Jared said quietly, drawing my attention. "But you two are cute together."

"Right? I told him that!" Billy agreed, grinning at us both.

My cheeks flushed and I shook my head. "If you're gonna make fun of me, I need a lot more bacon to endure this."

"All the bacon you could want," Ricky promised me, scooting over my lap. "I'll go talk to the kitchen."

I smiled at him, watching him head off to talk to his coworkers.

"Well, that was a dreamboat smile," Billy commented with a wicked grin. "Someone's head over heels, huh?"

I snorted and shrugged. "Maybe." But I was smiling way too much to deny it.

"Both of you are." Kev folded his hands under his chin. "How adorable. And he's finally coming out dancing with us!"

"He's never been before?"

Adam gave me a significant glance. "Not with us. Must have been on his own."

Poor guy. From everything he'd said, I could guess—he sat awkwardly in the corner, afraid to flirt with anyone. Or maybe he'd managed to flirt, but not to get any further, before running away again.

I'd make sure he had a good time, in every possible way.

"And as for job-hunting?" Billy leaned in. "We'll put our heads together at brunch tomorrow. Someone's gotta know about a good job for you. No more working for that asshole."

I rubbed my face for a moment to keep myself from crying. When I could trust my voice, I answered, "That'd be... great."

Two straight days of knocking on doors, brainstorming what kind of work I could do in this neighborhood, trying to hide the tremors that always made employers suddenly *have the position filled* when I walked in...

Yeah, life sucked, but it sucked less when there were friends on my side.

"Bacon on the way," Ricky told me, sliding in next to me and kissing my cheek.

I beamed at him and kissed him back. I wanted so badly to tease him for being so affectionate in public, but I also didn't want to scare him off.

"So, are you two an item?" Adam asked, leaning in.

Ricky grinned sheepishly and nodded. "Yeah. Boyfriends. Look at me. Got a boyfriend."

It was still funny to say, and even stranger to hear out loud—but in a great way. It made my chest warm, and I took his hand. I'd seen so many of my friends with these new-love butterflies and figured it would be months or years before I felt them again—if anyone ever *could* love me again.

Now I knew how much of that was bullshit, and not even my own baggage. Well, I was putting down Nathan's suitcases and walking into the sunset, hand-in-hand, with this man.

"Good job, man," Adam told Ricky, punching his shoulder across the table.

The others joined in the congratulations to us both, and someone toasted with their orange juice.

"A proper toast to follow as soon as we're done eating," Kev promised with a grin. "Hope you don't have to be up early. Oh, wait. Brunch. Oh, well. We're young and agile. Or some of us are."

Billy flipped him off.

"I'm gonna die," I moaned, but I was grinning. Suddenly, all my fears and stresses seemed miles away.

I had the sword of Damocles of this investigation hanging over my head, but it no longer felt so hopeless. From now on, I was going to make sure I had backup when I talked to the investigators… and I wasn't going to take this lying down.

If Nathan thought I was an easy target to pin his crimes on, he was going to think again.

Too long had I let him use me. Time to fight back—but first, time to celebrate the fact that I'd made it through all of that bullshit.

And I still had a hand to hold—this one warm, generous, kind, and surprisingly strong.

"Bacon's up!" announced Jess with a cheerful smile as she dropped off plates of food in the middle of the table. Like animals, we attacked the food with friendly cheers and laughter.

When my hand shook as I tried to grab bacon, Ricky plucked the strip from the plate and pressed it into my fingers.

I smiled at him and he smiled back, saying nothing. There was none of the pity I might have expected from other people on his expression. Not even a hint of annoyance that I was here being *extra*, as Nathan would have said.

Nothing but adoration on Ricky's expression, and it made a small part of me unfurl that had been tucked away for a very long time.

Love—for Ricky, and for everyone around this table who had my back, but most of all, for myself.

At the end of all of this, I deserved to be okay. Finally, I felt like I was worth the fight.

RICKY

I'd never seen Cedar so sunny and smiley. Despite the chilly winter air that breezed into the diner with everyone who entered or left, he stood by the door to greet people and welcome them to the LGBTalk drag brunch.

The place was full of drag queens—many I recognized from late-night breakfast sessions or next-morning brunches when they hadn't changed. At any given time, someone had the microphone and was making a contingent of patrons groan and others laugh.

"How are things going?" Jared asked, ducking into the kitchen and offering me a grin. "Want a break?"

"I wanna make sure Cedar's hands aren't freezing off." My poor boyfriend was bundled up in a coat, but he refused to come any further inside as he greeted people and chatted with them until they could be seated.

And he thought he was bad with people? Bullshit. Everyone was walking away from him with a smile. We'd had a great time last night, even without much alcohol, and I was glad for it today. No hangover made this morning fly by.

I wasn't even halfway across the floor when I saw the door fly open, catching Cedar in the side. Madison stood there imperiously, staring down her nose at all the little people in her way.

Oh, God. I should have known she'd come back, but I hadn't expected it to be today, of all days.

Cedar winced and grabbed his side but still managed a smile. "Eager to get out of the cold, hm?"

She cast him a withering look and I could guess what she was thinking: that he was so gay she shouldn't even have to talk to him. How the hell hadn't she been fired instantly?

"Madison." It came out as more of a snarl than I'd meant as I stormed toward the door. Hurting Cedar made me see red. Accidental or not, she should have taken more care, and she sure as shit should have apologized. Not that apologies were a thing Madison did.

I could feel the party mood sinking around me as people turned to look at us. *Don't cause a scene,* I coached myself. However pissed off I was at Madison, I wasn't going to ruin the drag brunch that Cedar had spent so long planning.

"I heard you're playing for the other team now." She sneered. "That explains… well, everything about our relationship." She just barely held in an ugly giggle.

"Yeah, it sure does." I smiled back at her, moving past her without even looking at her. I put my arm around Cedar and murmured, "You okay?"

He looked startled but relaxed under my touch. "Yeah. It just glanced off me."

"Good." I turned to face Madison and smiled at her, my shoulders settling. I was so used to there being tension and guilt in my chest that I half-expected it to be there. Instead, there was just… what? Confidence? Not quite.

I could do this… right? "What would you like to discuss?" That was a good start. Business-like.

She opened and closed her mouth a few times, staring between the two of us and then back at me. "What do you mean, *discuss*?"

"I assume you're here to discuss something with me." I kept my tone casual and friendly, knowing full well that she'd hate that. "You'd have no other reason to hang around a den of gays, as you like to call this place."

Madison stepped close. "I was going to *discuss* how your mama would feel about you being surrounded by all of this."

It made my chest tighten and my stomach drop from habit alone. Again, I was so used to being controlled that now that I was seeing *how* she did it, I was pissed. But she didn't have that control over me anymore.

"Why?" The more questions I asked, the more I was in control of the situation. It kept her on the defensive, and forced her to justify what she was doing.

"Because!" Madison exclaimed, throwing her hands in the air as she approached me. "I thought you were too good for this."

Because she wanted to blackmail me. *Nice try, honey*, I thought.

"No, this is too good for you," I told her instead with a wink. I didn't even need to be cocky and loud about it. It was pure fact. "But I'm flattered at everyone who's hitting on me this week. You all keep dreaming."

Madison's claws came out. "Oh yeah? At least *I* can fake it in bed."

I grinned. "Not really something to brag about, babe. Go live your best life and find someone who *wants* to ravish you. Presto. No faking needed. Just… stop trying to make me that guy, because I'm not and I won't ever be." I was shitty at faking it, so yeah, everyone around me knew I was for real. This was the moment I decided for myself how I was going to live, and I was going to be goddamn proud of who I was.

"You could have been my guy! Should have been!" Madison ran a hand through her hair. "Now what am I going to do for the wedding? Your mama *said* you should take me."

"That's before she knew you were using me for my money." Again, I kept it as calm and pleasant as I could. No way was I giving her an excuse to claim I'd flipped out at her. I'd learned my mistake from Nathan. "And that I'm gay."

She stared at me.

"Yeah, I told her," I added, grinning. "So don't go try to get the drop on her. Too late."

"And she's *fine* with all of…?" she waved around, looking stunned. "Even though she's…"

"Why wouldn't she be?" When Madison didn't answer, I grinned. "Get real. We stand by each other. A concept you wouldn't know anything about. Your homophobia doesn't belong here," I told her firmly and opened the door. "Bye, Madison."

She didn't seem to have a word to say to that. She just stormed out, darkly glaring at anyone and everyone nearby while I flashed her a peace sign.

Cedar sucked in his breath and looked up at me. "Babe? You okay?"

I just smiled at him and pecked his lips. "Never better. She's got nothing on me," I murmured. If I wanted to lead by example, I had to show him. I had nothing to be guilty of, so I wasn't going to act like it. "I've long since repaid any obligation to her."

"Now kiss the pretty boy again!" one of the queens called out. "But over here, where we can see better."

I flipped them off, but Cedar was laughing, his eyes sparkling as he looked at me. Whatever he said, I knew he wanted to be shown off.

And God, he deserved to be.

So I bent him over and kissed him again to the whoops and hollers of my friends and coworkers and patrons.

———

"That went so great!" Cedar twisted his hands together, his eyes on Jared. "I wonder how much we've got."

Jared was handling the cash bucket while Neil, Jess, Cedar, and I watched on. The more witnesses, the better, we reckoned. He was counting out bills, lips moving silently as he did so.

"Enough to be proud of yourself," I said quietly. The place had mostly emptied out now, the late afternoon lull striking at last— several hours later than a weekday, of course.

Before long, the pace would pick back up again as people came out to drink and dance and celebrate together.

I'd done all my own celebrating already. I'd gotten a lap dance from a drag queen, kissed Cedar several more times in front of everyone, and cooked until my feet wanted to fall off.

"I can't say how much I appreciate this," Neil said yet again. "Especially getting all the funds. You could hold back half like you were planning, if you're starting a new charity… startup funds can go a long way."

I nudged Cedar, but he just smiled and shook his head at us. "I don't want to own a charity anymore," he said. "I'm done with that headache."

"Well, I can't say I blame you." Neil chuckled and looked around at us. He'd come by late in the afternoon to thank everyone there for their support and explain more about the hotline. "It's a full-time job and a half, that's for sure."

"Speaking of full-time jobs," Cedar spoke up. "Are there any available at LGBTalk?"

Neil's brows raised, and then he rubbed his chin. "Well… I think I'd need to check with a few people first."

"I should say that Plant for the Future is currently under investigation," Cedar added, which was a ballsy move when he was asking to be considered for a job. But his voice was steady and confident. No more shrinking violet, and I loved it.

"Oh. What for?"

"Fraud. I'm certain the investigation is going to clear my name, but I don't know how long it'll take." Cedar bit his lip and sighed. "They said they'd get back to me as soon as they've gone through their bank statements. They expect it to be pretty open-and-closed, from what he danced around saying."

"Right." Neil drummed his fingers on Jared's desk as he leaned on it. "Tell you what. Give me a call when you know more. If nothing else, I'll see if anything comes up that doesn't require handling cash. But you were so great today—it would be a shame to waste your talent on paperwork."

Cedar's cheeks flushed. "Really?"

"Really," Neil said. I spotted Jared smiling and nodding as he bundled up the cash and scribbled numbers. "I'm surprised you weren't the face of your charity already."

"My partner…" Cedar trailed off and then rolled his eyes. "You know how it goes. Once this charity is dissolved, I'd be more than happy to work behind or in front of the scenes. Wherever you want me."

"We'll talk," Neil promised and reached out to shake hands on it.

Jared leaned in. "Not to interrupt, but I think we're clearing eight hundred in profits. Can someone check my math here and sign off on it?"

Cedar raised both hands to his mouth and squeaked, which made everyone else laugh. I grinned and wrapped an arm around him. "See?"

"I thought I was better with plants than people. Turns out I'm pretty bad at both, but I can fake it until I make it." Cedar grinned up at me. "I learned that lesson from someone smart."

"And handsome, and talented—"

"Don't go fishing," Cedar warned and elbowed me.

I snickered. "Fine, fine."

"Yep," Jess said, looking up. "Eight hundred."

"That will go a long way. I'll make up a giant check and give you guys a call when I'm ready to take a photo. Tomorrow?" Neil asked us. "You too, Jared."

Jared rubbed at the back of his neck. "How about Ricky on my behalf?"

"Works for me," Neil said with a smile. "Thanks, everyone."

I clapped his shoulder. "Our pleasure."

Something great had come out of all of this after all—and it was driven by Cedar. I was so damn proud of my boyfriend, and not just because it had been a success. Even if we hadn't raised a cent, I would have been proud of him for showing his face in public and doing this despite Nathan's best attempts to isolate him.

As we finally walked home, Cedar wouldn't let go of my hand, even when we had to dodge sign posts and pedestrians.

"You feeling okay about all that?" I asked, grinning at him. "That was a great thought, asking Neil for a job right after raising a bunch of money for him!"

"I think I could earn back my salary if they hired me to raise funds. I'm used to hustling," Cedar told me. His expression fell. "I just didn't know it was disappearing after I collected it. No wonder we were always broke... like this spring when I was trying to get supplies."

I nudged him gently. "You can't fix the past," I murmured. "But you can sure as hell fix the future."

"Yeah." He drew a deep breath and pecked my lips when I stopped to unlock the front door.

Our new friend wasn't outside the hair salon, but no doubt we were going to chat with him again soon. It was nice to have a friendly neighbor.

"On which note," I added, flicking on the light switch and leading him upstairs, "can I interest you in a moving day soon? I'd really like you to live with me until you get the job situation sorted out."

"Yes, please." Cedar beamed when I held the door for him and headed inside. "I'd live with you even longer than that, on one condition. Well, two."

"What's that?" I lit up. Anything he wanted. A better shower? I'd talk to my landlord. Supper every night? I'd make it work.

"First, that I split the rent as soon as I'm able." Cedar took my hand and swayed lightly. "It's really important to me."

"Of course," I murmured. In his shoes, I'd feel the same way. It would help me out financially a bit, too, but he needed to feel like he wasn't dependent on me. I wanted to make sure of that. "What's the other one?"

"That we ask if we can get the knobs changed to handles."

"Handles?" I let go of his hand and made a grab for his dick, and he swatted me away. "You've got one already."

"Perv! On the doors!"

I pretended to pout. "Well, fine. Ruin my fun." I kept trying anyway, walking my fingers up his thigh.

"That handle is gonna get a lot easier to grab if you keep it up," Cedar giggled breathlessly.

"Ooh!" I grabbed Cedar's hips instead and hauled him into me, not even flinching much when his hand hit my cheek as he tried to put his arms around my neck.

"Sorry, sorry."

I chuckled. "It's all right. You keep me on my toes, that's all."

Cedar let his breath out and rested his head on my shoulder. He was just an inch shorter, but it was enough that I felt like I was protecting him when I wrapped my arms tightly around him and swayed with him.

"You did it," I breathed out. "We're gonna be just fine."

And he'd agreed to move in now, so I could keep him safe much more effectively than worrying about what would happen if he went back around Nathan.

The investigators could come by my place all they wanted—I had nothing to hide. All I wanted to do was to call them and tip them off about Nathan's drug problem, but it wasn't my call to make. Besides, if Cedar didn't know...

"Do you think they know why Nathan's doing it?"

"Not yet." Cedar pressed his face into my neck. "You know him. He's always been good at hiding his money problems."

"Have you thought about telling them?"

"That just seems like a game of tattletale. He-said, he-said."

I guided Cedar to the couch and sat next to him. "But it's also helping clear your name. What's the real reason you don't want to tell them?"

Cedar looked startled for a moment. He finally pulled away from me, keeping one arm around my shoulders. "I guess... I'm afraid that if I get him in trouble, he'll just dive off the deep end into that life."

"He's already way off the deep end, baby," I told him gently, then pulled him to hug him. "I love that you want to save him, but you can't let him pull you into that orbit."

"Hell, no." Cedar scoffed. "I've done that for too long. Time for me to set my own course."

"Damn gay," I agreed, which made him laugh and hug me silently as we swayed into each other. Like magnets who had been turned the right way, I couldn't stop myself from falling for—and toward—him.

I believed in Cedar, down to my very bones. Now I had to pray that the investigation dug down to the truth, too.

CEDAR

"I could still ask them to meet me somewhere nearby." I anxiously watched Ricky as he made two mugs of coffee. At least that gave me something to do.

"Nuh uh." Ricky brought over the mugs and set them on the table in front of us. "You're not getting away that easily."

A guilty twinge made me frown at him. "Sorry. I'm not trying to run off on you again."

Ricky kissed the side of my head. "You're overthinking it," he told me gently. "I just want to be here to support you and act as a witness—that's all."

I was going to be sick if I had to wait much longer. I'd already been waiting all morning for Hal Jones and his cop sidekick to drop by, as they'd promised to do as soon as possible. Apparently they wanted to have a word with me, and I'd told them that in return, I had some information for them.

Ricky had taken the morning off work with Jared's blessing. He'd cooked me breakfast and kept me entertained with silly stories from the diner. Apparently the kitchen was the best place for gossip around there, and I'd almost forgotten what I was waiting for.

Until now, anyway.

I nearly jumped out of my skin when I heard the knock. Oh, God. They were here. Were they going to arrest me? Would they believe a word I had to say? And was I about to do the right thing?

If only anyone had the answers. I couldn't look to someone else, though. Not anymore. Ricky could guide me, but I was done letting other people run my life for fear of screwing it up. If Ricky was done *not* letting other people help, the least I could do was meet him halfway in hopefully a heathy balance.

"I'll get the door," Ricky told me, pressing me back into the couch as I rose to get it. "You wait here and be cool, all right? You've got nothing to hide."

I cast him a grateful smile and sank down again, trying to remain cool and calm. I was allowed to be here, and I was allowed to have Ricky here with me. I was allowed to be nervous, too. Last time I'd met with the investigators, it had ended with them grilling me on missing receipts that I knew I'd submitted.

But again, how the hell could I prove that when I'd blindly handed everything over to Nathan and trusted him to take care of it? This was a lesson I'd never forget in trusting people blindly—if I survived this lesson without getting my life destroyed.

"Ah, Cedar. Hello." It was Hal Jones again, in a slightly different boring suit but looking much the same as always. Slicked-back hair and a slightly hassled look. "Thanks for meeting with me."

"Hi." I gestured toward the couch like I owned it. Now that I was moving in, I had to pretend that I did, anyway. "Have a seat."

"That's fine, thanks. It won't take much of your time." Hal folded his hands behind his back as Ricky came to sit next to me. "What do you have to tell us?"

Oh, God. Here we were. I wanted to cradle the coffee mug for warmth and comfort, but I told myself to grow up. I could sit up straight, make eye contact, and stand up for myself at last.

"I have a tip-off about Nathan. If you go to his place any given weekend, you'll see where he's blowing all his money." My cheeks flushed. "I've never taken part, but… he holds parties. But he says he doesn't have money. Expensive parties."

"Not just top-shelf Champagne?" Hal pressed. "You're talking illegal activity."

"Sure am." I pressed my lips together and then shook my head. I couldn't believe I was turning him in. But I'd never sworn not to tell, and he was trying to get me put behind bars when he was the one getting himself into shit. Using my body as a life preserver was despicable. "Yes. I don't know if he's supplying other people, but he's got to be spending some of his own money on his activities, and I don't think he wants people to find out."

"Well, you'll be happy to know our findings corroborate your suspicions."

"What?" I looked up quickly. "You mean you… checked him out already?" They'd seemed so laser-focused on me that it was hard to believe they'd actually taken the time to check him out.

"We've already wasted a good week on a small-fry charity." Hal sounded frustrated, and I couldn't blame him. They weren't going to make national headlines or serve the public good by closing one teeny-tiny charity down. "Our main pressure was… political, shall we say. Turns out when we took a closer look at the source, it was rotten from the ground up."

"Oh, my God. His dad." Nathan's father had some political influence, I knew that. That was why he knew Jacob and other professionals—lawyers, accountants, politicians, bigwigs. Nathan was good at schmoozing with them.

So it wasn't so much that I was bad with people, but that I was good at talking to ordinary people. I didn't speak suck-up or WASP like Nathan did, though.

Hal didn't confirm it, but neither did he deny it, which was enough for me. Nathan's dad had been trying to get me into trouble then, or else he'd looked at the accounts.

Bingo. Jacob had called him and told him something was off with them. I'd bet anything that was what happened, and Nathan had realized we were under a microscope and thrown me under the bus instead.

"We were able to check out Nathan's apartment over the weekend, and… well, that changed the course of our investigation substantially," Hal said. "Needless to say, you have nothing to worry about."

I let out a long breath of relief. Despite Ricky's reassurance, I'd felt weird about turning Nathan in. It still felt like betraying him, and no matter how much he'd betrayed me, I didn't want to give him the satisfaction of having a vendetta against me.

"Does this mean he's in the clear?" Ricky leaned forward, taking my hand. He was here to ask the important questions when I couldn't, emotion clouding my speech.

"Yes. We have evidence of what's going on. Nathan's father has been giving him money through the charity to avoid gift taxes, and that's an IRS matter. Things will get complicated with this prosecution, but we'll make sure you won't be involved."

Ricky scoffed. "Was his dad in on this? Or was it Nathan blowing money and covering it up so his dad didn't get mad at him?"

That was an excellent point now that he brought it up. I wasn't sure if I'd have thought of it myself. "Oh, my God. Maybe he didn't know." I pressed my palm into my hair and slid it down to my forehead to facepalm.

It sounded exactly like Nathan to try to play everyone around him off against each other.

"We haven't yet confirmed everything," Hal told me. "We had Nathan in the station for a chat yesterday, though."

I winced. These days, Nathan was a wreck on Sundays. Long nights of partying did that to a person. He was always loudest and most obnoxious at the end of the weekend, and I couldn't imagine him responding well to questioning in those circumstances. "And?"

"He finally admitted that he's been making up the shortfall in his finances with money from the charity for some time. We have a confession. That's why we're so happy to eliminate you as a suspect."

A noise of relief slipped from my throat. I covered my face, propping my elbows on my knees as so much stress drained from my body in the space of a few seconds. "Oh, my God." With a confession, it was no longer he-said, he-said. Nathan was finally, *finally* telling the truth.

Probably only to get out of further trouble, but I didn't care. It meant I was safe.

Ricky rubbed my back gently, but his voice was tough. "So you've been barking up the wrong tree, so to speak."

I peeked through my fingers at him, my brows furrowing severely.

"Did you just make a name pun?" Ricky's lips twitched, and I smacked his thigh. "Not the moment."

Hal was hiding a grin, too. "Yes. It seems it was a clearcut case. I just have one question left."

Ricky and I both groaned. Thank God Hal was joining in the puns.

"Yeah?" I composed myself, pushing back the relief that threatened to flood me until I couldn't even think straight, and sat up again. Now that he wasn't looming over me and threatening me with prosecution, I was a lot more willing to help. If only they'd approached me like this the first time instead of as the lead suspect.

Hal stuck his hands in his pockets. "Nathan's finally admitted you didn't do anything wrong. But if you're not guilty, why have you been shaking like a leaf whenever we talk to you?"

"Oh, for fuck's—" Ricky started, but I cut him off with a tap on his chest. I had this one, and I didn't want or need him explaining and defending me. It was sweet that he wanted to try, though.

I let Hal see the tremor as I reached forward for the tissue box to blow my nose. "This shake? It's called cerebral palsy. I can refer you to my doctor if you're not familiar with the condition. But there are plenty of other reasons I might be nervous. Thinking I'm going to jail, for example. Especially if I'm being intimidated by a cop and an investigator. Or maybe I have anxiety, or one of plenty of other conditions that would do the same thing."

He deserved a bigger comeuppance than that for scaring the shit out of me for the last week, but I could barely believe my own courage. Even giving him even this much of a tongue-lashing was unusual for me. It was like I was channeling Ricky a little bit right now, and I loved it.

Hal looked flustered as hell. I wouldn't lie—a part of me greatly enjoyed seeing people get embarrassed when they realized they'd been an asshole. I wasn't ashamed of my condition, but a lot of people seemed ashamed *for* me. I didn't mind exploiting that to make sure they never made anyone else in my shoes feel like shit again. "Oh. Oh, my apologies," Hal muttered. "I didn't realize..."

"Most people don't." I made my smile as pleasant as possible, even if I wanted to throttle them. "A lot of people assume that if you can walk or talk, you can't be disabled. There's invisible—and hypervisible but relatively unknown—conditions galore out there. Look below the surface."

They weren't the first to think I was up to something because I *looked* healthy, or too young to be sick, or any of that shit. But this was the last time these particular people would make that assumption, at least.

"All right. That's everything for now. Have a good day. We'll be in touch if we need more information." Hal tipped his hat to me and headed for the stairs with great haste.

Ricky choked back his laugh until Hal was heading down the stairs, and then grinned at me. "Oh, my God. That was an epic burn."

"At least I'm giving and not getting it, for once," I giggled. I was riding high off this, my life suddenly stretching out ahead of me again instead of one big question mark. I hadn't done anything wrong, and I wasn't going to suffer even more for Nathan's actions.

I was grateful that Ricky hadn't butted in and tried to deal with everything for me. He'd clearly been worked up, but he'd let me defend myself, and that meant the world. He wasn't being brash just for the sake of it—and he respected me enough to know I could hold my ground.

So it turned out I hadn't needed to tattle on Nathan after all. He'd brought his downfall on himself, and he deserved it. Maybe whatever legal trouble this got him into, it would straighten him out. Maybe not. That was his problem.

With Hal gone, I breathed out a long sigh and leaned into Ricky's shoulder. It all felt surreal—like the last week had never even happened, and at the same time, like I'd been mired in this swamp forever with no hope of getting free, only to suddenly find myself on dry land.

"Wow." I reeled and leaned into him, closing my eyes. "I thought it was going to hang over my head forever."

"No way," Ricky murmured and smiled at me. "Not when there's only two suspects. What an idiot Nathan is. He could have waited for the charity to hire a few more people at least... muddy the waters."

"He's not dumb," I corrected him. I liked that Ricky thought that, though. "Not at all. He just didn't think he needed the extra protection. He didn't respect me enough to think I wouldn't just roll over and take the blame. And he couldn't wait—he was desperate for money now."

"Well, he judged you wrong." Ricky snorted. "You fucking kicked their asses, and his too. I'm just happy he's going down. This means we can start our new life."

My new life with him. Now that I wasn't terrified that they'd somehow think I was paying for anything in Ricky's place with stolen money, I might even help him buy a new couch. It would be nice to stretch out along it. For now, I'd stuck a pillow onto the spring as a reminder—mostly to avoid spontaneous piercings.

I beamed at him and snuggled into his hold. "I'm happy, too. Can we move me out this week? I want to be settled here way before Christmas."

"Sounds perfect," Ricky murmured. "What about all the plants?"

"It's supposed to warm up later this week. Perfect chance to move them." I grinned at him. "When I gave the investigators my bank records, they told me I can keep anything I hadn't charged to the charity yet. I'm not letting them wither away. We'll find space in here."

"There was never a question of that," Ricky said with a fond smile. "Besides, I could use the fresh air. Especially with two people here and winter sealing up the windows."

"And we'll be putting out a lot of carbon dioxide over the next few weeks," I told Ricky with a meaningful grin.

Ricky opened his mouth to say something and then shook his head, laughing at me. "You nearly got me there. We'll save that for after we move you out. Come on, let's go over to your place right now... before we get distracted."

I pouted for a moment. "But I'd love to distract you."

"Sure you can," Ricky winked and headed for his shoes. "The anticipation will only make it better, isn't that right?"

"Damn gay," I told him as I put on my boots and jacket.

I'd been packing over the last few days, any moment that I was at home. It had been surprisingly quick—mostly because I couldn't afford things, and my spare money had gone to the charity. All that was left was to pack up my old life, and I could blossom into something new.

2 7

RICKY

"Done."

Cedar laid his keys on the counter and smiled at me, then raised his hands and backed away from them like they were poisonous.

I laughed and pulled him into my arms, swaying with him. "Look at that. All done, and home in time for supper."

Sure, it had taken a few days to get everything packed as tightly as possible, and a few annoyed Uber drivers to move everything over to my place. My rating was going to take a ding from that.

Waiting around for people to pick up the old furniture had been a pain in the ass, but we weren't quite done with that, either. We still had one couch to get rid of—after the next payday, anyway.

But it was over now, and these were the last couple of boxes that stood between us and officially-moved-in status.

"Think the plants will be okay on the ride?" I asked. It was chillier today than it had been lately, with snow on the ground, but that was to be expected—we were just a week away from Christmas.

"As long as we don't linger outside, yes." Cedar pulled away and adjusted the cloth wrapping over the tray of plants, fussing with them like a mama hen.

I smiled at him and kissed his temple, taking the chance to annoy him a little while he was trying to move around. "You gonna give them a pep talk?" Cedar just snorted, but I grinned at him. I'd heard him talking to them when he didn't think I could hear. It was adorable. "Come on, little guys," I told them. "One cold snap and you'll be in a nice, cozy house for Christmas. Maybe I'll make Santa hats for you."

It worked: Cedar laughed and turned to face me again. "You're ridiculous, Ricky Rosa."

"No, you." I stuck out my tongue at him, tickling his sides for just a moment—until he squeaked and protested.

I loved that my last box was kitchen supplies. It was easy to see that Cedar did like to cook, whatever he said about it. He had a pepper grinder, a knife sharpener, the whole damn kitchen sink.

"So, are you making supper?" I teased. "Since you've got such a stockpile of cooking supplies here?"

Cedar fidgeted and frowned at me. "Maybe. I don't know."

"What's up?"

He glanced at his phone and I followed his gaze. Traffic was bad— five more minutes for the Uber to get here. No mercy for him just yet.

"You don't have to compare yourself to me," I told him. If that was it, I wanted to dispel that right away. I'd never expected to date anyone who'd been through the literal fires of culinary school at all, even if he'd dropped out early on. "I'm sure I'll love whatever you make. And I've seen your recipes you've given out for the charity, remember? If you can make those, you're good in the kitchen."

Finally, Cedar looked up at me, chewing his lip. "It's not that. It's just that… well, people try to wrap me in bubble wrap."

"Oh," I breathed out. "And you don't want to worry me?"

"I get that you don't want me to hurt myself, but sometimes I don't mind. I'm used to it."

I nodded as I listened, none of this surprising me. Cedar needed his independence, and I was going to be careful to respect that. "So I'll leave you alone if you cook a meal for us. I'll bandage you up if you need it, though."

Cedar breathed out a sigh of relief. "Thank you for understanding. It's not that I'm self-conscious about my body…" His hand shook as he raised it to cup my cheek, and I waited patiently for him to get it in just the right spot to succeed. "It's that I'm used to monitoring everyone else's reactions to it."

I leaned in and kissed him, then wrapped my arms around his shoulder. "Of course, baby. I think that's how I felt about being gay. I was more worried about other people's reactions to it than anything else."

Especially Mama. Now that I knew she just wanted me to follow my dreams, it all made sense. The only dream I'd expressed to her was that of having a nuclear family—so she'd pushed me because that was what she thought I wanted.

Well, now I wanted this man, and I didn't care what other people thought.

"It's good to be leaving that behind," Cedar murmured. "And all of this." He pulled away from me with one more peck of the lips. "Come on, it's around the corner."

As I followed him outside, I did one last sweep of the empty place. "All ready to say goodbye?"

"Fuck, yeah," Cedar said, shifting the plants just long enough to flip off the apartment while I shut the door.

I laughed as I followed him. "So good to be out, huh?"

"Yeah. Not just because…" Cedar glanced down the hallway at the next door down. I'd half-expected another confrontation with Nathan, but I had the feeling he had much bigger fish to fry all of a sudden. Cedar turned and led me down the hall instead. "But things were rough here. Good times, but lots of bad times. And I felt so lonely here, a lot of the time."

"Even though you've got all your friends?" I shook my head. I wanted to bump hips with him and cheer him up, but I might knock him off-balance. So instead, I led the way downstairs, taking it nice and slow.

"Yeah. It's different to have friends and actually… talk to them." Cedar gave me a rueful smile. "You know that, I'm sure."

Did I ever. Now that I'd unloaded the great secret on my mind, all these guys I'd thought of as just acquaintances or customers were becoming friends.

We scrambled into the Uber, balancing the boxes on our laps as we waited for the short ride back to my place.

"How about after this, we drop by the diner?" I suggested. "See said friends, and celebrate?"

"We've got a lot to celebrate," Cedar agreed, smiling at me. "Sure."

It wasn't just going into work on a day off when I came to Bubbles to chat with people now. The place meant a lot to me after years of working there, but far more from these last few weeks.

They'd had my back here, and that kind of place meant it was a home. A second home—well, since Mama's was my second home, maybe my third. If Cedar was right about his parents, maybe fourth.

It was a far cry from working my ass off as a scared sixteen-year-old suddenly learning how to make ends meet. I wasn't exactly rolling in dough now, but I was comfortable—with myself, with my living situation, and with my love life.

I couldn't ask for more.

"Hey, guys!" I grinned. I leaned in to hug Billy and Adam, and shook hands with a guy I vaguely recognized as a bouncer at Friction. He came in here sometimes after work.

Cedar jerked his head in greeting at everyone and scooted in next to me, putting his arm around me. "We're all done moving."

"Moving?" the bouncer asked. "You should be celebrating with pizza!"

I shook my head and grinned at him. "Nah. Nothing beats our bacon—I'd bet anything." I rested my hand over Cedar's on the table. "Am I right?"

"You're right," Cedar grinned. "As long as you aren't distracted. I guess that means I can't stop by work too often, even if I live closer now."

I winked. "Oh, stop by anytime. I'll do even better with you here to keep an eye on me."

"Gag me with a spoon, the honeymoon is strong with this one," Billy commented. He grinned at us. "Making me feel very single."

"Me too," agreed the bouncer, and I caught him giving Cedar an extra look.

Cedar tightened his hold on me and grinned. "Not Adam, though."

"No." Adam gave me a sheepish grin, and I grinned back at him. We'd spent one day cuddling—months ago now—after failing to hook up. Not long after that, he'd figured out who his heart lay with, and I couldn't be happier for them.

Especially now that I'd found a guy of my own, no Grindr needed.

"Hey, guys!" Neil ducked into the restaurant, shivering. "Lord, it's getting cold out there. I was hoping you'd be here, or I might have had to do something crazy like call you, Cedar."

Cedar laughed, but I could hear the nervous note in it. "Hi. Good to see you again."

Neil joined us and greeted everyone else, then turned to Cedar. "I talked to my bosses and, long story short, you can come in for an interview after Christmas. Is it okay to wait that long?"

Cedar frowned to himself and I could see him doing the math in his head—when the first paycheck would be, and how long he'd be living with me without paying rent.

I nearly interrupted to say it was fine by me, but I caught myself just in time. Even if my intentions were good, I wasn't going to make decisions in Cedar's life. When Cedar looked at me, though, I smiled and nodded, relieved that I'd realized what I was about to do just in time.

"That's fine, thank you. I can wait until after Christmas to attend an interview," Cedar told Neil with one of his dazzling smiles. "I appreciate the chance to get on board. I'd love to fundraise for you!"

Neil grinned. "Wonderful. I'm sorry to make you wait; I'd have you start tomorrow if I could. But everything's chaotic this time of year. The lines are so busy right now, like every Christmas."

It was a sobering moment when I realized why that was, and everyone around the table was quiet for a few moments, sharing a spontaneous and collective moment of silence.

So many LGBT people didn't have a home to go back to for Christmas, or family who wanted them there. It had to be a lonely, painful holiday season when you'd been thrown out of your home or community for daring to be yourself.

I might not have a dad around anymore, but I knew he would have accepted me. And I counted myself lucky as hell that I'd always had a mom who made sure I knew she loved me. Not everyone had one parent, let alone two.

And then some had both, but they were blinded by ignorance and hatred and were still hiding the truth from the people around them. Although I'd been hiding too, perhaps it was more from my own vision of myself than anyone else's.

Hotlines like LGBTalk gave people the chance to talk to someone who knew the truth about them, and to say it out loud to some-body who was safe to talk to. If I hadn't had Billy around, or Jared, or the other people who had sheltered and guided me, God knows... I might have been calling them, too.

"I can't wait to try and interview," said Cedar at last, his voice quiet and determined. "After everything that's happened, it feels good to find somewhere I know is a good place."

"I heard the investigation wrapped up, and your partner is... um..." Neil trailed off, wincing sympathetically. "Implicated."

"Guilty," Cedar corrected him simply. "I'm just thankful they got the right guy. It was scary to have that looming over my head. I'll be glad to work somewhere that people actually know protocols, too. We were pretty much making it up as we went along."

"All of us are to an extent. We don't usually get burned by it," Neil assured Cedar. "It's not your fault at all."

Cedar shook his head. "Maybe not, but it made me realize a lot of truths about myself. I'm a little nervous, I'm not gonna lie... but I feel like I can do this job."

"Damn gay," I murmured, and I caught everyone staring at me. I flushed with embarrassment. "I'm not—not as an insult! I mean, yes. Yes, he can do it. Oh, God."

"Damn gay means damn straight, only better," Cedar added, backing me up. He winked at me. "Isn't that right?"

"Sure is for me," I agreed.

Billy laughed. "Damn gay. Huh. I like it. Maybe it'll catch on."

"Donations slow down after Christmas for you guys?" Cedar asked Neil, folding his hands. "I know that's the normal pattern."

"Yep. Every year," Neil confirmed. "Honestly, if you can bring in even a little more than we pay you in that time period... hiring you will be a slam-dunk."

Cedar nodded. "I'll get a game plan together. Just call me when you've got a good time to talk."

Neil grinned. "Perfect."

"Now," Billy interrupted. "Let's talk about this moving-in thing. When's the housewarming?"

"I'm not sure there's supposed to be a housewarming party if it's not a new house..." I trailed off, catching the look Cedar gave me. "I mean... after Christmas. New Year's?"

"Great answer," Billy teased. "Pregaming spot, right? We'll bring the Champagne. If you're lucky, it'll be the *second*-cheapest kind, since we like you."

"You're on."

I brightened up at the thought of having our friends all over to celebrate with us—the new life together, the new year ahead of us, and hopefully the new job, too.

As conversation moved on, one lingering worry occurred to me. I leaned into Cedar and kept my voice down. "If you're getting a job... will you be moving out soon? Cause I'd hate to repeat all this gross moving stuff again." I knew my smile at him was hopeful, and almost shy... but I didn't want to get my hopes up for nothing. "I'll help you again if you do want to, of course."

"Nope," Cedar told me, grinning at me. "You can't get rid of me that easily. Literally. That key sticks to the inside of my pocket still, and I've already washed it."

I laughed and then leaned in for a kiss. "Good," I told him. "Cause I don't want to make you feel like you aren't the strong, independent man that I love... but I also don't want to lose you."

"Not ever," Cedar promised with a smile, and then winked. "Love."

I blushed and looked around. "Anyone want bacon all of a sudden? Just me? I'd better go order up."

If I could memorize the sound of Cedar giggling as I headed to the kitchen and replay that any time I felt stressed, my life would be so much easier. It brought a smile to my lips and a bounce to my stride.

Thank God we'd found each other. As long as the health and safety department never found out how, we were home clear.

CEDAR

"I'm so happy." I pressed my nose into Ricky's chest, hugging him so tightly I had trouble breathing.

"Ooof." Ricky gasped, but he laughed as he slid his arms around my waist and swayed with me. "Good. You deserve it."

I slid my hand up Ricky's shoulder blades to cup the back of his neck before pulling away and kissing him. "Thank you for sticking with me through all of this."

I couldn't say enough about how I appreciated him being by my side at the drag brunch, and while the investigation finished, and throughout the hell of moving out. And offering his own place for me to live was a step beyond what anyone could have expected from their new boyfriend.

But it was easy to see that Ricky was in it for the long haul, and I loved that.

It was gorgeous here now. I'd noticed that Ricky had washed the windows and even vacuumed before the move. My plants—*our* plants—were arranged around, catching the light and breathing fresh air into the small space. Sure, it was the same old couch, but with my blanket on the back, it looked like new; my rugs across the floor kept our toes warm.

The melding of our lives into one. It was a scary thought, but it felt so right. I'd fallen for him, and he'd caught me. This little apartment and the humble furnishings were all I needed, as long as he was here with me.

"So do you," I murmured. "Are you happy? Living here with me?"

Ricky smiled gently at me and pressed his lips against mine once. "I'm so happy I can't think straight."

"I hope you never think straight again," I teased, grinning at him. "I'll do my best to help with that cause."

"How selfless of you." Ricky winked and tugged me to the kitchen. "Coffee or water?"

"Water," I decided. "If I go with coffee, we'll be up all night."

"I will be, one way or another." Ricky ground his hips against mine, making the dirty intentions behind his words clear.

I squeaked and tried to break free, but when I turned around, I just presented the perfect opportunity for him to press his cock against my ass and shimmy left and right.

Fuck, he was already turning me on. The jerk had it down to an art. Living with him was going to present so many more opportunities for spontaneous love-making—or fucking—or maybe both at once.

"I love you," I whispered, my hands on the kitchen counter. "And not just in the *you're such a good lay* way."

"I'm your Christmas layaway?" Ricky teased, but he slid his arms around my waist and pressed his chest against my back, his lips against the back of my neck. "I love you too, hon."

"And I can't wait to bake Christmas cookies with you right here… naked." I giggled as Ricky caught his breath. "And make eggnog naked, and…"

"We'll leave the naked cooking to me," Ricky told me firmly, grinning when I managed a glance over my shoulder at him. "I know you want to cook and bake on your own, but I'd rather wrap you up in a few layers first. I can't stand seeing you get hurt." His voice was low and passionate.

That in itself was too sweet. I smiled to myself and pressed my head into his shoulder, sneaking a look up at him. "Yeah, I can compromise on that."

"You know what? We should rearrange this living room when we get the new sofa. Bring the bed out of the corner so we don't have to crawl down to the end of the bed all the time," Ricky said quietly, finally peeling himself away from me to rest his hip on the counter and look across the living room. He kept a hand on my back, like he couldn't bear not to touch me.

"Agreed." I smiled at him, visions of a cute, plant-filled living room already dancing in my head. I could keep some indoor flowers in pots, too.

"And we'll have to break in that couch one way or another," Ricky smirked.

"Is that how you broke the last one?"

"Shh." Ricky flapped a hand at me playfully. "We'll get a better couch that doesn't break."

I shivered with pleasure, way too distracted by wondering how hard and fast and deep I could get him to fuck me. "I want you inside me, baby," I breathed out. "Fuck the water. We can do that later."

Ricky moaned, his hold over my arms tightening. I felt like a caged animal, but for the first time, I liked it. I especially liked the way he hauled me over toward the bed, overpowering me easily when I wrestled back.

I growled playfully and he kissed me until my knees buckled, then scooped me up into his arms.

Okay, he could do that any damn time he wanted.

"Yes," I gasped as he dumped me on the bed. I even managed to scoot up the bed without feeling too undignified.

My adrenaline kicked in when he crawled after me on hands and knees, much faster than I could go. "Gotcha," Ricky whispered as he flopped onto me, pinning me face-first on the bed.

I pushed my ass up into his hips and rolled my body in slow waves, my nails digging into the pillows as I made a grab for anything I could.

He hauled my hips up just enough to unbutton my jeans and pull them off, wasting no time stripping me down. My shirt came off next, and feeling his fully-clothed weight on top of me did things to me that I hadn't even imagined existed.

It was a thousand times better than fucking because of boredom, or an itch to scratch. Knowing that it was Ricky, the sweetheart with a prickly shell who had swept me off my feet from day one, made it all the better.

I wanted to make him feel good, and it occurred to me that he was the first guy to make me feel equal in that desire. I wasn't just giving in, letting him have me, and hoping it felt good for me along the way.

I *wanted* pleasure for myself, and I wanted it with the desperation of dried grass sucking up water in a summer heat wave. The heat all around me, enclosing me in safety, let me push myself further than ever before—and do so with joy.

"Fuck me," I whispered. "Hard and fast, baby. Make me forget this whole damn week." I grinned. "And our tests came back clear, so… no condoms. I want you *marking* me."

"Yeah, baby." Ricky kissed my shoulder. The sound of a zipper grinding down its track made me catch my breath. "I'll second that."

I pushed the pillows around until one was under my stomach and folded my arms under another that covered my face. I hugged it tightly as wet, cool fingers slid along my thigh and up to my waiting hole.

"Fuck," I mumbled into the thick fabric, my voice muffled even to my ears. I pushed up into those fingers as he gently eased them inside, opening me up with the care I'd been craving without even knowing it.

"I want to be inside you every day," Ricky whispered. "Some days I'll take it slow until you beg me for more. Some days I'll pin you down and screw you until the mattress begs us for less. Some days I'll just hold you and frot. I wanna do everything you've shown me and then some."

Ricky had found my prostate, rubbing his fingers along inside me until I was sparking with pleasure, a fire of need roaring inside me. *More* and *now*.

It was never gonna get old that I was Ricky's sexual awakening. That did so many things to my ego. I grinned and turned my face to the side to make sure he could hear me as I murmured, "We have a hundred more things to do."

"Make a list and we'll do it," Ricky promised. His fingers slid out and I moaned a sharp protest.

"What?" Ricky caught his breath as if worried he'd hurt me. "You okay?"

I smiled, twisting to try to look down my back. Totally worth the effort. I could barely handle the gorgeous sight of that hard cock jutting from Ricky's pants, veined and throbbing with need for me.

"I'm perfect," I whispered. "I just need you in me."

"Here." Ricky knelt further down the bed and turned me over, a hand on each hip.

I moaned again and pouted, trying to resist. "I want you to go hard, though."

"I can get deep in you this way, too," Ricky promised, stroking my thigh. The gentle touch calmed me, and I found myself smiling again. "But I want to see you, too. And kiss you. And let you see me in you…"

I gulped and nodded, shoving the pillows out of the way and settling on my back as he nestled between my thighs. Instantly, it felt like the right decision. I liked being able to wrap my arms around his broad back.

Ricky wrapped a hand around himself and pressed against me. The soft gasp that he gave when he slid inside was easy to miss, but not when I was so wrapped up in him that I had to pay attention to his every sound and move.

And then he was inside me, inch by inch, stroking my bare skin all over my body like he was soothing me, praising me in a steady, low whisper. "You're so beautiful," Ricky murmured. "You're so tight around me. I dream of this, you know. Love being in you.

Love *you*. Never thought I could love someone this hard, or… hell, or stay this hard while making love… or any of it."

My eyes blurred and I swiped my hand across them. "Damn it," I whispered. It felt like a puzzle piece of my heart had just slid into place.

Ricky smiled fondly at me and cupped my cheeks, staying so deep inside me that he filled me up completely. "I mean it. I'll try to keep saying it out loud, you know."

That meant the world to me. I only managed a watery grin and nod.

"Aw, baby," Ricky whispered. When he leaned down to kiss me, his cock shifted inside me too, making me squirm and moan. "Oooh," Ricky whispered, his lips warm and wet against my mouth. "You ready?"

"Please," I begged. I hitched up my legs carefully until they were around his waist, and Ricky thrust inside me.

Stroke by stroke, we relaxed into this rhythm together, even our breathing coming into sync. Every moan and gasp filled the living room of this cozy place, and when I tipped my head back, I could see evening setting in through the window above the head of the bed.

It was beautiful, crisp, and clear, and so were my feelings right now. No more confusion or trying to hide from them.

When this slow, deep rhythm wasn't enough, Ricky hooked my knees over his shoulders and sped up, pressing one hand against my chest to keep me flat on the bed while he pinned my wrists above my head with the other hand.

"Yes!" I gasped. I couldn't touch myself, and that should have meant I was going to last longer—but it looked like I was going to come pretty damn quick.

"You're squeezing me so tight," Ricky gasped. "I can tell you love this." He kissed my jaw. "I'm so hard it hurts. I'm gonna blow my load right inside you, claim you as mine."

"I'm yours," I gasped, my voice barely a whisper. I meant it, too. From head to toe, every inch of me wanted to be Ricky's, and was glad that he was mine.

"You're my beautiful boyfriend," Ricky whispered. The hand on my chest slid down toward my cock. The moment his palm brushed sensitive skin, I gasped, but he soothed me with kisses against my neck.

My cock twitched in his hand as I clenched hard, and he gave an approving moan before stroking.

I lost myself in that moment and found someone better: the man Ricky deserved, the one strong enough to let go of himself for a moment and let Ricky be there for and with me... in every moment, forever.

"Ricky!" I gasped in warning, but I barely had any myself. I came hard, throwing my head back and crying out as he twisted his hand around my shaft and milked every last drop.

I wasn't prepared for Ricky's orgasm to hit him just as fast. He kissed me so hard my lips stung, letting go of my cock and digging his nails into my hips. Then he grunted and squeezed his eyes shut. I felt him shudder and swell inside me, and I got to watch bliss spread across his face as his warm passion filled me up.

"Yes," I gasped, tingling with pleasure. "You're so fucking beautiful."

Ricky chuckled throatily, his lips finding the sensitive spot behind my ear as he slid out of me. "No, you are."

"No, you." I stubbornly stuck out my tongue at him.

Ricky sucked it into his mouth and flicked the tip of his own along it. He poked me in the chest, and it took me a moment to realize he was continuing the argument.

I laughed, my head falling back against the pillow. "I'm glad I found someone as damn stubborn as me."

"Yeah," Ricky whispered, rolling onto his side and running his hand down my side. "So am I."

Already, I couldn't wait to see Ricky keep growing, and I was eager to be better and better myself. This felt like the beginning of our story rather than the end.

Together, we could do whatever we dreamed.

CHRISTMAS DAY, RICKY

"And now we get our own celebrations." I was almost dizzy with happiness as I unlocked the front door and once again saw the decorations we'd put up in the hall.

The supports of the bannister were threaded with garland, though I'd avoided the bannister itself so Cedar could safely grab it if need be. We'd put sparkling Christmas lights up in the hallway; the changing colors were visible through the glass above the door.

There was a wreath on the interior door, and once we made our way up the stairs to open that door, I took in the rest of it: a tabletop Christmas tree, more garland everywhere I could justify sticking them on with masking tape, and dangling bits of tinsel from all the shiny new door handles.

"I'm so glad you said yes to meeting my parents," Cedar told me, giving me another giddy little smile.

"It's only fair," I told him, pulling him into my arms and pushing the door shut behind him. I kissed him a few more times. "You met my mom already, after all."

"Mmm." Cedar rested his cheek on my shoulder and then offered me the Tupperware of Christmas cookies. Even though we'd baked together, his mom had insisted we bring them home after Christmas lunch.

Supper was just ours, and I had big plans for it.

"I'm going to have to start cooking now," I told him, my brain already switching into gear. "I've left things marinating, and I've done some pre-chopping…"

"Can I help?" Cedar asked softly.

We'd taken turns cooking over the last week, and it was working remarkably well. When we worked together, I handled the prep for him. It was kind of like demotion in kitchen terms, but as far as I was concerned, it was a promotion in life.

Cooking for him was my idea of romance, but I'd set everything up so that I could give him something that satisfied his own need for romance.

"I'd love you to," I told him. "Stuffing?"

"I'd love to stuff you." Cedar blinked innocently at me. "For you, I mean."

"You sneaky little bastard," I grinned. "Don't think I don't see what you're doing there."

"Oh, I hope you see it." Cedar grabbed my ass and squeezed. "Or feel it."

"I'd better open the wine now, then." I grinned at him. "We have a lot of celebrating to do. And then presents."

We'd stuck with a twenty-dollar limit, since he hadn't yet started his new job.

I was so damn proud of him—he'd been so eager that Neil had

managed to sneak him into the LGBTalk office for an interview two days ago. He'd passed with flying colors. The job was his, as of January second.

Meanwhile, most of my spare money this month had gone to Christmas decorations, but it was totally worth it. The cozy warmth of our little place seeped into me, calming me the moment I walked in from work every day.

Christmas with my own family—not just Mom, but my aunt and at least a dozen extended relatives and neighbors—had been yesterday. Cedar's family had claimed today.

New Year's Eve was for our housewarming—more of a *welcome home* party for Cedar—and all our friends were going to come over before we headed out to Friction together.

But tonight was ours.

I poured glasses of wine and beckoned him into the kitchen with me. "The recipes are there," I pointed them out. "All the plastic containers are the pre-chopped ingredients. What do you need me to do, chef?" I saluted him and winked.

I'd bought new wine glasses, too—goblets that were easier to handle and harder to tip over, but still looked fancy and crystalline.

I didn't expect Cedar to tear up and throw his arms around me. I held him tightly and rubbed his back. "Oops?" I offered, guilt immediately setting in.

"No," Cedar whispered. "It's perfect. Thank you."

I smiled at him and kissed his cheek. "And over the next year, we'll work on setting things up so you can do most of the prep yourself, too. I'll teach you things I learned. Maybe we can see about a cooking school that can work with your needs."

It was scary to tell him my plans out loud. I didn't want to patronize him; after all, Cedar had been getting along just fine before meeting me. He didn't need a caretaker. But if I could help him rekindle an old love, why the hell not?

Cedar was trembling in my arms—I was used to feeling his hands shake, but this was his whole body. Before I could be alarmed, he just gave me a beaming grin that told me I'd read the situation right.

"I can't wait."

"Me neither," I murmured as I picked up a goblet half-filled with wine and offered it to him. "Here's to us."

"To us," Cedar whispered and clinked his glass against mine.

Meeting each other's families was nice, and going out together was fun, but there was nothing like being alone together in the home we now shared. I couldn't be prouder to spend my Christmas cooking with this man who had made me the happiest guy in the world.

I couldn't resist adding, "And to many more Christmases to come."

Cedar's grin was so big it lit up my whole world. He set down his glass and wrapped his hands around my hips to sway with me. "A lifetime of Christmases."

A lifetime had once seemed insurmountable. But now, this new life, with him?

I couldn't wait.

Dear reader,

Thank you for reading *Boiling Point*, the third book in the Brooklyn Boys series!

I'm tremendously grateful to those I'm lucky enough to count as my family and friends. Without you, I don't know what I'd do. Same goes for my betas, editor, and proofers. Thank you, thank you, thank you. And to every one of you beautiful flowers just itching to burst through the cracks and bloom: however grey your surroundings, yes, you can. The world needs you.

Last, but not least, my love to the boy. You've taught me more than you know.

Don't forget to check out *Electric Sunshine* (Brooklyn Boys #1) for Kev and Charlie's story, and *Live Wire* (Brooklyn Boys #2) for Darren and Adam's story! (Both books are also available in audio, and *Boiling Point* will follow suit in April 2019.) To get to know Shay and Jared, check out the short story "Wind Tunnel" (you can grab it for free by subscribing to my newsletter). If you've caught up already, I recommend diving into the Significant Brothers or Riley Brothers series next!

Make sure you follow me on Amazon to hear about new releases only, or subscribe to my newsletter to hear about new releases and sales, get sneak peeks at upcoming books, and hear about audiobook releases, event appearances, and other exciting news as it happens!

I also have a reader group on Facebook here if you want to tell me what you loved about this book, see cute bee and flower photos, and keep on top of my upcoming releases with a whole bunch of fun, lovely readers: https://www.facebook.com/groups/edavies

Last but not least: always be you!

~Ed

ABOUT THE AUTHOR

Gay romance author E. Davies grew up moving constantly, which taught him what people have in common, the ways relationships are formed, and the dangers of "miscellaneous" boxes. As a young gay author whose role models were characters punished for their sexuality, Ed prefers his stories lightly dramatic, full of optimism and hope.

Now out and proud, Ed writes full-time, goes on long nature walks, tries to fill his passport, drinks piña coladas on the beach, flees from cute guys, coos over fuzzy animals (especially bees), and is liable to tilt his head and click his tongue if you don't use your turn signal.

For exclusive release notifications and a free copy of my novel Buzz, sign up for my newsletter below!

Newsletter: www.edaviesbooks.com/subscribe

facebook.com/edaviesbooks

twitter.com/edaviesauthor

instagram.com/thisboyisstrange

bookbub.com/authors/e-davies

ALSO BY E. DAVIES

Brooklyn Boys series:

Electric Sunshine

Live Wire

Boiling Point

Significant Brothers series:

Splinter

Grasp

Slick

Trace

Clutch

Tremble

Riley Brothers series:

Buzz

Clang

Swish

Crunch

Slam

Grind

F-Word series:

Flaunt

Freak

Faux

Forever

After series:

Afterburn

Afterglow

Aftermath

Hidden Creek books:

Shelter

Adore

Miracle

Coauthored with Zach Jenkins:

Sugar Topped

Just a Summer Deal

Audiobooks:

The list is growing rapidly! You can see all my books available in audio
on Audible.